*S*omebody sewed a child up in the camel's belly." Detective John Mazeroski took a toothpick out of his pocket and looked around Stewart's office for the reaction.

"WHAT?" gasped Samantha Mayer, thrusting her body forward, her face ashen. "That's impossible!"

Preston Stewart, President of the Carnegie Institute, kept the stony composure expected of CEOs.

"Okay, this is why I wanted you here, Przewalski. Lemme tell you what you don't know, but these folks do." Mazeroski nodded at Mayer and Stewart. "A month and a half ago, December 6th, about three in the morning, someone smashed the front glass panel of that camel driver exhibit, at the back of the second—"

"Detective," Stewart interrupted. "The exhibit, formally, is called *Arab Courier Attacked by Lions*."

Mazeroski nodded, maintaining his patience. "The perp knelt into the case—there were knee imprints in the sand. Then he slit open the camel's belly. Back to front if he was right-handed. He used a sharp blade. Probably a box cutter. We haven't recovered it. Then he pulled the stuffing out. Old straw."

Mazeroski eyed Harry. "Okay, Przewalski, now it gets interesting. The perp pulled something else out of the camel's belly. We think it was wrapped in a rough, linen cloth. Likely old and frayed. We found strands lying in the straw. Also, bits of hair, plant fibers … and skin. Maybe the tips of fingers. DNA says it's human. Female. Size says a baby, or small child. Maybe mummified. The flesh—"

Mayer suddenly bolted from her chair, hand over her mouth, and ran into the bathroom off Stewart's office. "Sorry," she sighed when she returned, her face drained, her hair spidering out like electrified wire. "It's been hard. First this. Then Anna."

"Anna?" Harry looked at her, questioningly.

"Anna Storck. Our physical anthropologist. Tragic. She committed suicide. It was two days after the vandalism." She looked at Mazeroski for confirmation. He nodded.

"That's about it," Mazeroski continued. "The perp walked off with whatever shed the bits of cloth and skin. We're guessing a mummified kid wrapped in a bundle. If we're right, we're stumped! Hell, if we're wrong, we're stumped!"

"What do you mean?" Stewart asked.

"What we mean is," Mazeroski declared, "what's a mummified kid doing in the goddamn belly of a camel that was stuffed over there in France over a hundred years ago for a camel driver diorama?"

To Molly and Zack

THE
CAMEL
DRIVER

Also by Leonard Krishtalka

Dinosaur Plots
The Bone Field
Death Spoke
The Body on the Bed

THE CAMEL DRIVER

LEONARD KRISHTALKA

Anamcara Press LLC

Published in 2020 by Anamcara Press LLC
Author © 2020 by Leonard Krishtalka
Book design by Maureen Carroll
Caslon Pro and Octin Vintage, Lucinda Sans Unicode.

Printed in the United States of America.

Book Description: New Hard-Boiled Detective Series Uncovers Bones, Bodies and Murder. Paleontologist turned private investigator, Harry Przewalski, excavates the dirty underbelly of people's lives, unearthing sexual betrayals, treachery, fraud and murder buried beneath the science of petrified shards, skin and bones. Ultimately, he must face a brutal killing in his own past, when he fled to a desert war and came back with a gun and a license to detect.

ANAMCARA PRESS LLC
P.O. Box 442072, Lawrence, KS 66044
https://anamcara-press.com/

Ordering Information:
Quantity sales. Special discounts are available on quantity purchases by corporations, associations, and others. For details, contact the publisher at the address above.
Orders by U.S. trade bookstores and wholesalers. Please contact Ingram Distribution.

Publisher's Cataloging-in-Publication data
Krishtalka, Leonard, Author
The Camel Driver / Leonard Krishtalka

ISBN-13: 978-1-941237-43-4 eBook
ISBN-13: 978-1-941237-42-7 hardback
ISBN-13: 978-1-941237-32-8 paperback

[1. FIC022060 FICTION / Mystery & Detective / Historical.
2. FIC022010 FICTION / Mystery & Detective / Hard-Boiled..
3. FIC022090 FICTION / Mystery & Detective / Private Investigators]

Library of Congress Control Number: 2020933939

BOOK ONE

THE TAXIDERMIST

1

Pittsburgh, Saturday, December 11, 3 AM

The museum guard lay on the splinters of glass, face down, one eye open, staring at the camel's hooves. Blood burbled from a small cut on his throat, a rivulet of red trickling onto the fine desert sand. His body was half in the desert, half on the cold marble floor. A small pool of urine crept down his black pants, pooling at his shoes.

On the sand, a Barbary lioness lay dead beneath the camel. The rifle that killed her, a one-ball flintlock, rested across her hindquarters, spent. Her attack had been camouflaged, a low, yellow dune ferociously come to life. She had sprung on them from the front, an Arab courier astride his dromedary, crossing the Tunisian desert in the sulfurous heat of midday. Until that moment the courier had been comfortably cool in his burnoose, the long, loose, black-hooded cloak, and the red Berber headdress under the hood. Until that moment his rifle had been lashed to the saddle, and his jambiya, the dagger with the sharply curved blade and enameled handle, sheathed under his burnoose.

The lioness had hurtled herself toward the camel's neck. The courier pulled back on the reins, fighting to control the camel's frenzied bucking. He fumbled for the rifle, raised it to the lioness' head and shot her through the skull. Almost immediately, her mate, a powerful male with a massive mane, leapt on them from the side. He sank his front claws into the camel's hump and shoulder and anchored his right hind leg into the camel's shinbone, until he hung there, slowly pulling them down. The camel bellowed, lips splayed back in pain. His legs began to buckle.

Frantic, the courier drew the dagger from under his burnoose and plunged the steel blade toward the lion's neck. With an immense roar, the lion lunged up at the courier, jaws agape, his massive carnassial teeth about to rip off the courier's arm.

The assailant calmly took a box cutter, needle and thread from a duffle bag, knelt in the sand under the camel, made a small, careful slit with the box cutter along the sewn seam of the belly, removed the straw stuffing from the cavity, reached in, and carefully extracted a small bundle wrapped in a brown-stained cloth. It shed bits of fiber and flesh onto the straw and sand. As the assailant threaded the needle, a siren wailed in the distance. Police.

The assailant slipped the box cutter, needle, thread and bundle into the duffle and carried it away.

2

Paris, 1864
6 Rue de Montmartre

Verreaux's journal

By the time I was eleven, my father had taught me to cut through skin and blood and bone. I smelled them in my bed at night, acrid yet somehow sweet, like the devil's bouquet. The knotted floorboards in my bedroom were good at carrying weight. But the gaseous odor defeated them, diffusing from dismembered carcasses below through the wood and into our rooms. It was as if the beasts were anaesthetizing our sleep, embalming our dreams.

We lived above Maison Verreaux. In the workshop below my bed were the animal cadavers, saws, straw, scalpels, knives, dissection pans, wire frames, and apothecary jars with turpentine, alum, sulfur, and arsenical soap. Along the front of the maison, the long, curved panoramic window looked out onto Rue Montmartre. I would crouch behind the glass in the jungle foliage by the leopard, or under the lion in the desert, or in the savannah between the crocodile and hyena. I would squat in the midst of our zoological theater, still, stiff, in rigor mortis. Like the skulls, bleached white, their teeth and empty eye sockets staring out from the horrors of death. I lived amid the stuffed animals, the bluebirds, warblers, finches, cranes, gulls, eagles, flamingos, herons, a penguin, a bird of paradise, a crocodile, hedgehogs, hares, zebras, wildebeest, giraffe, monkeys, kudu, gerenuk, gazelle, tigers, an elephant, a whale, a hippopotamus, all staring out onto Montmartre. And I sat at the feet of the jungle savage, beside the end of his spear. All who passed on the street would gawk at the taxidermied boy who blinked.

I, Jules Verreaux, lived here with my brothers, Édouard and Alexis. Both were younger. My father, Jacques Philippe, started Maison Verreaux seven years before I was born. He was the finest taxidermist in France, people said, perhaps in all of Europe.

For me and for him, it began with the fifty birds—solving the plague of taxidermy. No sooner would a bear or heron be mounted, then the insect pests would devour it, ravaging the fur and feathers in tiny unseemly patches until the poor animal died a second death.

I helped him with the birds. I was seven years old when he took me into the woods, armed me with a potato sack, and shot fifty birds, one after another, boom, boom, boom. The deafening sound ricocheted from tree to tree, shaking the birds from their perch.

As each bird fluttered to the ground, I ran into the underbrush, retrieved the little body, and put it in the sack. I remember how the birds would float down, not fall, as if they were descending to heaven. How life ebbed out of the little red and brown and green bodies in my hand. And how the sack with the birds was warm against my skin.

Fifty birds were heavy. My father carried them out of the woods straight to the workshop in our maison. We laid them carefully on the long wooden table and skinned them out. It wasn't difficult. He showed me how to separate the feathers, slit the belly open along the midline of skin, eviscerate the organs and bones, stuff the cavity with fine cotton, and sew it up so that the soft underdown hid the incision. My first bird was badly misshapen. The second had unsightly lumps. The third, more symmetrical, somehow lacked the grace of life. The fourth was flawless, resting motionless for a moment before taking flight.

My father arranged the fifty birds, now embodied with cotton, in two rows, neatly, orderly, side by side, their heads flopping over to the right, a tiny, colorful corps de ballet, feet frozen in the first position, turned out, en pointe. He was meticulous in his life, as if every action had a predestined perfection. To my mother it was a mania so unbearable that she abandoned the kitchen and never descended the rear staircase to the taxidermy workshop. It was not that she minded cooking or seeing the animal bodies. It was my father's exactitude. To him, kitchen and workshop were chemical laboratories that demanded unwavering precision. To him, creativity was formula.

I counted out fifty paper tags, numbered them, and tied one around the right foot of each bird. My father lined up fifty glass beakers beside the birds, each with a different chemical potion. Magically, it seemed to me, the brown bird refracted to a liquid yellow through the translucent glass, and the yellow bird to a trembling green, and the green bird to a convulsive blue. The chemical fumes were pungent. They burned my eyes and made me tear. I turned away so that my father wouldn't notice. I didn't want him to think I was pitying the dead birds, which I was not.

He brushed each bird with its test chemical potion. Then we placed them outside on the ground, daring the beetle pests to attack the fifty skins. During the following weeks, my father painstakingly recorded the results. He had four leather notebooks. One for the experiments. One for the finances of Maison Verreaux. One to catalogue the plants and animals that our expeditions were bringing back from southern Africa and Asia—their genus, their species, their locality, the date they were shot. And one notebook to record their ultimate destination: the head of the white Oryx, sold to Baron LeGaré for a wall in his chateaux; the head and pelt of the Indian tiger for a rug on the cold stone floor beside Mdm. LeGaré's bed; the kudu and the leopard from Kenya, fully mounted, purchased by the Muséum National d'Histoire Naturelle for an exhibit; the plants, pressed and dried, sold to the Muséum des Plantes for its systematic herbarium collections.

My father was pleased with his test of the birds. Five of the fifty chemical potions appeared to ward off the beetles, though weakly: camphor, ground arsenic, soap, potassium carbonate, and powdered calcium hydroxide. So, he combined the five chemicals into a new compound—arsenical soap. It proved potent. When rubbed on the skin of a taxidermied mammal or bird, it shielded the body against insect infestation.

Word spread. Mounts from Maison Verreaux would last forever. Hunters brought their trophies. Zoologists—the great Georges Cuvier himself—brought their collections. Museums placed orders for specific wild animals to be hunted down on our expeditions and prepared for their tableaux, their dioramic exhibits. Competing taxidermy concerns went bankrupt. Maison Verreaux became the pre-eminent natural history emporium of Europe and America. My father made me swear to keep the formula a secret. I did.

When I finished preparing that fourth bird, my father looked at me and said that I, Jules Pierre, was a magician. I knew. I knew I could take a life, then wrest it back from the dead. I could give immortality. Especially then, at the age of seven, when life and death were fairy-tale forms of being. And later in the Cape, when I skinned the savage from Betchuana, I knew I could resurrect the skin, the face, the body, even the soul, until it seemed that in his black skin, he could stalk the baboon in the pitch of night, frighten the springbok into flight across the veldt, elude the python dropping from the tree, and provoke the grass owl to screech at the moon.

When I inherited Maison Verreaux as the eldest son, I continued using my father's ledgers. I remember the final entry: A dromedary camel, two Barbary lions, male and female, and the skin, skull and skeleton of a Berber tribesman, all from North Africa. I placed them in the most thrilling theater the world had ever seen: "Arab Courier Attacked by Lions." I entered it in the 1867 Exposition Universelle in Paris. It won Le Grand Prix d'Or, the Gold Medal.

3

Pittsburgh, January 19

Still taste like an ashtray, Przewalski?"

Harry groaned into the phone. "No one's complained, Liza." He coughed, then added, "okay, truth is, last kiss I had was yours. No one else has been tasting."

"The offer still stands, detective," Liza chuckled.

Harry hadn't forgotten her offer. It was their first evening a few years ago, the day he took on the Marchand case at the Carnegie Museum of Natural History. She was assistant to the director. They'd had dinner, driven slowly along the Monongahela to his house on Orkney Street on the South Side, then listened to Coleman Hawkins seduce the night air over coffee and scotch. He rolled a Drum, lit it, and pulled her to him. She bit his lips, kissing him deeply, viciously.

Abruptly, she rose from the couch, kicked off her heels, peeled off her skirt, blouse and bra, and faced him, front on, a long, lithesome five-eleven. She put one hand on her naked hip, another on her breast and licked her lips. "Until you quit smoking those cancer sticks, this is what you're missing."

Then, nonchalantly, she slipped her clothes back on, kissed him on the cheek, and skipped down the narrow stairs and out the door into the night. Harry grimaced at the memory. And at the can of Drum tobacco sitting on his office desk.

They'd kept seeing one another, prospecting the terrain ahead, mapping their contours of intimacy. Dinners, spur of the moment. Long walks by the river. A few Pirates games. The pro bike race up Mount Washington. Pittsburgh opera. They arrived and left separately, she in her red Jeep, he in the yellow Corolla rustbox. There were no nocturnal retreats to his walkup on Orkney Street, or her loft in Shadyside. It was deliberate, this stepping back from an erotic threshold so easy to cross. They'd sensed the emotional promise, wary of losing it to nonchalance.

She'd told him that none of her relationships had proved to be preferable to solitude. He understood. We keep looking for that holy trinity of fulfillment, he'd told her. The physical, the emotional, the intellectual. But the odds were low. Most people got one out of three. Some, maybe, got two. Sure, there were substitutes—books and such for the intellectual; porn and such for sex. But there was no stand-in for the emotional. Except liquor, for those driven to drink. And religion, for those driven to believe. Maybe that's why religion was so pervasive.

"What's the punch line, Harry," she'd asked.

"You are," he'd told her. "Somehow I don't see you hurrying off to the local meeting of the Unitarians."

She'd laughed.

A barge on the Monongahela River outside his office window sounded two sharp, baritone bursts. It shook Harry out of his reverie.

"You sound good, Liza. But the detective in me says this isn't a smoke-out phone call."

"No, Harry, it's not. It's a formal request. President Stewart and Director Mayer are meeting with the Pittsburgh police this afternoon at the museum. Detective John Mazeroski—you know him. He asked that you be here. One-thirty. Apologies for the short notice." She dropped the formalities. "Say yes, Przewalski."

"What's this about, Liza?"

"Harry!" She sounded surprised. "Read the newspaper lately?"

"Hold the sarcasm. Yeah, I read the paper. The last time the Carnegie made the *Post-Gazette* was about a month ago. Someone threw a brick through the camel driver exhibit. That's too smash-and-grab for Mazeroski."

"Apparently it's more than a smash-and-grab. Mazeroski told Mayer and Stewart that it has become complicated. Anyway, punch the Arab sensitivity button. It's not the 'camel driver exhibit.' It's officially, *Arab Courier Attacked by Lions.*"

"What're the complications?"

Liza sighed. "Show up Przewalski. Then come tell me about it. Better yet, tell me over dinner tonight." She hung up.

He'd done the Marchand case for the Carnegie a few years back, but he avoided the place. It made him feel like a chimera, in the dioramas peering out, in the galleries peering in, a visitor to his own life. He'd spent good years there among the cabinets of fossils in the backrooms of the museum, detecting the stories petrified in the bones of extinct beasts. None of it mattered after Nicole.

If Liza knew about it, she never said. Nicole's murder had been splashed across the *Post-Gazette* and the television news: patient cages his social worker in a rural barn north of Pittsburgh; rapes her, tortures her, butchers her body; stuffs the parts into a rusting fifty-gallon drum. Harry's name had appeared twice in the paper, as Nicole's friend, and as a doctoral student in paleontology at the museum. It would have appeared a third time, but Harry just missed killing the psycho. The Pittsburgh cops—Mazeroski—got there first.

By the time of the trial, Harry had fled to the violent solitude of a desert war. It was not cathartic. It never answered Job's lament: why me, why her, why now. He came back with a gun and got a PI license to execute meaning in venality. He didn't return to his desk at the museum, to detect the intrigues petrified in bones and teeth. Now the intrigues were fresh, the raw, messy entrails of their moral dilemmas just beginning to rot. He'd kept his service gun. He might have to do something as a PI that he hadn't done in the war: kill.

Another barge hooted on the river, a long, sonorous tone muted by the gray mist. He stood at the window and looked out through the layers of grime. His office was on the fourth floor of an extinct steel mill on South Carson Street, above the old furnace, long cold, rusting to red metal dirt along the banks of the Monongahela.

Across the river, the blue glass of the PPG building hung in a dirty rime over Pittsburgh's downtown triangle, a peninsula of concrete between the Mon and the Allegheny. Snow was falling on the water. The wet flakes merged into chunks, hit the murky currents, and perished into the Ohio.

4

Pittsburgh, January 19

"Somebody sewed a child up in the camel's belly." Detective John Mazeroski took a toothpick out of his pocket and looked around Stewart's office for the reaction.

"WHAT?" gasped Samantha Mayer, thrusting her body forward, her face ashen. "That's impossible!"

Preston Stewart, President of the Carnegie Institute, kept the stony composure expected of CEOs, an impassiveness groomed gray by aristocratic entitlements and moneyed gravitas. He leaned back in the upholstered red-leather chair behind his desk and propped two fingers against his temple. On Stewart, Harry thought, it looked like a desperate impersonation of a thinker.

"Okay, this is why I wanted you here, Przewalski. Lemme tell you what you don't know, but these folks do." Mazeroski nodded at Mayer and Stewart. He was in his late fifties, fleshy and balding. He had long tired of his name being engraved in Pittsburgh lore. In the 1960 World Series, game seven, bottom of the ninth, score tied 9-9, Pirates second baseman, Bill Mazeroski, smacked the second pitch from New York Yankees hurler Ralph Terry over the left field wall of Forbes Field, winning the series.

"A month and a half ago, December 6th, about three in the morning, someone smashed the front glass panel of that camel driver exhibit, at the back of the first—"

"Detective," Stewart interrupted. "The exhibit, formally, is called *Arab Courier Attacked by Lions*. We would appreciate it if you referred to the exhibit by its official name. Our communities in Pittsburgh expect us to be culturally respectful of their traditions. Referring to Arabs as camel drivers can be interpreted as demeaning."

Harry half expected Mazeroski to tell Stewart to "go piss up a rope." A few years ago, during the Marchand business, Mazeroski had told Stewart to do just that in the basement of the museum. Now, he put the toothpick in his mouth and managed to restrain himself.

"Okay, the night guard was doing his rounds and heard the perp break the glass—"

"The what?" Stewart broke in again. "Perp?"

Mazeroski nodded, maintaining his patience. "Perp … perpetrator." He wiggled the toothpick with his teeth and waited, staring Stewart into submission.

"The night guard probably surprised him. He bopped the guard on the head with some instrument. Probably the same one he used to smash the glass. Probably a hammer. We haven't recovered it. The guard fell into the exhibit case. He cut his throat on the glass. Lucky, he didn't die. Just a concussion and a bad gash. The perp knelt into the case—there were knee imprints in the sand. Then he slit open the camel's belly. Back to front if he was right-handed."

Mazeroski grabbed a ballpoint pen from his shirt pocket, took the cap off, and dragged it slowly through the air, nib up, as if he were slicing the underside of a cadaver levitating in front of him. Mayer buried her hands in her thicket of white hair.

Mazeroski waved the pen. "He used a sharp blade. Probably a box cutter. We haven't recovered it. Then he pulled the stuffing out. Old straw."

Mazeroski eyed Harry. "Okay, Przewalski, now you're caught up. And now it gets interesting. The perp pulled something besides straw out of the camel's belly. We think it was wrapped in a rough, linen cloth. Likely old and frayed. We found bits of the cloth lying in the straw. Whatever was wrapped in the linen cloth was also coming apart. We found bits of hair, plant fibers … and skin. Maybe the tips of fingers. DNA says it's human. Female. Size says a baby, or small child. Maybe mummified. The flesh—"

Mayer suddenly bolted from her chair, hand over her mouth, and ran into the bathroom off Stewart's office. They heard retching, the toilet flush, and the splash of water into the sink. Before being appointed director, Mayer had been the museum's curator of mammals, leading expeditions into Peru to census its rich bestiary of rodents, bats, marsupials, monkeys, tapirs and other denizens of the Amazonian rain forest. She'd trapped and killed thousands of animals, sliced open their bellies, eviscerated their bones and guts, snipped bits of their heart, muscle and liver into tiny alcohol tubes for genetic sequencing, stuffed the skins with cotton, and sewed up the incision. Apparently, Harry thought, that had not prepared her for human taxidermy.

Mayer returned, her face drained, her hair spidering out like electrified wire. "Sorry," she sighed. "It's been hard. First this. Then Anna."

"Anna?" Harry looked at her, questioningly.

Mayer's shoulders sagged. "Anna Storck. Our physical anthropologist. Tragic. She committed suicide. It was two days after the vandalism." She looked at Mazeroski for confirmation. He nodded.

Stewart paid her no attention. "Go on, detective."

"That's about it, Stewart," Mazeroski shrugged, moving the toothpick from one side of his mouth to the other.

Stewart flinched. He was used to being addressed as 'President'.

"The perp," Mazeroski continued, "walked off with whatever shed the bits of cloth and skin. We're guessing a mummified kid wrapped in a bundle. It's taken a month for the lab work to come back—the DNA and the strands of cloth. We've told them to do more testing. The hair, the plant fibers. Anyway, if we're right, we're stumped! Hell, if we're wrong, we're stumped!"

"What do you mean?" Stewart asked.

"What we mean is," Mazeroski declared, raising his arms, "what's a mummified kid doing in the goddamn belly of a camel that was stuffed over there in France over a hundred years ago for a camel driver diorama—"

"It's Arab Cour—" Stewart began to interject.

"Okay, forget it, Stewart," Mazeroski said, his voice calm, stern, as if he were instructing a child. "Between us here, it's the camel driver exhibit. To Pittsburghers, it's the camel driver exhibit. Always has been. Always will be. Live with it. Y'know, it's like trying to undo time. Way too late for me. Anyway, there's no insult here. Save the politics for real issues. Us cops have to, every day."

He took the toothpick out of his mouth, examined it, and put it in his shirt pocket, somewhat embarrassed at having exposed a philosophical side.

Stewart reddened, sat up, and cleared his throat. "I'll be speaking with the police commissioner."

"Okay, you do that." Mazeroski wasn't worried. He was a couple of years from retirement. "I briefed the commissioner this morning. He says the Pittsburgh police don't have the time or people to track this camel driver business back a century and a half to some French outfit. That's why I wanted Przewalski here. Anyway, there's no evidence of a crime. Who knows how that stuff got into that camel back then? If there was a mummified kid bundled up in there, chances are it died a natural death. Kids died like flies then in France. Plague. Typhoid fever. Common flu. Maybe it was the taxidermist's own kid, preserved and touring the world. In body, anyway. Maybe in soul, if the spirit's all it's cracked up to be. If I was the father, I'd do that. Better than putting the kid in the ground."

Stewart resumed his imitation of a thinker, immune to Mazeroski's detour into the sensibilities of a corpse on a world trek. "Does that mean the police won't investigate the matter?"

"Right," Mazeroski nodded. "We don't care about that. Like I said, that's why Przewalski's here. If you care about that, hire him. But someone assaulted one of your guards. And that same someone vandalized one of your museum exhibits. Those are crimes. And we care about that."

Mazeroski stood up, shuffling his feet in the puddle of slush around his boots, as if he could make it disappear into the green and red flecked marble floor.

"We'll do our business. We'll nail the bozo who whacked the guard, bust into the exhibit, and snatched whatever bundle was inside the camel. If it was a bundle. You hire Przewalski here to work the French end. We'll work this end. When we meet, he might have the motive. And we should have the perp."

"Any feelers on the guy?" Harry asked. "ID by the guard? Can't be too many possibilities. Either someone from the inside—an employee. Or someone who hid out in the museum after closing."

Mazeroski chuckled. "Good to see your brain can still earn a living, Przewalski."

Mayer broke in. "We were pretty crowded that week. Pitt and the Museum hosted the annual meeting of the American Association of Physical Anthropologists. We had seven hundred of them here. Mostly in the archaeological collections. And in the lecture hall during the sessions. Some in the galleries."

"The same week Storck ..." Harry asked, gently.

"Yes," Mayer half mumbled. "So tragic. We organized a quick commemorative session ... her students ... colleagues."

Harry changed the subject. "The camel driver exhibit. Anything special about it?"

Mayer shook her head. "No. Nothing we know of. At least nothing that would invite this vandalism. It was created for the 1867 Paris exposition by a taxidermist and naturalist, Jules Verreaux. He worked in the Paris museum. It won the gold medal. I asked Liza to check our archives for any information on the exhibit. And to dig up everything she could find about Verreaux. She'll brief you, Harry."

Harry nodded, guardedly. Mixing business with personal was unsanitary, he thought, exposing both to infection. They were best kept quarantined. With Liza he preferred the personal.

"What about the DNA?" he asked Mazeroski. "Race or ethnicity on the kid?"

Mazeroski shook his head. "Negative. At least not yet. We should have more details in a few weeks. From the FBI lab. They told us they need to run alignments, whatever that means."

"It means," Mayer said, some color returning to her face, "they're comparing the DNA run to standard human types, such as they are. Marker genes. Or different proportions of genes. They might point to a racial or ethnic group."

Stewart's chair creaked as he leaned back, impatient with the science.

"Not likely here," Harry noted.

"Right," Mayer agreed. "Genetics of race works best for peoples that haven't interbred much. Like indigenous peoples. Or extinct ones, like Neanderthals. DNA from Neanderthal bones was just sequenced. Turns out that Europeans are part Neanderthal." She looked pointedly around the room. "As are each one of us. We're carrying about three percent of their genes. Neanderthals might have been a separate species, but when we met up with them around fifty or sixty thousand years ago in Europe, we mated with them. Then they became extinct. So far, DNA says that our females slept with their males."

Stewart shuddered at the thought of cohabiting with a Neanderthal. He stood up, clearly exasperated. "This science is all well and good. But, Detective Mazeroski, I hope I can count on you and the police department to keep your findings and conjectures confidential. We expect the story to the press to continue being a simple act of senseless vandalism. Meanwhile, we will have Przewalski here look into this camel business ... the bundle ... whatever. I will confirm this with the police commissioner when I speak with him."

Mazeroski grabbed his blue police parka from the coat rack in Stewart's office. "Yeah, okay, do that. Until Przewalski turns up something worth telling, there isn't any story." He yanked a pair of heavy gloves from the pockets of his parka and tromped out.

Stewart turned to Harry. "I don't need to impress upon you too the importance of discretion in this matter. We have just invested tens of thousands of dollars in promoting *Arab Courier Attacked by Lions* as one of America's cultural treasures, on par with the skeletons in Dinosaur Hall. We are about to launch an entire series of products based on the image—towels, shower curtains, fruit bowls. Even a snow globe ... actually a sand globe."

He tightened his jaw, leaned forward, and put his hands on his desk, knuckles down. "If word gets out of a mummified baby moldering for 150 years in the camel's belly, this Institute will become a circus, a monstrosity. I will not have one of the museum's most respected and venerable exhibits turned into a … a … fr … a freak show!"

Stewart folded his arms across his chest, quickly checked the placement of the square gold cuff links on his shirt, and turned to Mayer. "Sam, we will do as the police say. They will investigate the vandalism. Przewalski will investigate the meaning of this … this … confounded bundle."

It was an order. He'd been raised on one of the estates near the Rolling Rock Club north of Pittsburgh with the blue-blood branding of class, privilege and the expectation of obedience. He sat down at his desk and pulled a file from his credenza.

"I'll think it over," Harry said, guardedly. "You might not like what I find. A dirty business, taxidermy. Not much cultural respect. Graves robbed. Bodies stolen and sold. People murdered. Humans stuffed."

Stewart's face twitched. "I can deal with it." He went back to his papers.

5

Pittsburgh, January 19

Mazeroski was waiting for him in the Carriage Drive entrance to the Carnegie Institute. The half-circle driveway off Forbes Avenue was a vestige from when wealthy patrons would arrive in their horse-drawn buggies. Harry had parked his Toyota rust bucket there illegally, behind Mazeroski's police cruiser. A white parking ticket was iced to the Toyota's windshield. Mazeroski saw it, stomped over through the snow, ripped it off, and stuffed it in his pocket.

"Okay, Przewalski, this won't happen often. I'm gonna save you the ninety bucks." He waved at Stewart's office window. "It's just that I don't want the city to feed off that arrogant sonofabitch. Anyway, stop in downtown. I didn't mention it in there, but the perp could'a been female. We found some longish hair in the exhibit case. Hell, could'a been you, Przewalski, with your mop."

"Very funny. The suicide. Storck. Any connection?"

"Nah," Mazeroski said, dismissively. "That would be too easy. Just lousy timing. Coincidence." He wiped a swath of snow with his big glove from the windshield and climbed into the cruiser.

Harry grabbed the door before Mazeroski could close it. "Yeah, well, in our business coincidence could be a fact just waiting for an equation."

"Congratulations, Przewalski. You just reminded me you got an education. Listen, you want a connection? Storck did it in style. First thing in the morning, she's drinking her coffee, she walks out of her office to the third floor gallery and dives over the railing into the open atrium. Almost hit the camel driver case on the first floor. Landed on the marble just in front of it. There's your connection."

"Didn't see anything in the paper."

"No, you didn't. Museum kept it quiet. A museum anthropologist going splat in an exhibit gallery is a downer for the paying public. That, Przewalski, is an economic fact just waiting for an equation."

He slammed the door, started his beater bar flashing, and fishtailed the cruiser through the deep slurry into the traffic on Forbes.

Harry scraped the ice and snow from the windshield and climbed into the Corolla. The engine was cold. It coughed, then stalled. The muffler belched a small cloud of blue-black smoke that vaporized in the slush. Some of the exhaust began diffusing into the car through a heater vent. Harry rolled a window down and aired his lungs.

Four maintenance men in black boots, gray parkas, and mitts came out of the Institute. For a moment Harry thought they were going to pick up the Toyota, carry it off Carriage Drive, and dump it onto Forbes Avenue. Instead, they picked up brooms and began brushing the snow off the four massive bronze statues arrayed along the front of the Institute: Galileo, Michelangelo, Bach, Shakespeare—Andrew Carnegie's noble quartet, his archetypes of Science, Art, Music, Literature. Each one sat in an oversized, bronze, upholstered armchair. Bach and Shakespeare flanked the massive doors to the Music Hall, Galileo and Michelangelo the entrance to the Natural History Museum.

Bach wore a ruffled blouse, a jacket, and a drape over his legs. He was studying a piece of sheet music, inventing endless variations on the same fugue. Shakespeare sported a long coat over a high-collared shirt and thick boots. He was reading a huge tome, material for his next play on the perfidy of princes. Michelangelo, in boots, vest, and shirt, had rolled up his sleeves, ready to sculpt, wedging a chisel into his unfinished masterpiece, the Dying Slave. The marble original was in the Louvre. Galileo, in frock coat and sandals, was taking a compass measurement on a globe of the Earth. He seemed to be brooding on the mathematical music of the heavens, two fingers pressed in thought against his temple. That's where Stewart had picked up the pose, Harry thought.

Harry turned off the engine, got out of the car, bounded up the snow-covered steps between Galileo and Michelangelo into the marbled foyer of the museum, and stepped through a pair of tall, mahogany doors into the main office. Liza was behind her desk. She looked up, registered surprise, then smiled at him—tight white teeth, hair still short, almost punk, blonde replacing auburn.

"Harry!" She quickly looked around the office to make sure they were alone. "I was hoping you would stop in before this evening."

Harry winked and pointed to a manila file folder on her desk labeled VERREAUX. "Is that on the menu? Samantha Mayer said she unleashed you on this guy. And his camel driver."

"Yes," Liza said, putting on a pair of red-framed, round bookish glasses. She held up the folder and waved it at him. "Romantic dinner conversation."

Harry frowned. "Seven-thirty? Le Pommier?"

"Perfect. It's French, like Verreaux. We haven't been back there since our inaugural evening, Harry."

"I like reruns. With new endings. Don't like being a prisoner of history. I cranked my office window open, let the snow blow in, and tossed out the can of Drum. True confession. It's rolling around with the other litter at the edge of the Monongahela."

Liza nodded, approvingly. "Some vagrant will pick it up. They'll think that Dutch tobacco falls from heaven, like manna. I bet that's how most mythology got started."

Harry liked her wit. "I'll pick you up. But I can't change all history. You get to ride in the yellow Toyota shit box again. It's sitting out there in Carriage Drive. Has a bit more rust. Won't start in the cold without a few rehearsals. And there's a smell coming from the heater that isn't Dior."

She laughed. "Forget it. I'll take the Jeep and meet you there. It's got Dior's Poison Girl pumping out of the defrost vent."

Harry circled the grand staircase in the museum's opulent foyer on his way out. Carnegie had it built as a palace of culture, knowledge enclosed by massive blocks of Grecian marble, each slashed with streaks of geologic red and green and white, glinting flecks of gold. Large, heroic murals on the walls romanticized Pittsburgh at work in the early 1900s: coal-laden trains chugged steam along the rivers; steel mills belched an innocent smoke; workers muscled iron in the foundries. This was Carnegie's manifest industrial destiny, his 'Gospel of Wealth' rendered incarnate and in color. Hard manual labor made wealth. And wealth made culture and the cultured. Missing, Harry thought, were the street lamps burning at midday, the dirty yellow light, and the thick soot-suspended air blocking out the sun. The murals, the art, were illusion, layers of paint perjuring the coke-smudged lungs and souls of a blackened city.

The Toyota had another $90 ticket on the windshield. He'd charge it to Stewart. Harry engaged the clutch, turned the key in the ignition, and floored the accelerator. The Toyota shuddered to life. He spun the tires in the dirty wet snow, coating the rear window with brown muck, and slid slowly onto Forbes Avenue.

6

Pittsburgh
January 19

Here's to Jules Verreaux, a real son-of-a-bitch." Liza Kole picked up her glass of wine and clinked Harry's.

He'd waited on the sidewalk in front of the restaurant on the South Side. She drove up in her red Jeep Cherokee, pulled in two cars behind his Corolla on the other side of West Carson Street, swung her long legs out, hopped over a puddle, and strode purposefully across the gray-slushed road, hips swinging under her long black wool coat.

He helped her slide it off her shoulders in the restaurant, and had the sudden urge to nuzzle the back of her neck, a long sinuous line below the short blond cut. Instead, he just touched the warm skin above her black velvet choker, pretending to adjust it. She quickly glanced at him with friendly suspicion. Her puffy chartreuse blouse was tucked into black slacks, which were tucked into deep purple boots, Cossack style. Very Slavic. She was a Kolacevic from Eastern Europe, chopped down to Kole by her parents. Immigrant surnames evolved like genes, Harry thought, the individual letters mutated, shuffled and lopped until they became new species fit for the new linguistic terrain. For Harry's father, Przewalski was immutable.

They sat at a table by a window. She nodded at the simple, rustic, white lace curtains adorned with doves. "Verreaux was a bird man." She handed him a folder of papers. "There's not much on him out there. Mostly his scientific articles describing lots of new species. And almost nothing on the camel driver exhibit. We've owned it since 1899. Carnegie bought it for fifty bucks from the American Museum of Natural History, who had bought it from a dealer, who had bought it from Verreaux after the 1867 Paris exposition. It had won the gold prize. We're not sure when Verreaux put it together. Likely in the early 1860s. Notes in the archives indicate that the two lions, the camel, and the Berber clothing came from a Verreaux expedition to the Sahara, likely Tunisia. Maybe the Berber himself!"

"You mean his body," Harry prompted, suspecting the answer. He browsed through the folder—copies of old newspaper clippings, a couple of Verreaux obituaries from ornithological journals; a short bio from the national museum in Paris; a few articles on an exhibit called 'El Negro' from the University of Botswana.

"Right," Liza said, emphatically. "It's likely he robbed a grave for the Berber, and used the guy's skin, skull and limb bones for the mount. Listen, he had practice. He started young. He was born in Paris in 1807. He was eleven when his uncle took him on his first expedition to South Africa in 1818 to make collections. He was already a taxidermist, trained by his father.

She reached for the folder and took out a yellowed piece of newsprint. "This is from a French newspaper. They returned to Paris in 1821 with a whopping 131,405 animals and plants—288 mammals, including a whale; 2,205 birds; 322 reptiles; 265 fish; 3,875 shellfish." Liza looked up from the newspaper, her face soured. "Also, two dozen skulls and skeletons of Hottentots, Namaquas and Bushmen that uncle and nephew Verreaux ransacked from old Cape Town cemeteries. Imagine! He's only fourteen!"

"Yeah," Harry nodded, "inhumanity came young those days. Nowadays too, in some places."

Liza grimaced, and slipped the newspaper article back into the folder. "Anyway, here's what we know. Verreaux had two younger brothers, Édouard and Alexis. They worked for the family business in Paris, Maison Verreaux. At the time it was the largest natural history emporium in the world. Expeditions to Africa, Australia and Indochina. They brought back hundreds of thousands of animals and plants. Sold them to museums and private collectors. Carnegie Museum has quite a few Verreaux birds in its collection. So does the Smithsonian. But most are in the museum in Paris. He worked there off and on till the 1860s ... instructor, taxidermist."

"The Muséum National d'Histoire Naturelle."

"Oui," Liza joked, admiringly. "Your accent is good."

"Thank my father," Harry quipped. "He told me to take either French or Italian. So that I could read the original articles about the great cyclists. Coppi, Hinault, Bartali, Merckx. I chose French. He'd quiz me on the French towns and cols—the climbs in the Alps and Pyrenees. Alpe d'Huez. Le Galibier. Le Tourmalet. Then he'd reminisce."

Liza put her wine down, and raised her eyebrows. "Your father was a bike racer? In Europe?"

"Yes." In his mind he still is, Harry thought. "He rode with Eddy Merckx—wanted to name me after him. He has a bike shop in East Liberty. *Velo Europa*. He imports classic old bikes and refurbishes them. He's old guard. He hasn't emigrated from the past."

"That's pretty judgmental, Harry. Maybe that's where he's most comfortable. What about your mother?"

"Art historian." Harry paused. "Now she's in her own history. In a nursing home, on the other side of dementia."

Liza clasped his hand. "I'm sorry, Harry. I ... I can't imagine what it's like."

"Nor should you." Harry moved a wisp of blond hair off her forehead. Every visit, he thought, is like watching a metronome slow its swing, gradually, imperceptibly, through the friction of a dense cognitive fog, until it stops.

"My father sees her every day. He tells me he can feel her brain erode, slowly, atom by atom, losing its radioactivity, until it won't pulse anymore."

Liza squeezed his hand, then raised her glass. "Here's to your mother, Harry. And your father. I'd like to meet him, see the bike shop. Hey, maybe get one of his classics. I hear it's easier on the knees than running."

Harry imagined her long legs loping down the road, the rhythmic rocking of her body between the strides. Her face was oddly unsettling, a fluid alchemy of the pure and the impure. It stirred him. Perhaps, he thought, it was what he wanted to see, that camouflaged duality between the chaste and the wanton, drawing the graph of desire.

He leaned across the table to kiss her. She held up her finger. "Not yet. Impulse is good. Anticipation is better. Anyway, this is Pittsburgh, not Paris." She nodded at two young couples sitting at a nearby table with their heads bowed.

Harry grinned at her and raised his glass. "Yeah, they're praying. Or texting on their cell phones. Either way, they're sending messages into the cloud—and expecting an answer." Harry motioned to the folder. "What's the El Negro business?"

Liza frowned. "Here's where the son-of-a-bitch comes in. Jules returns to Cape Town alone in 1825 to make more collections for Maison Verreaux. He's eighteen. His brother, Édouard, joins him about four years later, around 1829. On one of their expeditions they rob the fresh grave of a Botswanan chieftain, skin him, ship his skin, skull and bones back to Paris, and mount him in a diorama wearing a loin cloth and holding a spear. It was displayed all over France. Then at the Barcelona World's Exposition in 1888. Then in some small museum in Spain. That's El Negro."

Harry shrugged. "Not surprising. Like the human zoos at the world's fairs. In the early 1900s an anthropologist imported six Mbuti pygmies from the Congo for the St. Louis Fair. They were trotted out every day—a living example of a primitive, ape-like stage of human evolution. Hell, anthropology then said it was so. It was born a racist science. After the fair closed, the Bronx Zoo got one of the Mbuti natives, shoved him in a cage with a chimp, and hung up a sign: 'Missing Link.' A lot of folks still think that."

Liza scowled. "Exhibits tell the bigotry of their time, Harry. I also turned this up." She pulled a copy of a newspaper clipping from the folder. "A circus owner bought four Uruguayan natives—

three men, a pregnant woman—took them to Paris in 1833, and paraded them around as an example of a nearly extinct race. They were among the last of the Charrúas. Three months later three of them were dead. Plus a baby daughter born to the woman. Cold. Tuberculosis. The circus owner got the bodies taxidermied, then sold them to Verreaux's Paris museum. They were on display until a few years ago."

"What happened to the baby?"

Liza shrugged. "Don't know. Probably in some basement storeroom in a big glass jar, swimming in alcohol. But, hey, our pal, Verreaux, had nothing to do with this."

Their food arrived on large white plates with silver chargers—lamb chops with mint sauce and roasted potatoes for her, salmon and frites for him. Harry ordered two bottles of Bière de Paris. She picked up a chop by the rib and ripped into it, talking while she chewed.

"Forget manners, Harry. I'm hungry. And I eat, mouth open, so I can talk. Food for itself is boring, no matter how culinary. It needs chatter. Food is conversation's reproductive act."

Harry laughed. He ate a couple of frites. They were soft and undercooked, the equivalent of treason in Belgium.

"About El Negro, Liza, as revenge goes, the motive is pretty thin. It's 180 years after the fact."

Liza tugged at her short hair and shrugged. "Yeah, implausible. But not impossible. Could be a descendent of the Botswanan. They read about the exhibit. Maybe even see it in that museum in Spain. They find out Verreaux did it. They decide to exact retribution on his Camel Driver."

Doesn't jibe with snatching a kid from the belly of the camel, Harry thought. Mayer hadn't told Liza about the bundle. "Okay, anything else on Verreaux?"

"Yeah, a side reference in one of the bios. A woman. Happened in Cape Town around 1827, two years into his stint there. Before his brother Édouard joined him, before the Botswanan business.

"So, he's what? About eighteen or nineteen?"

"Right. Between collecting expeditions, he had a romance with a young Dutch woman, Elisabeth Greef. Turns out he was just trying to get into her fine Dutch underpants. And she let him. He got her pregnant, then abandoned her."

Harry sat up. "What happened? Did she have the baby?"

Liza shrugged. "Presumably. Details are sketchy. I checked for christenings in one of the Cape's paper for those years, the *South African Commercial Advertiser*. Funny name for a newspaper. Anyway, no christenings for Greef or Verreaux."

"Deaths?"

She shook her head. "No, no death notices."

Damn, Harry thought, Mazeroski might have called it. The mummified kid in the Camel Driver could be Verreaux's daughter touring the world. Maybe she was stillborn. Maybe they just wanted to make her disappear. Verreaux would have had to pickle her in alcohol, take her back to France, keep her in a jar for 34 years, then sew her into the belly of a camel he was preparing for the Paris Exposition. It reminded him of the deformed babies swimming in formaldehyde in the old glass tanks in one of the cellars at the Paris museum.

Harry pushed his plate away. He'd lost his appetite. "Anything else?"

"One thing," Liza noted. "The newspaper mentions a trial in the Cape Supreme Court involving Verreaux."

"Oh, yeah?" He tossed his napkin on the table. "What about? Child murder?"

"No. Newspaper only says breach of contract. Could be related to his collecting and taxidermy there. But if you want to find out, the court archives are in Cape Town." She opened the file folder to one of her notes. "On Roeland Street. I checked. It's a long flight. Via Amsterdam. Seven hours over the pond. Then eleven and a half to Cape Town. It's summer there now. I can book it tomorrow."

Harry grunted. "So, Verreaux made enemies when he was a young lad in Cape Town. First a Botswanan body desecrated. Then, maybe, a business deal gone sour. Then a Dutch woman, bedded, impregnated and deserted. And you think the vandalism might be payback."

Liza held up her glass of beer. "Yup, could be. A Greef relative discovers Verreaux was the father—and a deceiving bastard. He does some research, up comes *Arab Courier Attacked by Lions*. Bingo. Payback."

Harry raised his hands. "Hard to believe. Someone six generations down the road decides to get even by desecrating an exhibit Verreaux put together 150 years ago. Grudges are like species. They eventually die off."

"Oh yeah?" Liza raised her voice, animated. "Ever hear of the Balkans, Harry? Or old Marshall Tito? Every fucking Serbian and Croatian slight from the past 1000 years has been archived for revenge."

Harry laughed. "Yeah, okay."

"Listen," Liza blurted, suddenly animated, leaning over the table. "My family came from there. Tito sat on that tribal powder keg for as long he could. But he couldn't live forever. He tried, though. The doctors kept amputating small pieces of him at a time, like running him through a microtome. He stayed in power as long as some piece of flesh kept metabolizing." She sat back and glanced around, as if she were checking the restaurant for Tito's spies.

Harry signaled for the check. "Anna Storck. You guys kept that quiet."

Liza tossed the last rib onto the plate, picked clean. She wiped her hands and swiped the napkin over her lips. "So, they told you about that. We kept it out of the news. Stewart didn't want the publicity. And out of respect for Gideon ... Gideon Gould ... her husband. He's the ornithologist at the museum. He's devastated. They were ... having difficulties. He blames himself."

Harry remembered his own devastation after Nicole. He'd fled to a war. Gould stayed put.

"I talked to him today," Liza continued. "Gould. About Verreaux's birds in our collection. He showed them to me. They come from all over—South Africa, Asia, Australia. He said he's using Verreaux's field notes to try to pinpoint the localities ... where he collected the birds. He wants to see how much the geographic ranges of the birds have changed in the past 150 years, when global warming began to skyrocket. It's called biogeography. Impressed?"

Harry grinned. "Yeah, more than impressed."

"Right answer, Harry. Let's migrate to your place," she said, her voice suddenly husky.

Liza followed him in her Jeep to Orkney Street. The row of walkups had been built for the steelworkers in the early 1900s, three stories high and one room wide—a kitchen off the landing, a living room on the second floor and a bedroom on the third. The two flights of stairs were too narrow to haul up anything large enough for two people. Harry's furniture was bolt-together. Two singles for the bed. Two sectionals for the couch. And a fold-out breakfast table in the kitchen.

"Still living like a grad student, Harry," Liza observed, folding her legs beside him on the couch. "Except for the scotch." She clinked his tumbler of Highland Park. "And the bike." A sleek, carbon black Calfee hung from a hook on the opposite wall. "And the stereo. We should dance."

Buck Clayton was jamming Basie's "Blue and Sentimental," the tenor sax throating through the loneliness of longing.

"It's enough to make any Dutch girl take her underpants off. Or a Slavic girl." She winked at him. "Dance with me, Harry. It's time."

She pulled him off the couch, put his arms around her neck, held him close and tried to nestle her head in the crook of his neck. "Won't work," she whispered, "we're the same height."

"Sure it will," Harry said, pulling her face to his in a long, unruffled kiss as they moved to the sax's melancholy lament. She took his hand and ran the nicotined forefinger slowly under her nose, as if she were sniffing a cigarette hand-rolled from the finest Dutch tobacco. Abruptly, she pushed him back on the couch.

"Watch," she mouthed, silently. Slowly, deliberately, she shook out of her puffy chartreuse blouse, unhooked her light purple bra, let it fall onto the floor, and slipped out of her black slacks.

"Slavic underpants, not Dutch," she whispered. She wiggled out of her panties and stood before him, hands on her hips. "Come take the choker off. Unless you want to play with it."

BOOK TWO

THE TRIAL

7

Cape Town
Monday, January 25

The library tables at the Cape Town Archive were venerable oak trestle affairs, with elegant tongue and groove joints at either end. Harry opened the thick, red, leather-bound ledger. The spine and front cover were embossed, "GREEF v. VERREAUX, Cape Supreme Court, March, 1829." A faint smell wafted up from the pages, earthy, slightly sweet. The transcript of the trial, Harry thought, had captured the words. It had also captured the scents of the people, their sweat, their perfume, that had suffused the courtroom.

The file began with seven exhibits—seven letters, six from Jules, one from Elizabeth. Reading them, Harry felt the suffocation of Victorian manners, the words stiff, stilted, deliberately circuitous. But, there was no suffocating the passions: first, love; then deceit; then hate.

Exhibit No. 1
Letter from Jules Verreaux to Elisabeth Greef,
9 March 1827
[Translated from the Dutch]

Dear Friend

It is with very much sorrow that I have learnt all the disagreeableness and sorrow which you undergo on the account of Margaretha, your sister. As I have heard, it will oblige you to leave your father's house to go with your brother, and his wife into the country. But I hope you will however be so good as to give a friend some information as to your intentions before your leave him. For since he has had the happiness to know you, he has never ceased to love you with a burning affection, and to respect you.

Thus, I hope the more to obtain from you, for it would be a death-blow to me in case this came to pass. I pray you do your best, in case it be possible, that this do not take place. Endeavor to entreat your mother that you may remain in the Cape, that I may have the happiness to convince you of my constancy, once to render myself worthy of you, that I may be the faithful man [also means husband] of whose heart you are the only object which I have chosen.

Remaining forever
Your loving
Jules Verreaux
Cape Town, March 9, 1827

Exhibit No. 2

My dear friend,

I have, from your letter, which I have read with much attention, comprehended your upright and true intention, and as I can perceive your good heart, in every respect, I must declare that I love you from the bottom of my heart, wherein you shall always remain loved, and respected—yes—until death closes my eyes. I pray you then, in God's name, not to go into the country, but I even request of you to grant me the favor to let your dear Father and Mother read this letter, and to beg of them, in my name, to leave you in the Cape, that will do my duty to your Father as an honest Man.

But my dear friend of my soul it is a steadfast truth, that I certainly and truly wish to marry with you and to divide my worldly lot with you, whereupon I give you my heart, and my word. But, according to my circumstances, it may be six, and at the utmost eight months, before I shall be able to fulfill my wish regarding the marriage. However, relying upon your constancy, as you may on mine, we shall continue to see each other as often as possible and remain loving and true.

Wherewith I live and die,

Your true friend,

Jules Verreaux

The 14th March, 1827

Exhibit No. 3

Much loved Friend

From your answer, I see your upright heart, so that I swear to you by all that is holy that you are the only one upon earth who is in possession of my heart, and that I will live and die for you alone, but not as a low and base man to leave you, and to make you unfortunate. No—God hears and sees everything, and He knows my good intentions.

Thus live at rest, in this assurance that I will, as much as is in my power, endeavor to make your life agreeable, pleasant and happy, and rather to take care of you than myself. This is my word and my oath, which I give you in writing.

And if you love me, as I do you in my heart, we shall always remain true to each other, and live happily. With regard to the consent of my parents to the marriage, I have again written to them, and I am certain that my parents, who know me, will be perfectly satisfied with my choice.

Thus, fear nothing, be contented and remain true to me. This is all that your true lover expects from you.

Jules Verreaux

The 17 March, 1827

Exhibit No. 4

Dear Friend!

I seek not to make any person unfortunate, much less you who I love. I persist in my request, and in case you will not grant it, I am certain that you do not love me as you say, and also place no confidence in me, for why should you not do it.

There is nothing for you to fear or to lose, for I shall love you much more on that account. I believe you in everything, therefore, I also hope to be assured of your word and promise. And as quickly as possible, not to let me droop as a flower in the fields, which you will certainly be the occasion of—which I expect otherwise from your affectionate heart.

Until death,

Your true love

J. V.

The 11 April 1827

Exhibit No. 5

Dear, and tender friend,

It is with great grief that I find myself obliged to delay the happiness of my life, but motives which I cannot express to you at present, as your heart would thereby be pierced. But a little patience, and our unison will be accomplished, and we will live as happy as two turtle doves until the end of our lives.

Receive a thousand kisses upon your vermillion lips. Your friend,

Jules Verreaux

8

Cape Town
May 13, 1827

Verreaux's journal

Cape Town. 13 Mai, 1827

I looked at her, the African moon rising across her skin, the last beautiful woman I would see in the tawny light of morning, seeping into the nocturnal blood.

I knew the end had begun. I knew she had conceived in the night, that hours after our uncontrollable pleasure the milky seed would plow its inexorable route, intent on consummating the act. I knew it when we became unentwined, when the mind was no longer the fevered prisoner of abandon. So did she.

Now I see Elisabeth dreams of it, her face in tortured pilgrimage to a life lost through a life begun. She knows I will leave her with child alone.

Édouard tells me I will never marry. It is a disease afflicting my psyche, he says, the one that slowly constricts the throat, suffocating the permanent breaths I might share with another.

Édouard has avoided infection. He is already married, his wife with child in Paris, in the rooms upstairs above Maison Verreaux, above the tableaux in which nature is now illusion, safe not to threaten or move, but free to pretend it could at any moment. He says I inhabit a series of tableaux of my own making, capturing passion, making it a still life, then proceeding to the next.

9

Cape Town
Monday, January 25

Exhibit No. 6
Letter from Jules Verreaux to Family Greef,
4 June 1827
[Translated from the Dutch]

To Mr. & Mrs. Greef together with their daughter, Miss Elisabeth Greef.

I doubt not but that you will all feel for the sincere utterance of my heart, which I must make known to you and whereto I am to my sorrow forced. It is very well known to you that with your consent, I spent some time in paying visits to your daughter Elisabeth, and owing to the great respect I did and still do bear for her, I promised in a certain time to marry her if I got my parents' consent thereto, and also some means of subsistence were sent to me by my parents.

But alas! Everything goes against me, receiving no intelligence whatsoever, and also not the least assistance, either in money or anything else. I have thereby fallen into poverty, and am loaded with more debts than I can pay. On that account, I do not see any mode of subsisting myself, much less a wife, and also not the least of carrying on my business here, for disbursements must be made which I can neither obtain, nor furnish.

Thus as I have always conducted myself in an honorable and upright manner towards your daughter, without making her unfortunate or contemptible in the eye of the public, I find myself obliged from regard to you, as well as for the happiness of your daughter, to make you acquainted that I thank you all for your good reception and kindness, that to my sorrow, I, from poverty, entirely decline the marriage with her, which resolution will be the most advantageous for the happiness of your daughter, and of myself, that we may not for our lifetime both be plunged and remain in an abyss of poverty, and misery; and therefore I also send you the three rings back which she gave me.

Let your hearts thus be touched for the welfare of us all. Consider the wicked consequences which would arise from a wretched marriage. And doing this, I am assured you will not take my refusal of the marriage ill. For it is our duty to reverse misfortune, which has not yet taken root, & is still in its birth.

And further to assure you of my continued regard, I wish you all every prosperity, happiness, and blessing, and am with all affection. Yes. As not finding any means of subsistence here I have resolved to quit this colony for ever.

Mr. & Mrs. & also Miss E. Greef,
Your true servant,
Jules Verreaux
Cape Town
the 4 June 1827

10

Cape Town
Monday, January 25

**Exhibit No. 7
Letter from Elisabeth Greef to Jules Verreaux,
5 June 1827
[Translated from the Dutch]**

Sir

Your unexpected letter of yesterday has reached me and from it I have learnt that I have unfortunately fallen into the hands of a dishonorable man without character, who after having been betrothed to me for four and a half months dares, without any cause, to use the business shamelessly to decline fulfilling his engagement. I, on the contrary, thank you for your unfeeling conduct about my person. Do you pretend to be obligated to do so in consequence of poverty?

Were you not about 4 months ago equally well acquainted with the state of your affairs as at present, or have you been dishonorable enough to extort from me my consent to marry you under a cloak of shameless hypocrisy. If so I wish you a very quiet conscience about your noble conduct shown to me. I shall, I hope with God's assistance, be able to endure that penetrating grief, but know also that the almighty God, whom you called to witness, when, in your own handwriting and letter, you assured me of your fidelity till Death, cannot leave the author of such grief unpunished.

If you have feeling enough you will, I hope, remember that I have rescued you from Death. What gratitude! You have nearly reduced me to the Tortures of Death. Do you imagine that you will pass a more happy life without me. Take then this advice from me, never to act in a similar manner towards another of my Sex or you will be sure to experience the Vengeance which is the consequence of such a deed.

For the rest, I wish you many quiet moments, provided you no more think of me or of this letter, which I conceive might otherwise cause you a few unpleasant moments.

Your poniard [knife] and pistol bullet you will, I hope, allow me to keep in remembrance of you. Conversations which we have held together I shall hide in my heart, but as to the conscience—yes, the conscience once awakened—I shall put the good God as judge between you and me.

I am who calls herself,
E. H. Greef.
5 June, 1827

11

Cape Town
Monday, January 25

Harry pushed his chair back, his eyes clouded over with the faded ink from the seven letters. Verreaux had penned five to Elisabeth Greef. Then a sixth to her parents, withdrawing his promise of marriage. Elisabeth answered Jules the next day. She had sent him other letters. But they hadn't been introduced at the trial and weren't in the court records.

They had written to one another in Dutch. Verreaux, Harry surmised, had picked up the language during his few years in the Cape—at least enough to seduce Elisabeth. For the trial, the court had apparently used two scribes to record the English translations, one for Verreaux's letters, one for Greef's. It seemed to Harry that the scribes had become infected by the words on the page, charting the lovers' emotional valence. The handwriting on Verreaux's letters leaned forward, beckoning, a rococo flourish offering a honeyed bait. On Elisabeth's, the serpentine script was snarled, a labyrinthine fury choking the breaths between the lines. Script was psyche, Harry thought, the cursive revealing the accursed, as if the pens were needles hooked to a smoked kymograph.

Harry carried the thick, leather-bound archive over to the woman behind the long wooden counter. "It is possible to get the trial record copied?"

"Ah, the Verreaux trial," she observed, flashing a knowing look at the volume. "Yes, of course." Her soft-spoken alto accompanied large, friendly eyes, strings of woven-black hair, and a full mouth that seemed to be set in a perpetual state of mysterious grace. "Our charge is five rand for each page."

Harry wondered about her apparent knowledge of Verreaux. He'd ask her later. "Do you have a bulk rate?" he joked, pointing to the bound volume.

"No, I'm sorry," she laughed, resting her palm on the archive as if she were about to take an oath. "I'm afraid it will be expensive. Please fill out this request form. List the items and number of pages you wish to have copied."

Harry wrote the case reference on the form: Cape Supreme Court record 2/1/1/6, No. 13, Greef vs. Verreaux. The case documents and transcript in the archive were chronological:

Seven letters: written during March, April and June, 1827.

The Denunciation, November 21, 1828: Elisabeth's attorneys begin legal proceedings against Verreaux a year and a half later, threatening suit.

The Plaintiff's Declaration, February 2, 1829: Elisabeth files suit for breach of contract against Verreaux.

The Defendant's Plea and Answer, February 10, 1829. Verreaux responds to the Plaintiff's Declaration with his statement of defense.

The Plaintiff's Replication, February 16, 1829: Elisabeth counters Verreaux's Plea.

The trial, Greef vs. Verreaux, proceedings of day one, Friday, March 20, 1829: argued in front of the Cape Supreme Court.

The trial, proceedings of day two, Saturday, March 21, 1829.

The Judgment, Greef vs. Verreaux, July 6, 1829, read in the Cape Supreme Court.

The letters between Jules and Elisabeth had thrust Harry into the uncertainty of a time past and foreign. So had the travel. He'd flown into Cape Town two days earlier, arriving just after midnight, fifteen minutes into Sunday. Liza had booked him a room at a hotel on Roeland Street, near the Archives. She'd also arranged for rental of a road bike. The shop had dropped it off at the hotel Saturday afternoon. A Cannondale, aluminum frame, Shimano drive train. Fifteen hundred rand for the week, about a hundred and fifty dollars. He'd charge it to Stewart.

On Sunday morning, hot winds blew bedraggled, humid clouds off the sea. Harry spun down Adderley Street through the thick traffic, past the Slave Lodge, a long, low rectangular building with a white colonial façade. He rolled up onto the sidewalk to read the historic marker. For a hundred and fifty years, more than 500 slaves of the Dutch East Indies Company lived in the Lodge's open, dirt courtyard. They ate there, slept there, made love there, birthed their children there, fouled themselves there, and died there. One Sunday a month they were allowed into the Company Gardens beside the Slave Lodge. In 1811, with the lodge overcrowded, the slaves were moved to pens on the outskirts of the city. The lodge's inner courtyard was gradually built in with government offices. A wooden rotunda, added in 1825, housed the new Cape Supreme Court. Four years later, Jules Verreaux would stand trial here for breaching the marriage contract with Elisabeth Greef.

Harry wound the bike through crowded downtown streets, conscious of sticking to the left side of the road. Only Canada, Harry thought, had sensibly spurned this sinistral scourge that Britain had imposed on the roadways throughout its colonial commonwealth. At the Cape Town waterfront, the ocean was hidden behind a boardwalk of high-rise, upscale hotels, and a modern mall. Throngs of people milled in and out with bags and baggage, clogging the pavement. They seemed bored with oceans, no longer enthralled with the edge of the terrestrial world where the Atlantic and Indian waters meet and mingle.

Harry cycled south into the wind along the narrow ocean road, winding in and out of the shadows of Table Mountain to the east. At Hout Bay, a picturesque rocky amphitheater facing the ocean, he turned east up the steep, narrow, two-lane highway through the notch in the mountain. Semis blared at him, forcing him off the tarmac onto the dirt strip along the road. Over the summit, Harry descended fast through the S-curves on Rhodes Avenue, past the Kirstenbosch Gardens, a botanically manicured World Heritage

Site. The road back to the hotel narrowed through wealthy residential areas, houses hidden behind high walls topped with barbed wire. Suburban internment camps, Harry thought, fenced with the same, unbiased architecture designed to keep whites and blacks in or out.

At the hotel, Harry parked the bike in his room, showered, put on jeans, a black T-shirt, and sneakers. He disregarded the advice of the matron at the front desk not to walk the streets of Cape Town at night. At a fast food stand on Waale Street near the Company Gardens he grabbed a couple of African style fish tacos and fried potatoes. The street was pedestrian thin. Two prostitutes lounged at the Gardens gate. A third, in a red miniskirt, tight white tank top, and blue high-heels, leaned against the Slave Lodge. Visions of America, Harry thought. Her face was hawkish, hope long deceased.

He wondered whether Jules and Elisabeth had strolled along Waale and Adderley and through the Company Gardens on a cool March evening in 1827. Had he pulled her behind a tree for a secretive kiss, a promise, and a sexual caress?

12

Cape Town
Monday, January 25

USHER OF THE SUPREME COURT
DENUNCIATION

In the name of the undersigned Attorney acting for Elisabeth Helena Henrietta Greef, duly assisted by her Father Hendrik Greef, repair to and in the presence of Jules Verreaux, residing with Christoffer Lenage, No. 59 Long Street Cape Town, and denounce to him that he cannot be unaware of his having seduced the said Elisabeth Helena Henrietta Greef by holding out promise of marriage to her, and that in consequence thereof she has had a child by him.

After having made this denunciation, demand of the said Jules Verreaux by way of insinuation whether he be ready and willing to enter into the bond of matrimony with the said Elisabeth Helena Henrietta Greef.

In case of an evasive or unsatisfactory answer, inform the said Jules Verreaux that an action at law will be immediately instituted against him.

Insinuate duly and report your occurrences in writing.

Cape Town
J. P. de Wet
November 21th 1828
No. 32 Berg Street
Cape Town
Attorney for E. H. H. Greef

13

Cape Town
Monday, January 25

COURT ORDER

GEORGE THE FOURTH, by the grace of God, of the United Kingdom of Great Britain and Ireland, King, Defender of the Faith

To the Sheriff of the Colony of the Cape of Good Hope, or his lawful deputy—greeting:

Command

Jules Verreaux residing with Christoffer Lenage of No. 59 Long Street Cape Town that justly and without delay, he enter into the bonds of matrimony with Elisabeth Helena Henrietta Greef, who he had seduced under promise of marriage, and who had had a child by him, the said Jules Verreaux

and unless he shall do so, then summon the said *Jules Verreaux* that he appear before our Justices of the Supreme Court of our said colony, at Cape Town, on the First day of December next, at 10 o'clock in the Forenoon, to shew wherefore he hath not done it, and return you then there this Summons, with whatever you done thereupon.

Witness—SIR JOHN WYLDE, Knight, our Chief Justice of our said Colony, at Cape Town, the 27th   day of *November* 1828 in the *Ninth* year of our Reign.

J. P. de Wet
No. 32 Berg Street
J. H. Bowles
Cape Town,
Registrar of the Supreme Court
Plaintiff's Attorney

14
Cape Town

Monday, January 25

*In the Supreme Court of the Colony of
the Cape of Good Hope*

**Elisabeth Helena Henrietta Greef,
assisted by her Father, Hendrik Greef, Plaintiff**

vs

**Jules Verreaux, Defendant
In the Fourth Year of
the Reign of King George the Fourth**

PLAINTIFF'S DECLARATION

Cape of Good Hope.

Jules Verreaux was summoned to answer Elisabeth Helena
Henrietta Greef, assisted by her Father, Hendrik Greef, in a plea
of promise of marriage, and subsequent seduction, and thereupon
the said Elisabeth Helena Henrietta Greef, by Jacobus Petrus de

Wet, her Attorney, complains, for that whereas the said Jules Verreaux, during the months of March, April and May in the year of
our Lord One Thousand Eight Hundred and Twenty Seven did,
by subtle wiles, and promise of marriage, as well written as verbal,
entice the said Plaintiff, and induce her to depart from the paths of
duty and virtue, and that the said Jules Verreaux, having, under the
aforesaid promises of marriage, prevailed upon the said Elisabeth
H. H. Greef, to allow him to have carnal knowledge of her person,
did beget a child by her, which child was born on or about the
eighteenth day of February, in the year of our Lord One Thousand
Eight Hundred and Twenty Eight, and the said Plaintiff brings
into Court here the said written promises of marriage, under the
sign manual of the said defendant (marked from No. 1 to No. 5)
which gives sufficient evidence of the aforesaid promises of marriage.

Yet the said defendant, altho often thereto requested, hath
hitherto refused, and under a false pretext, doth still refuse to marry
with the said Plaintiff, in proof whereof she brings into Court here
a letter under the sign manual of the said Jules Verreaux (marked
No. 6) as also an insinuation, and the answer of the said Defendant
thereto (marked No. 7) wherefore the said Plaintiff says that she is
injured beyond the possibility of retrieval by any mode whatsoever,
save and except by the said defendant's compliance with his aforesaid promise to marry her. And therefore she brings her suit, and
prays this Supreme Court to condemn the said Jules Verreaux to
marry with her in facie Ecclesice aut coram Judice according to the
laws of this Colony and to cohabit with the Plaintiff as becomes
married people, and to pay the costs of suit.

Filed February 2, 1829
J. P. de Wet
No. 32 Berg Street
Cape Town
Plaintiff's Attorney

15

Cape Town
Monday, January 25

*In the Supreme Court of the Colony at
the Cape of Good Hope*

**To His Honor Sir John Wylde, Knight, Chief Justice
and either of the Judges of the Supreme Court of
the Cape of Good Hope
Elisabeth Helena Henrietta Greef,
assisted by her father, Hendrik Greef, Plaintiff
vs
Jules Verreaux, defendant**

DEFENDANT'S PLEA AND ANSWER

Jules Verreaux the Defendant in the case, by Henry Cloete his Attorney at Law, comes and defends the wrongful complaints by the Plaintiff, and states: that the defendant is a native of France and a young man who has now barely attained his twenty-first year of age; that admitting that the Defendant did inscribe certain letter or letters addressed to the plaintiff in or about the month of March 1827 which may have contained certain offers of marriage; that those letters were written in a language which the Defendant did not understand; and that the offers or promises therein contained were entirely conditional and dependent on the approval & consent of his parents and Guardians, the defendant having then been and still being under age, and therefore requiring such a consent or approval to make any promise of marriage by him valid in law.

The Defendant moreover avers that he has never obtained such a consent but on the contrary that a marriage with the Plaintiff would be directly in opposition to the wish of his parents & Guardians; and that consequently the Defendant is not bound by such promise; that the same is moreover null and void at law having been made without such a consent while the Defendant was under age and incapable lawfully to contract such a promise; and finally that the Defendant having communicated to the Plaintiff and her parents the dissent of his parents and Guardians. The retraction of the Defendant's conditional promise was formally accepted and acted upon by the Plaintiff who already at that time and subsequently has been in habits of the most intimate friendship and courtship with other young men; and now only institutes this action two years after she had herself approved of the Defendant declining all further intercourse with her (Vide Exhibit No. 7).

The Defendant finally avers that no action having been instituted against him for the defloration of the Plaintiff and alimony of her child, the Defendant is not bound to answer on that averment contained in the Plaintiff's declaration.

For which reasons the Defendant prays that judgment may be given against Plaintiff with costs.

Filed February 10, 1829
Henry Cloete
Defendant's Attorney

16

Cape Town
Tuesday, January 26

The archives were closed on Tuesday. Harry woke early, put a couple of waffle wafers from the breakfast table in his jersey pocket, and biked south down the peninsula toward the Cape of Good Hope. He didn't need a map. There was only one road, a four-lane job leading out of the city lined with car lots, fast food joints and cheap furniture stores. No shoulder. Glass and garbage along the curb. Battered minibuses, packed with people, swayed passed him belching diesel smoke. They tore in and out of lanes of traffic to pick up passengers, their doors open, a hawker hanging out the window barking the routes to go from here to there. They were the people's transport all over Africa: 'matatus' in Nairobi; 'da-la-dalas' in Arusha; 'tro-tros' in Accra; 'fula-fulas' in Kinshasa; 'blue donkeys' in Addis Ababa. They also had their own social castes. Mzungus—whites in Swahili—didn't ride matatus or dala-dalas.

After twenty miles the road narrowed to two lanes of tourist traffic wedged between Table Mountain to the west and False Bay to the east, an arc of rocky ocean. Liza's notes said that Verreaux was eleven when he and his uncle collected a 75-foot whale that washed ashore here in 1819. They also grave robbed skulls and skeletons of Namas, Bushmen and Hottentots. Then, in 1830, during his second expedition to the Cape, Verreaux and his brother, Édouard, dug up the Botswanan chief, who became El Negro. Was it motive enough for one of the chief's descendants to vandalize the camel driver exhibit? Improbable. Hell, it was just as likely that some radical African environmentalist decided to take retribution for Verreaux's wholesale slaughter of the Cape's biota.

Further south, at Simon's Town, Harry joined a group of high school students trooping down the boardwalk to the colony of African Jackass Penguins nesting on the boulder-strewn sands. Verreaux and his brother had captured ten adults and fledglings for Maison Verreaux and the Paris museum. Harry knew the penguins were miniature. But here, live, they seemed comical—cloned, hunched gnomes in tuxedos. The mothers were viciously territorial, attacking any fledgling that waddled by accident into the wrong nest. It reminded Harry of the homeless living in cardboard boxes under the Fort Pitt Bridge. One a month would turn up badly beaten. In the night, drunk, they'd misread their address on the cardboard box—Sony, Sears, Ikea—and crawl into the wrong one.

Near Cape Park, the land began to fall away to the ocean. The road abruptly turned inland and climbed onto a windswept escarpment. Harry was alone on the barren landscape, an austere heath spreading away to the flat, blue horizon. Scrub grasses and flowers grew amid granite rocks sprayed red and yellow with lichens, all hunkered down to the earth to keep from being blown asunder.

Harry descended to Cape Point, an enormous field of round, massive sea-worn boulders where the water lapped onto the land. He made his way to the outermost of huge gray stones, the same one that James Cook had sailed past on the thirteenth of March, 1771, and Da Gama before him in 1497. Overhead flew the descendants of the petrels and albatrosses their crews had seen, shot, and eaten.

Harry wondered whether Verreaux had ever taken Elisabeth here, to seduce her at the edge of the world. They wouldn't have known that they were making love on a rocky memory of Gondwana, an ancient continent on an ancient Earth. That 300 million years earlier, the geologic gods rumbling beneath the molten crust were not pleased. At least not enough to keep the land from being rent and rifted into two voyaging terranes, an Africa and a South America, ever since drifting apart an inch or so a year across a new water, an Atlantic sea. Elisabeth wouldn't have known that Verreaux was drifting her into abandonment with child.

Harry turned and started pedaling back, his world somehow forever altered. Perhaps it was just his language of the mind.

17

Cape Supreme Court
Cape Town
Friday, March 20, 1829

"In the matter of Greef versus Verreaux, all rise for the Court." The bailiff's booming baritone reverberated through the courtroom.

Elisabeth Greef stiffened. The gallery, though crowded with spectators, had been strangely still, like the charged air before Sunday mass, fearful that the slightest twitch might derail the imminent spiriting of body and blood. Oak panels circled the courtroom in long, thin horizontal strips. Justice strangling crime, she thought. The reddish brown wood matched the tint of the bailiff's handlebar mustache.

Light from the austral sun burned through the high arched panes. Despite the heat, the windows were shut in the courtroom and throughout the town. Sweat was a lesser evil than locusts, which had swarmed in from the north. They'd cloaked the sky, then settled to the ground, blackening the buildings and the burnt yellow veldt. The women in the gallery had come armed with fans.

The correspondent for the *South African Commercial Advertiser*, a broad-faced, sandy-haired man in brown trousers and a rumpled white shirt, was using his notebook to cool the sweat streaming down his face and staining his chest. He had arrived early to take a seat in the front bench of the gallery, equidistant between the plaintiff's and defendant's table. He wanted an uninterrupted view of Miss Greef and Mr. Verreaux and their emotional demeanors.

He and his colleague, Thomas Pringle, had started the *Commercial Advertiser* five years earlier to expose private and public corruption. The paper did not concern itself with most crime, just cases of murder and moral turpitude. Months earlier it had covered the trial of a wealthy horse breeder accused of killing his young, second wife. The husband had chanced upon his wife and his eldest son in the horse stable, breeding on the straw in one the empty stalls. In his defense, he claimed that one of his high-strung Arabian horses had become spooked by his wife's amorous moaning and kicked her in the head. The son, however, finally taking revenge for being regularly beaten as a child, willingly told the court that his father had pummeled his wife's skull with the shin-bone of an ox until she was dead.

The Greef trial, to the paper and the community, reflected the insidious ruination of Cape Colony society by unscrupulous foreigners. The Greefs were high society. Hendrik Greef was owner and president of the Dutch Standard Bank of South Africa. Elisabeth was the toast of Cape Town's chaperoned Saturday dances. Jules Verreaux was a Frenchman, come here with his brothers to pillage the land of its wildlife for the amusement of Europe.

The judges appeared from behind the raised bench, three black robes silently ascending like resurrections from a privileged underworld. They took their seats on the dais, Chief Justice Sir John Wylde in the center, Justice William Menzies on the left, and Justice William Burton on the right. All three had recently volunteered for the British colony's new Supreme Court of the Cape of Good Hope, attracted by a good salary, an agreeable climate, and a ready escape from personal misadventures. Wylde, beset by rumors of incestuous peccadillos, was fleeing his wife in Australia. Menzies had allegedly killed a man in a duel. Burton was a sailor turned lawyer, chased by a trail of smuggling and adulterous affairs on five con-

tinents. Still, they brought judicial respectability to the new court.
All three were well-educated, thoroughly versed in the law, and un-
afraid of flamboyance, panache and spirited debate. Months earlier,
Menzies, after convicting the horse breeder of murder, asked him
whether he had ever consulted Shakespeare before taking a much
younger woman for his second wife.

John Wylde belied the visage of a chief justice. He was short,
almost scrawny, with thinning hair and a squeaky voice. His chair
had been modified to raise him high enough above the bench to
see the plaintiff, defendant, and the public gallery. He motioned to
Elisabeth Greef and Advocate de Wet at the plaintiff's table on the
right side of the courtroom.

Elisabeth sat erect, stoic, her hands clasped on the table, her
simple white frock dappled in pink and blue flowers, brushing the
floor and covering both arms. De Wet had approved. Only your
face should be exposed, he had cautioned. It would put to rest
any suspicions of tempting flesh or amorous seduction. Two white
ribbons caged her blond curls from their normal wild abandon, one
above her forehead, the second at the back of her head, restraining
her hair from springing down to her shoulders. De Wet had told
her to look straight at the justices, never at Verreaux, never at the
defendant's table. All eyes in the courtroom were on this young
beautiful woman, poised, confident in the manner of indignation.

She did not need his coaching. She would never again acknowledge Jules, a passion poisoned to hate. The trial was revenge.
Should the justices rule for her, Jules would be bound to her, but he
would never again know her bosom, or lie between her thighs, or be
consumed by the heat of her skin.

"Mr. Advocate de Wet," Chief Justice Wylde prompted, "you
may begin."

"Thank you, your Lordship." De Wet was short, rotund, and
wore spectacles. His face, disarmingly humorous, belied a dramatic
demeanor and skill for verbal dissection. He walked slowly in front
of the defendant's table and stopped.

"This case," he began, pointing a finger at Jules Verreaux, "concerns a breach of promise of marriage. Our young plaintiff, Miss
Greef, not yet of majority age, together with her father, Mr. Hen-

drik Greef, both of whom live here in Cape Town, have taken this action to compel the performance of a contract of betrothal. As we will prove, that contract was made in writing to Miss Greef by the defendant, Jules Pierre Verreaux." De Wet pointed at him again.

Verreaux shook his head. He leaned over, whispered to his counsel Advocate Cloete, drew something on a sheet of paper, then sat back. Verreaux was tall, lean, with black hair to his shoulders, a broad forehead, darting deep-set brown eyes, and a wide mouth frozen in a perpetual smirk. After their first kiss, Elisabeth had confided to him how that smirk had attracted her, how it advertised a rebellious adventure. That, and his profession, the expeditions into the wild to wrestle with Nature.

"He is a foreigner, a young French naturalist," de Wet continued. "He has come here from a distant country to seduce our animals into his traps, or to shoot them, and to abscond with these collections of our birds and reptiles and elephants and butterflies into the commerce of museums and private natural history emporia for stuffing and display and sale."

De Wet paused and waved at Elisabeth. "He also came here from France to seduce one of our innocent daughters, Miss Greef, into his amorous trap. And, in consequence of his assiduous attention and false promises, he made her the mother of an illegitimate infant."

In the first row of the gallery, the woman next to the correspondent leaned over to him and whispered, "Where is it—the child?"

The reporter glanced at her, intrigued. She was smartly dressed in a feathered hat despite the heat. Her left hand, though not unsightly, bore the veins of middle age, but no ring. He wondered whether she had spoken to him or merely murmured to herself.

De Wet turned to face the bench. "Your Lordships, Mr. Verreaux's behavior has not only violated his contractual obligation of marriage to Miss Greef, but every moral standard of our society." He walked back to his table, picked up a sheaf of papers, and waved it at the defendant's table.

"In this brief, my learned counsel for the defense, Advocate Cloete, makes four excuses for Mr. Verreaux's dishonorable and unconscionable act. Each will be offered by the defense to your lordships and the fine citizens of Cape Town in this courtroom. Each is groundless.

Firstly, the defense will claim that Mr. Verreaux was a minor when he promised marriage to Miss Greef, and therefore the contract cannot be binding. Secondly, that Mr. Verreaux was ignorant of our language—Dutch—in which his letters, containing the promises of marriage, had been written. Thirdly, the defense will argue that Mr. Verreaux was unable to obtain the consent of his parents to wed, which is required of a minor, thus annulling the promise of marriage. And fourthly, that Mr. Verreaux's letter retracting his offer of marriage had been accepted and acted on by the lady, Miss Greef, who had subsequently permitted the intimacy and courtship of another young gentleman."

De Wet paused, turned to Verreaux and his counsel, and abruptly let the sheaf of papers clatter onto the floor of the courtroom, as if he were disposing of refuse. Startled, people in the gallery craned their necks to see documents scattered in front of the defense table.

"Your Lordships, we intend to ensure that Mr. Jules Verreaux, having seduced Miss Elisabeth Greef with contemptible and vile misrepresentation, will not seduce the justice from this court or this case."

He bent down, gathered up the papers, neatly placed them back on the plaintiff's table, and faced the bench. "I call Mr. P. J. de Villiers to be sworn."

18

Cape Supreme Court Cape Town, March 20, 1829

The bailiff ushered a short man in his late twenties with curly, reddish hair to the witness box. He wore his black trousers high on the waist, suspended above a small paunch, so that the pant legs ended above the ankles, exposing white socks and black shoes. With his black jacket and dark gray shirt, he could have been mistaken for a minister of the Dutch Reformed Church.

"Mr. de Villiers," de Wet approached him with a friendly smile. "What is your relationship to the plaintiff, Miss Greef?"

De Villiers cleared his throat. "I am Elisabeth's brother-in-law. I am married to her older sister, Margaretha."

He glanced quickly at his wife, a plain woman in a long dress, seated beside her father in the front row of the gallery behind Elisabeth.

"And did you have occasion to reside in the home of Mr. Greef and his two daughters?"

"Yes, I did, for almost one year. From December of 1826 to September, 1827."

"And why did you reside there?" De Wet asked, leading de Villiers as they had rehearsed..

De Villiers reddened and began fidgeting with a button on his jacket. "I was betrothed to Margaretha. I had only recently gained suitable employment as an accountant with a shipping concern. My father-in-law," he pointed nervously at Hendrik Greef, "was gracious enough to provide quarters for me before ... before Margaretha and I were married ... and with sleeping quarters for us after our wedding. Once we accumulated a sufficient sum from my earnings, we afforded our own accommodations in September, 1827."

He smiled weakly at his wife. She looked, de Villiers thought, like a young nun, the wire-rimmed spectacles resting on her sharp nose, the blond hair parted in the middle and in a tight bun under a kerchief. Their life, as he had wished, had become a proper certainty. He'd sought marriage into convention, a genteel family, and fortune. But soon after he took lodging in the Greef house, Elisabeth had thrown his propriety into turmoil. Daily she would mock his manhood and manner. She deliberately tempted his flesh. She would linger in the doorway to her bedroom in her underclothes, seemingly innocent, all the while shamelessly brandishing her ample bosom at him. She knew he could not keep himself from staring at the heavy outline of her breasts and nipples under the thin cotton gown. She would raise her nightshirt, suggestively, to expose the long beckoning flow of her thigh that he knew led to the furnace of hell. Now, he felt, judgment had finally given Elisabeth the righteous sums of life—a bastard child, and a spinster's sentence.

"And Mr. de Villiers," de Wet prodded, "during your nine-month residence in Mr. Hendrik Greef's home, did you have occasion to see the defendant, Mr. Verreaux?"

De Villiers looked at Verreaux at the defense table. "Yes, quite often. He visited regularly. They were courting, he and Elisabeth." De Villiers reddened again.

"Can you inform the court as to the precise time period you witnessed this courting?"

"Yes, during winter and spring of 1827, from February to June."

"You are certain the visits ended in June?"

De Villiers suddenly seemed uncertain. "Why … why yes. Mid-June I believe."

"And where in the house would the visits proceed?"

De Villiers reddened further. Despite rehearsing this testimony with de Wet, he was uncomfortable with the memory and the words. Elisabeth and Jules had been disgraceful in their behavior, freely exhibiting sexual proclivities that dismayed him and Margaretha. He was proud that he and Margaretha had not touched before marriage. And after, it was infrequent and quick enough to suit Margaretha's dutiful spousal obligation whenever he would wake and mount her. She never reached for him.

"Most often in the parlor of the house," de Villiers answered, "but, when Elisabeth was confined to her bed-chamber by indisposition, he would visit her in her private quarters."

"Were those visits to the bed-chamber appropriately chaperoned by other persons?"

"Yes, usually," then on cue, "but other times they were there alone."

A buzz of whispers spread through the gallery. Justice Wylde cracked the gavel to quiet them.

"I see," de Wet declared, raising his eyebrows in feigned surprise. "And can you relate to the court an incident that you witnessed during one of Mr. Verreaux's visits?"

"Yes," de Villiers nodded, now more comfortable. "Elisabeth and Jules—I mean Mr. Verreaux—were in the parlor alone, sitting on the sofa, while the family was at supper in the dining hall. Suddenly, we heard the report of a pistol from the parlor. Mr. Hendrik Greef, along with Miss Greef's brother, Willem, and I immediately rushed to see what had transpired. We found Mr. Verreaux kneeling on the floor, at the foot of the sofa. He was holding a pistol. Miss Greef was standing a little distance from him. Mr. Verreaux begged Mr. Greef's pardon for firing the pistol. He confessed that he had tried to kill himself out of sorrow that Mr. Greef would likely not give his consent for him to marry Elisabeth."

De Wet swiveled around to look at Hendrik Greef in the gallery. "Did Mr. Greef respond?"

"Yes, most assuredly," de Villiers nodded. "He said he was not aware of having been asked for his consent, or refusing it. Verreaux then leapt up and contended he wished to marry Elisabeth, to which Mr. Greef responded, 'it is good.' Verreaux then took Elisabeth into the dining room where her mother was sitting. He asked Mrs. Greef for her consent to the union, which she gave."

"Very intriguing," de Wet stated. "Tell us then, Mr. de Villiers, from your observing of this scene, was it your impression that the defendant, Mr. Verreaux, had staged this pistol play? Perhaps as a piece of melodramatic theater to gain Mr. Greef's consent and Miss Greef's admiration?"

"I believe—"

Before de Villiers could finish his answer, Advocate Cloete rose from the defendant's table and held up his hand. Cloete was tall and rail thin, almost sinister, with the pinched, deep-set eyes of a necromancer. His black hair, brushed severely back over his scalp, accentuating a broad forehead, a pointed chin, and a thin scythe for a nose.

"We must object, your Lordships." His soft, raspy voice was unnerving, as if it could pierce the camouflage of errant testimony. "My learned and crafty opponent is asking for a conclusion of intent to which he has goaded the witness, and which Mr. de Villiers does not have the industry to make."

Chief Justice Wylde quickly conferred with justices Menzies and Burton. Both shook their heads. Wylde smiled at de Wet.

"We rule for the objection, Mr. de Wet. Your point, as intended, has registered with the justices, although we will disregard it. Nevertheless, your allegation will not be hidden from the jury of public opinion, courtesy of the esteemed editor of the *South African Commercial Advertiser*, Mr. Robert Fairbairn. I daresay he will choose to speculate on it in his forthcoming account of these proceedings."

Justice Wylde nodded at the reporter in the sweat-stained shirt. Fairbairn put down his notebook, wiped his forehead with his sleeve, nodded at the Chief Justice, and turned to wink at the lady in the feathered hat beside him. She cocked one eyebrow, handed him a handkerchief from her handbag, took the pencil and notebook from his hands, and quickly scribbled a few words: "Hmm. I hear there is rot behind those robes."

Fairbairn stared at her. Who was this woman. What did she know about the Wylde affair? Or was it just her fortuitous intuition? He'd find out.

"Malodorous rumors," he wrote in the notebook below her scribble.

She leaned over, flashing a short, self-satisfied grin. "Follow the scent, Mr. Fairbairn."

De Wet bowed to the court. "Mr. de Villiers, here is a question that does not involve a conclusion of intent. In what language did the defendant address you, or Miss Greef, or her father?"

"Why ... Dutch."

"Did he also understand Dutch when it was spoken to him in response?"

"Yes. He comprehends the Dutch language and speaks it well enough to be understood."

"And, from your association with Mr. Verreaux, what is your knowledge of his profession?"

De Villiers looked over again at Verreaux, who had slouched down in his chair. "He described himself as a professional naturalist. He says he makes collections of animals and plants in the wild to take them back to Paris and sell them to museums and fanciers of nature."

"And, to your knowledge, is Mr. Verreaux residing here under any species of guardianship."

De Villiers shook his head. "No, not that I am aware. He has appeared to me to be of independent means, without responsibility to another."

"So, for all intents and purposes, Mr. Verreaux appears to you to be completely self-sufficient in our society?"

"Yes, absolutely." Then de Villiers added, as they'd rehearsed, "As much as any adult would be."

De Wet let the last answer hang in the air. "Thank you, Mr. de Villiers. Your Lordships, that is all for this witness."

19

Cape Supreme Court Cape Town, March 20, 1829

Chief Justice Wylde motioned to the defendant's table. "Cross examine, Mr. Cloete."

"Thank you, your Lordship," Cloete grunted, pushed back his chair, and approached de Villiers.

"Do you remember when the pistol scene in Miss Greef's house took place?"

De Villiers thought for a moment. "Yes, it was during the Spring, April or May I think, while they were still courting."

"You testified that Miss Greef and Mr. Verreaux were alone in the parlor while the rest of the family dined at supper. Had Mr. or Mrs. Greef objected to this situation?"

De Villiers looked over at Hendrik Greef, somehow seeking the right answer. "No," he replied, finally. "No objection was made by Miss Greef's parents."

Cloete picked up a one page letter from the bailiff's table, and waved it at de Villiers.

"Did you at any time become knowledgeable of this letter, dated June 4, 1827, received by Mr. Greef from Mr. Verreaux?"

"Yes ... bbbut I was not shown its contents."

"I see," Cloete remarked, stroking his sharp chin. "Nevertheless, I presume, living in close quarters in the Greef household, you were made aware of its contents—that Mr. Verreaux had formally withdrawn his offer of marriage, with explanation of the withdrawal."

"Objection!" de Wet yelled out quickly from across the courtroom. "Your Lordships, my learned opponent is asking the witness for hearsay."

Chief Justice Wylde nodded. "Yes, we agree," he pronounced, without checking with Menzies and Burton. "Witness will not answer."

Cloete grunted again and lightly ran his fingers over his hair. "Mr. de Villiers, are you acquainted with a Mr. Jan de Vages?"

"Yes," de Villiers stated without hesitation. "I saw him frequently at Mr. Greef's house."

"During what period of time did you see Mr. de Vages visit the Greef house?"

De Villiers thought for a moment. "In the winter. A month ... perhaps two ... before Margaretha and I left to our own accommodations."

"In other words," Cloete concluded, "during July and August of 1827?"

"Yes."

Cloete pressed on. "One month after Mr. Greef had received Mr. Verreaux's letter withdrawing from the marriage—"

"Mr. Cloete," Chief Justice Wylde interrupted, his voice stern, "we have already ruled on this matter."

"Excuse me, your Lordships." Cloete turned back to de Villiers. "Did Mr. de Vages begin visiting the Greef household in July, 1827, one month after receipt of the letter?"

"Yes."

"And after Mr. Verreaux was no longer a visitor to the Greef household."

"Yes."

"And for what reason was Mr. de Vages a frequent visitor?"

De Villiers began fidgeting with a button on his jacket. He glanced quickly at Elisabeth. She remained stiff, as if she had been starched in her chair, but allowed the slightest of smiles.

"To see Elisabeth," de Villiers half mumbled.

Cloete nodded. "And did she receive him willingly?"

"Yes."

"I see. And in which room would Miss Greef receive Mr. de Vages?"

"In the parlor."

"Alone?" Cloete raised his voice in pretended astonishment.

De Villiers cleared his throat. "Well … yes … sometimes … bbbut not often."

A loud murmur spread across the gallery. Wylde hit the gavel. "This court will observe decorum and respect. This is a trial, not titillation."

The lady in the feathered hat placed her finger on Fairbairn's open notebook, leaned over, and whispered, "Cloete has elicited the desired effect. Our Miss Greef will be perceived as an adventurous woman, perhaps even promiscuous. 'Titillation.' Write down that word, Mr. Editor. Your readership too will be titillated, as is the audience here."

Fairbairn turned to the woman beside him, intrigued by a stranger whose boldness was accompanied by an articulate wit. He saw gray-tinged blond hair escaping from under a feathered hat, a strong, mannered face made deeply sensual with age. For the first time since escaping to the Cape Colony from England, he felt beguiled by a woman.

"Thank you," he whispered back, smiling wryly. "I will. 'Titillated' is one of those words that excites two senses at once. Hearing. And touch." He brushed her finger briefly, as if he were demonstrating the word, but it was long enough for insinuation.

Cloete abruptly grasped the railing of the witness box and leaned close to de Villiers. "Can you tell us then whether Mr. de Vages was just visiting Miss Greef, or paying his addresses? Was it conjugal courting? Physically amorous?"

De Wet shot up at the plaintiff's table. "My learned opponent, having previously objected to a conclusion of intent from this witness, is now, without shame, demanding the same!"

Chief Justice Wylde shook his head. "Good effort, Mr. de Wet, but I'm afraid not. Witness might have learned from Mr. de Vages or the plaintiff the intent of the visits, or witnessed acts that would reveal intent. The witness will respond."

"Y ... y ... yes sir," de Villiers stammered, then turned to Cloete. "I ... I cannot say. They did not confide in me ... Mr. de Vages and Elisabeth. Perhaps they were courting. But Mr. and Mrs. Greef were at home most evenings."

"Naturally," Cloete said. "Did you witness acts of affection? A kiss of love, perchance? An embrace? An entwining of hands? Remember, you are under oath, Mr. de Villiers."

De Villiers looked anxiously at Elisabeth, then at Hendrik Greef, as if he were seeking their forgiveness for an imminent betrayal. "Once," he whispered.

"Can you say that louder for the court?" Justice Menzies instructed.

"Once!" de Villiers blurted. "I intruded on them once ... in the parlor ... in the midst of an embrace ... of intimacy." His tone suddenly turned judgmental. "Such as one Margaretha and I had never done before marriage!"

Fairbairn noticed de Wet, at the plaintiff's table, shake his head at de Villiers' impulsive pronouncement.

"Thank you, Mr. de Villiers," Cloete said, smiling, and walked back to the defendant's table. He noticed Verreaux completing an unflattering pencil sketch of the witness.

De Wet stood. "Redirect, your Lordship!"

De Villiers had already stepped down from the witness chair. Wylde waved him back.

"Mr. de Villiers," de Wet began, amiably strolling toward the bench, hands clasped behind his back. "When you witnessed Miss Greef receiving Mr. de Vages in the parlor of her house, was the parlor door kept open or closed?"

"It was always open, sir. Wide open."

"And, at all other times did they behave properly?"

"Yes, most properly, sir."

"Good," de Wet nodded. "Mr. de Villiers, apart from Mr. de Vages, did you see Miss Greef keep acquaintance with any other gentlemen?"

"No," de Villiers shook his head. "I did not see her in the company of any other gentlemen."

"Do you know whether or not Mr. de Vages was a friend of the defendant, Mr. Verreaux?"

"Yes, I knew they were acquainted."

"So you would know whether or not the attentions Mr. de Vages paid to Miss Greef—" de Wet paused, turned, and pointed an accusing finger at Verreaux "were conducted under the explicit guile of the defendant to cast aspersions on Miss Greef."

Cloete raised his arms in exasperation. "Your Lordships! This is unscrupulous! Mr. de Wet, with calculated innuendo, has slandered both Mr. de Vages and Mr. Verreaux."

"Indeed," Justice Menzies bellowed from the bench. His angry tenor matched his burly, angular head. "Advocate de Wet. Needless to say, we will disregard your unseemly theatre. Do not try the court's patience further."

De Wet bowed. De Villiers noticed Verreaux's sketch as he left the witness box and hurried past the plaintiff's table to a seat at the back courtroom.

"He seems anxious," the lady with the feathered hat murmured to Fairbairn. "Perhaps with good reason. There is rumor about him that may be revealed here."

20

Cape Supreme Court Cape Town, March 20, 1829

De Wet's next witness, Reverend Frederick Wagener, removed his large-brimmed hat on entering the courtroom. He had a gleaming bald pate, bushy eyebrows and cheeks that sagged to slightly below his jaw. In his favorite sermon, he admitted that his cheeks had begun to droop immediately after he had given his life to God. He ascribed it to a sign from the Almighty that as a worthy man of the cloth he should suffer a corporeal incarnation of man's original fall from grace.

"Reverend," de Wet began, are you acquainted with Miss Greef?"

Wagener nodded. "I am, from having seen her either at church or on visiting the Greef home. I am not sure."

"And Mr. Verreaux, do you know him?"

Wagener took a long studied look at Verreaux seated at the defendant's table. "I am quite certain that I have never met him. I would have, had he intended to marry Elisabeth Greef."

Verreaux grinned, grabbed his pencil, and began sketching the reverend on a fresh piece of paper.

"What do mean?" de Wet asked. "Please explain."

Wagener nodded. "Well, it is apparent that Mr. Verreaux had not taken any of the requisite formal steps preceding marriage. He had not published any banns of marriage—a proclamation in the Church of intent to marry. And he had not sought a certificate to do so from the Matrimonial Court."

"So, Reverend Wagener," de Wet raised his hands. "It is your conclusion that Mr. Verreaux never intended to marry Miss Greef despite his prom—"

"Objection," Cloete called out, almost wearily. "The witness is a reverend. He might have the ear of the Lord, but he is not a diviner of intent."

Justice Burton burst out laughing, surprising Menzies and Wylde, who looked askance at him as if he had lost all decorum. It was the first sound Burton had uttered in the courtroom that morning.

"I withdraw the question," de Wet said, smiling. He strolled back to the plaintiff's table, checked his papers, looked up at the three justices, and called the next witness. Sarah Bishop was a nurse and midwife, with a small, ruddy face and a thin, pursed mouth. For court, she'd rolled her gray-speckled hair into a prim bun at the back of her head. At the defense table, Verreaux began sketching Bishop with quick, deft pencil lines, removing the large black clasp from her bun and letting her hair cascade to below her shoulders.

"Miss Bishop," de Wet said, motioning toward Elisabeth, "did Miss Greef send for you on the morning of February 18, 1828?"

"Yes, she did." Bishop's voice was surprisingly low pitched and full-throated.

"And what was the reason she sent for you."

Without hesitation, Bishop stated, "to assist in delivering her child?"

On a fresh sheet of paper, Verreaux penciled the outline of a baby with a large, bulging head, somewhat misshapen, wispy hair, short pudgy arms and legs, wrinkled skin, and closed eyelids.

"And did you in fact do so—deliver the child?" de Wet asked.

"Yes."

"And that very afternoon, Miss Bishop, after the birth of the child, did Miss Greef send you on another errand?"

"Yes ... well," she hesitated, fingering the bun at the back of her head. "She sent me to Mr. Verreaux's lodging. I was to deliver a message to him. That she was the mother of a healthy child. And that he should come to see them that evening.

"And did you deliver this message and request?"

Bishop nodded, "I did so. Mr. Linage ... Mr. Verreaux is his lodger ... acted as interpreter." She pointed to an elderly gentleman sitting in the second row of the gallery.

"Thank you," de Wet said. "What was Mr. Verreaux's response?"

"It was in French. Mr. Linage translated it. Mr. Verreaux said that Miss Greef would be bringing up the child without him. He indicated he would not go to her that evening."

"Thank you," de Wet bowed slightly. "That is all."

Cloete stood up at the defendant's table "I have only one question, Miss Bishop. How did you know to recognize Mr. Verreaux, or the place of his lodging?"

Bishop frowned. "I was led there by Miss Greef's little slave girl, Roosje."

Verreaux picked up his pencil, shaded a thin swaddling blanket around the sketch of the baby, then drew a knotted bow around the shrouded body, as if it were a gift-wrapped package.

"Thank you," Cloete said, and sat down. He saw the drawing on the table, scowled at Verreaux, and quickly reached over and turned it face down. But not before Fairbairn and the lady in the feathered hat had caught a glimpse of the sketch. She nudged his elbow, grabbed his notebook and pencil, and quickly scrawled, "Is it the devil's stork?" Fairbairn grimaced.

De Wet cleared his throat and announced, "your Lordships, Miss Bishop's mention of the girl Roosje is timely, as she is the next witness for the plaintiff."

The bailiff left the courtroom to fetch Roosje. In the back row, de Villiers repeatedly craned his neck toward the double doors. He appeared to be sweating profusely. After a few minutes the bailiff returned with a message for de Wet.

"It appears, your Lordships," de Wet announced, reading from a slip of paper, "that plaintiff's witness has absconded. She has been sought, but she has not been found."

De Villiers, seemingly relieved, took a handkerchief from his pocket and wiped his face.

Chief Justice Wylde glowered at de Wet. "Does the plaintiff, Miss Greef, have knowledge of the girl's disappearance or where-abouts?"

De Wet scowled, then tried to wrench it from his face. He leaned over to Elisabeth, placed a reassuring hand on her back and whispered in her ear. She shook her head.

"I'm sorry your Lordship," de Wet responded. "We are as puzzled and disappointed as is the court. It is our experience that Khoikhoi slave girls are affrighted of our legal proceedings."

At the defendant's table, Verreaux chuckled out loud, muttered something to Cloete, turned to the gallery, and abruptly held up his sketch of de Villiers. The paunch was larger, the pant legs shorter, and de Villiers' face was blotched in embarrassed discomfort.

De Villiers reddened, opened his mouth as if to protest, thought better of it, then hurriedly brushed past the people in the aisle and ran out of the courtroom.

Amid the commotion, the lady in the feathered hat again leaned over to Fairbairn and touched his shoulder. "I did mention rumors, Mr. Editor," she whispered, "Surely you will record that something is amiss between that man and the slave girl."

Margaretha de Villiers did not look behind her, or acknowledge the sudden tumult. Instinctively, she adjusted the bun of hair pinned above the nape of her neck. She suspected her husband had taken liberties with Roosje in the house. Assuredly, it had been against the slave girl's will. No woman would willingly stand the advances of a man so oblivious to womanhood. His mechanics of coital consorting was done almost before it was begun. For him, her body was a vesicle for grunting entry and deposition.

Wylde hammered his gavel and turned to Verreaux. "Put down that drawing, Mr. Verreaux. We will have order, here. I have been to France. I have seen what passes for beaux art. Need I remind you that you are now in a courtroom in the British Cape Colony, not in some second-hand Parisian gallery!" Wylde's attempt at sternness and sarcasm was defeated by his squeaky voice. He heard a few titters in the gallery.

Cloete jumped up and placed a hand on his client's shoulder. "Mr. Verreaux apologizes, your Lordship. He is still a minor, ruled by the imprudent precipitousness of youth." Verreaux bit his lip to kill the mischief in his face.

"Precisely." Justice Menzies interjected, "It is precisely his imprudence with Miss Greef that is before the court in this action. Mr. de Wet, in the absence of the Roosje girl, proceed with your next witness."

De Wet held up a folder of handwritten letters. "Your Lordships, we have entered into evidence the five amatory letters written by Mr. Verreaux to Miss Greef. The defense stipulates that they were written by the defendant. Four of the letters are dated as having been written on March 9, 14, and 17, and on April, 11—all 1827." De Wet added a sarcastic edge to his voice. "The fifth letter our suitor forgot to date—no doubt in the ardency of passion. Each of these missives declares love. In the one on March 14, it is love and betrothal. In the letter of March 17 he declares that he has sought permission to wed from his parents in France, which might be received in six to eight months. And the letter of April 11," de Wet waved at Verreaux with a flourish of his hand, "our French suitor declares what he has already declared in the first three."

The gallery broke into laughter. Justice Burton joined in, covering his mouth. Chief Justice Wylde glared at him and pounded the gavel for quiet.

"This fervid affection, your Lordships," de Wet continued, in a mocking tone, "appears not to have been long of duration. It is evident from the final letter we have entered in evidence, dated June 4. Mr. Verreaux, herein and without shame, withdraws from his written declarations to Miss Greef: first he pleads poverty and non-consent of his parents to his marriage; second, he retracts the promise of matrimony he had made; third, he announces his determination to leave the Colony; and fourth, he returns, with many thanks and compliments, three rings that seem to have been gifted to him by the plaintiff."

"So noted, Mr. de Wet," Wylde acknowledged.

"Finally, your Lordships, we place into evidence affidavits from colleagues and acquaintances of Mr. Verreaux that he understands the Dutch language, contra his claim that—"

Cloete raised his hand. "Your Lordship, the defendant withdraws that plea from his defense. We stipulate that he has sufficient comprehension of the Dutch language."

Wylde nodded. "Anything further, Mr. de Wet?"

"No, your Lordship, the plaintiff's case is closed here."

"A short recess then," Wylde declared.

The three justices disappeared below the bench, descending magically to the hidden enclave from where they had emerged. Most of the gallery remained seated on the crowded benches, fearful of losing their place. So did Fairbairn, and the lady beside him. She put a hand on his arm.

"Suffer me graciously, Mr. Fairbairn. I am a curious woman of human affairs. I trust you are curious why Mr. de Villiers so abruptly scurried out of the courtroom at the mention of the slave girl? Perhaps his rules of conduct are … colored—that brown or black skin on a woman signals free rein. Perhaps Miss Roosje knows that there is safety in running from revelation."

21

Cape Town
Cape Supreme Court,
March 20, 1829

"Advocate Cloete." Chief Justice Wylde motioned to the thin, hawk-nosed barrister at the defendant's table. "Proceed with your opening statement."

Cloete rose, put his hands in the pockets of this trousers, and walked slowly toward the bench, head down, as if he were in deep thought. He stopped, abruptly, and looked up at the three justices.

"Your Lordships. My remarks are without complication because this case is without complication. My client, Mr. Jules Verreaux, was a youth of a mere nineteen years in the Spring of 1827, when his Gallic blood, being too warmly excited, dictated his letters of passion to Miss Greef. He was a minor in body—and in mind. Miss Greef was also a minor, and her parents were not ignorant of that circumstance. Your Lordships, amorous letters between two minors, whose emotions enflame mature judgment, are not the stuff of binding contracts. It is the wisdom and word of the law that this honorable woman, Miss Greef, and this equally honorable man, Mr. Verreaux, cannot and should not be held accountable for their actions until they are of majority age, that is, twenty-five years old."

Cloete pointed at Verreaux, slouched in his chair, twirling his pencil. "The defense will show that, being a minor from France, Mr. Verreaux required the consent of his parents to marry under French civil law, the Napoleonic Code. That consent was never forthcoming."

He turned and pointed at Elisabeth. She remained perfectly still, a stone totem witching a spell on the enemy.

"The defense will also show that Miss Greef, in honorable fashion, willingly released Mr. Verreaux from his impetuous promises. Subsequently, she behaved in a manner … shall we say … in keeping with this release."

Cloete walked back to the defendant's table, picked up a document, and pretended to study it. It bore the imprint of a crown at the top, with the words "Au Nom Du Roi" centered below, followed by declarations in cursive script, and a number of signatures.

"The defense calls Christopher Linage to be sworn."

An elderly man used his cane to lever himself up from his chair in the first row in the gallery. He had a dark stubble beard, stooped shoulders, shabby trousers, and a shambling gait. The bailiff helped him into the witness box.

"Tell the court how you know the defendant, Mr. Linage," Cloete began.

Linage coughed, cleared his throat, then declared in raspy voice, "Mr. Verreaux has lodged in my quarters for four years. Since he arrived from France."

"And do you recognize this document?" Cloete handed him the paper with the imprint of a crown.

"Yes, it is Mr. Verreaux's French passport. I examined it on his taking up lodging."

"Will you read the date and place of birth?"

"August 24, 1807, Paris, France."

"Thank you." Cloete turned to the bench. "Your Lordships, I enter this into evidence of the minority age of Mr. Verreaux when he wrote of betrothal to Miss Greef in his letter of March 14, 1827. He was nineteen years old." Wylde nodded.

"And, Mr. Linage," Cloete continued, "did you have occasion to see Miss Greef at your place of lodging?"

"Yes, three times. The first was an evening in April, 1827. I saw Mr. Verreaux escort Miss Greef to his quarters."

"Was she alone or chaperoned?"

"Alone. She spent the evening with Mr. Verreaux. I heard her leave his lodging and descend the stairs in the lateness of night."

A murmur spread through the gallery. The lady in the feathered hat nudged Fairbairn. "Two deliberate implications," she whispered. "Only a seductress would go to a man's quarters not chaperoned. And that evening is when she conceived. There are few venues for trysts in the Cape."

She noticed Fairbairn redden. He shifted in his seat to avoid looking at her. She smiled to herself.

"What was the second occasion, Mr. Linage?" Cloete prompted.

"It was November or December, 1827. I came home after nightfall. I observed a woman in the shadows near my house. She was attempting to conceal her person behind a pillar. When I opened the door, she quickly approached me from behind, laid a hand on my shoulder, and inquired whether Mr. Verreaux was at home. I checked his lodging and informed her that he was not. She asked for writing materials. She left a note for Mr. Verreaux of her intention of calling on him again the next evening."

"And is Miss Greef the woman in question?" Cloete asked.

Linage looked at her and raised his hand to his forehead, as if he were tipping his hat to her in respect. "Yes."

"And is this the note she gave you?" Cloete handed him a small, creased piece of paper with a handwritten line.

Linage examined the writing, turned the slip of paper over, and looked up at Cloete. "Yes, it is."

"Read it, please."

Linage cleared this throat again and surveyed the gallery. "It is written in Dutch. 'You know, Jules, I am with child. It is yours and no one else's! Please see me tomorrow!'"

The gallery erupted in gasps of shock. Elisabeth stared straight ahead, motionless.

Fairbairn turned to the lady in the feathered hat, his lips almost brushing her cheek. He caught the mild scent of a lavender wash. "As a reader, do you think the editor of the *Commercial Advertiser* should speculate on the paternity of her child? Cloete is implying loose morals—that she had more than one lover."

She placed a hand over his and turned to face him, lips pursed, eyes narrowed in stern judgment.

"I hope, Mr. Fairbairn," she breathed, "that I have not misjudged your character from your editorials. Intelligence, wit, and courageous words are rare among gentlemen in Cape Town. That is the reason I deliberately sought out this seat. I expect you will ask your readership to demand from the man the same morals that society now demands from the woman."

Fairbairn turned to her, suddenly urged to kiss her red lips. "You have chosen your seat well," he whispered.

Chief Justice Wylde quieted the gallery and nodded at Cloete.

"What was the third occasion, Mr. Linage, that you saw Miss Greef at your lodging?" Cloete asked.

"It was the very next evening. Miss Greef returned as she had promised in the note. Mr. Jan de Vages was then with Mr. Verreaux in his room. Mr. Verreaux instructed de Vages to go outside and deliver a verbal message to Miss Greef that he would not see her or have anything more to do with her. Mr. de Vages went down to the entryway, which was in darkness. Miss Greef, supposing Mr. de Vages to be Mr. Verreaux, ran to embrace him in an amorous fashion. When she discovered her mistake she immediately withdrew, refused to hear Mr. Verreaux's message, and left."

"Thank you, that is all."

De Wet placed a hand on Elisabeth's arm and stood. "Cross-examine your Lordships." Not waiting for permission, he strode over to Linage.

"Did it not seem to you, Mr. Linage, that Mr. Verreaux staged the entire scene with Mr. de Vages to place Miss Greef in a compromising—"

"Objection," rasped Cloete, rising from his chair. "I thought we had agreed to leave conjecture outside the walls of this courtroom. Learned counsel is asking the witness to read the defendant's mind!"

"Yes," Justice Burton said, quietly, "enough of that, Mr. de Wet." Burton had trained himself to speak very softly, yet firmly, convinced that his voice would carry more authority if the listener was forced to strain to hear him. "To the court," he continued, "conjecture is idle. It tells tales beyond the facts. At best, it foments canards. At worst, it leads to lawlessness." He had learned the speech from this father, the clergyman. It had been his daily admonition.

De Wet bowed slightly and sat down.

"Thank you your Lordship," Cloete nodded at Burton. "We can easily dismiss Advocate de Wet's insinuation. The defense calls Mr. Jan de Vages."

22

Cape Town
Cape Supreme Court,
March 20, 1829

A young, short, slightly portly man with very fair skin and thinning blond hair took the witness stand. He nodded politely at Elisabeth and adjusted the collar of his shirt.

"Mr. de Vages," Cloete walked slowly toward the witness box, "please tell the court how and when you came to be acquainted with Miss Greef?"

De Vages glanced quickly at Elisabeth. "It was March ... two years ago ... 1827. She and her friends were at a subscription dance in Keerom Street. After that, I saw her twice a week at the dances. She appeared to be in the company of Mr. Verreaux. When that ... er ... ceased in June, I would see her home ... er ... out of compliment. Because I had danced with her." His ears turned red. It made them seem larger than they were, set against his ashen complexion.

"Was Miss Greef chaperoned at these dances by her father or mother?"

"No." De Vages looked up, seemingly puzzled, when this elicited murmurs from the gallery. "But Miss Greef," he added quickly, "might have been accompanied to the dances by other relatives without my knowing it."

"Yes, quite," Cloete said. "And I understand that you and Miss Greef continued your romantic assignations at her home."

De Vages, indignant, began to stand up in the witness box. "They were not romantic assignations, sir," he asserted. "We were friends."

"Very well," Cloete nodded, "how often did you, as friends, see one another at the Greef house?"

De Vages looked at Hendrik Greef sitting on the first bench in the gallery directly behind his daughter. De Vages remembered Elisabeth telling him that her father was unlike others in the community. Hendrik had encouraged her independence, her defiance of convention. He wanted her to be a woman of fortitude, a leader. He'd confided to her once, when he'd had too much drink, that she had not inherited this maverick trait from her mother. Rather, the animalcules of personality had diverged in her mother's womb—his rebelliousness to her, her mother's complaisance to Margaretha.

"Well," de Vages said, "about … uh … about three times a week."

"Are you certain?" Cloete raised his voice, slightly, insinuating he knew otherwise.

De Vages looked down at this hands folded in his lap. "Perhaps sometimes five," he mumbled.

"Indeed!" Cloete exclaimed. "You visited Miss Greef at her house five times a week. That's quite a friendship!"

The gallery audience laughed. Justice Menzies tried but could not stifle a grin.

Cloete pressed the point. "Were these evening visits? Till what hour?"

De Vages, now flushed, began stuttering. "Yyy … yes. I visited in the evenings. Ttt … till eight or nine o'clock."

"And how long did this friendship, as you call it, continue with Miss Greef?"

"Until November, I believe. Or early December."

"That same year, 1827?"

"Yes, 1827."

"So," Cloete summarized, "you carried on your friendship with Miss Greef for approximately six months? Why did you discontinue your visits?"

De Vages squirmed in his seat and adjusted his collar again. "It became clear ... uh ... that she was with child—Mr. Verreaux's child."

Cloete paused, looked down at his shoes, then directly at de Vages. "I see. From your certainty on paternity, I take it then that you were present when the child was conceived."

De Vages began blubbering. "No ... of course not ... I mean ..." He looked up at the justices for relief. Wylde, strangely embarrassed, was staring down at the blotter in front of him. Menzies, with a wry smile, declared, "Point made, Mr. Cloete. Continue."

"Mr. de Vages, how well did you know Mr. Verreaux?"

"I had seen him with Elisabeth at the dances in March and April. Then, later, she appeared at the dances unaccompanied. I visited Mr. Verreaux to inquire whether his intentions with Miss Greef had ended. He confirmed they had."

"And did Mr. Verreaux engage your services on a certain evening in November, 1827 to relay an oral message to Miss Greef outside his lodging?"

"Yes, he did."

Cloete nodded. "And what was the message you were to deliver to Miss Greef? Verbatim please, as well as you remember."

De Vages looked quickly at Verreaux. "He asked me to affirm to her that his intentions had ended the previous June."

"And he told you to go outside his lodging and deliver that message—for that and no other purpose?"

"Yes"

"Not to lure Miss Greef into a compromising amorous behavior?"

"No. He did not ask me to do that."

"Thank you, Mr. de Vages."

De Wet moved quickly to cross-examine. "Mr. de Vages, is it not true that your relationship with Miss Greef was of utmost respectability?"

"Yes." De Vages sounded relieved.

"Were the subscription dances at which you had become acquainted with Miss Greef attended by very respectable people?"

"Yes, they were. The dances continued for two or three months. Several respectable young ladies had been in the practice of going to those dances and returning from them unattended by their parents, as Miss Greef had done."

"At the Greef house, were you not always received in the parlor, with the door wide open, and with the parents present. Or Miss Greef's young slave girl, Roosje?"

"Yes."

"Were your ever with Miss Greef in her bed chamber?"

"No."

"Did you ever pay your addresses to Miss Greef—offer marriage?"

"No."

"Or make love to her?"

A hushed gallery waited for the answer. De Vages, his ears jutting out like red beacons, glanced at Elisabeth with seeming regret, and at Hendrik Greef with seeming assurance.

"No, I did not. I swear it."

De Wet nodded. "One more question, Mr. de Vages. You joined Miss Greef at the subscription dances after the defendant, Mr. Verreaux, abandoned her in June, 1827—"

"Objection!" Cloete bolted up from his chair. "Your lordships, the young lady was never abandoned. Mr. de Wet would turn this court into an amalgam of hyperbole and melodrama. Mr. Verreaux did not leave Miss Greef alone in the middle of the veldt, or on Robben Island off the coast. He terminated a relationship with utmost sincerity and honesty, according to his parents' wishes—"

"The scoundrel abandoned a woman with child!" De Wet thundered. "His child! In the midst of a betrothal!"

Justice Menzies cleared his throat. "That will do. Both of you, reserve the speeches for your summaries. Go on, Mr. de Wet."

"Thank you, your Lordship." de Wet turned back to de Vages. "After the beginning of June, when you were with Miss Greef at the subscription dances, did you see the defendant, Mr. Verreaux, there?"

"Yes, I did."

"And was he squiring a woman at these dances?"

De Vages winced, seemingly perplexed by the question. "Yyy … yes," he stammered.

"And do you know this woman by name?"

De Vages gaped at de Wet, as if they had not rehearsed this testimony. "I … I … believe so." He turned his head to look up briefly at Chief Justice Wylde.

"With whom was Mr. Verreaux keeping company, Mr. de Vages," de Wet pressed.

The lady in the feathered hat grabbed Fairbairn's notebook and wrote, "Her initials are J. W. It spells the rot behind the robes." Fairbairn raised his eyebrows. How much did this lady know about Wylde?

De Vages hesitated. He scanned the courtroom, his head jerking nervously from left to right, as if to check whether the woman was in the gallery, then began fidgeting with his shirt collar. He looked pleadingly at de Wet.

"I'd rather not say, sir," he whispered, but not softly enough to keep from being overheard by the justices on the bench.

"Answer the question, please, Mr. de Vages," Wylde ordered.

De Vages hesitated, shrugged, then blurted out, "Jane Wylde, sir."

A muffled roar rolled through the gallery. Chief Justice Wylde got off his chair. His head could barely be seen above the top of the bench. He stared straight ahead, seemingly half-conscious, not hearing the crowd, not aware that de Wet had walked back to the plaintiff's table and sat down beside Elisabeth. He opened his mouth to speak, then closed it, turned to look at Menzies and Burton, and retreated from the bench.

At the defense table, Verreaux appeared dismayed, whispered something to Cloete, and returned to his sketchbook.

Cloete, unperturbed, waited till de Vages left the witness box. He took a document from a folder, held it conspicuously in front of him, and approached Justice Menzies and Justice Burton.

"Your Lordships, the defendant submits this request to the court that the Chief Justice be recused from these proceedings because of an apparent conflict of interest."

Menzies nodded. "Duly considered, Advocate Cloete."

Cloete bowed slightly. "We end our case by placing in evidence this letter. It was written by the plaintiff, Miss Greef, to Mr. Verreaux in response to his letter of June 4, 1827 to Mr. and Mrs. Greef and Miss Greef, in which he withdrew his promise of betrothal. Miss Greef's letter is undated. But its first sentence implies that it was written the next day, June 5, 1827. Plaintiff has stipulated the authenticity of this letter in which Miss Greef acceded to and accepted Mr. Verreaux's reasons for dissolving his pledge—that being of minority age, he had not, as required by French law, obtained the consent of his parents, and that he had not the means to support—"

Without warning, Elisabeth Greef shot up with such violence that her chair flew backward and clattered noisily on the polished wooden floor. She tore the ribbons from her head and shook out her hair, allowing it to spring untamed over her forehead and down to her shoulders. She turned to face Verreaux across the courtroom, lips trembling, hands at her sides clenched into fists.

Verreaux stood up, deliberately picked up his chair, and slammed it to the floor. He held up his sketch book for her to see. It was a freshly drawn portrait of Elisabeth—asleep, hair tousled, eyes closed, face shadowed in pain in the long oblique light of the African moon.

The gallery was stunned into silence by the exchange. They stared first at the portrait of Elisabeth and then at her, as if to check her likeness from a previous time. Justice Menzies looked at Burton, rose from the bench and banged his gavel.

"For this day, this court is adjourned!"

The lady with the feathered hat stood up. "I sense you are unattached, Mr. Fairbairn—Robert, if I may. And you may call me Auriana. Auriana Brouwer. Daughter of a brewer. Here in the Cape. You are likely familiar with him. And like the beer he brews, you may rightly perceive that I am headstrong. Even potent. And also unattached."

She smiled at him. "Perhaps, over one of my father's ales, we can discuss this trial and Chief Justice Wylde. And discrete inquiries I could make on behalf of your investigatory newspaper."

23

Cape Colony
Friday, March 20, 1829

Auriana Brouwer and Robert Fairbairn left the Cape Supreme Court and crossed the Heerengracht canal, which was carrying water from Table Mountain to the city. On Waale Street, beside the Dutch East Indies Company Gardens, surveyors were staking out the foundation for St. George's Cathedral, the new Anglican church. Company slaves had swept up the dead locusts in the street into large, brown skeletal mounds and set them on fire. The pyres hung a fetid, gray pall on the late heat of the autumn day. A block and a half down Waale Street, Brouwer's Ale House stood back from the street, a brown brick building with two white pillars on the portico. A Dutch flag clung to a high pole anchored in the garden.

Inside, Auriana Brouwer removed her hat, revealing blond hair metamorphosing to gray. Fairbairn thought it sharpened her face, the narrow blue eyes, pointed chin, and the thin, straight nose that angled high out of her skin like a bayonet. She scrutinized him across the polished wooden table, and he her, as if they were conducting surficial autopsies for clues to their psyches beneath.

"Who are you, Miss Brouwer?" he asked. "Apart from being the daughter of Jan Brouwer?"

She reached between the glasses of ale and placed her hand on his. "What you mean is, who is this lady in the feathered hat who sought out the seat beside you at a court trial?"

Robert liked the way her lips pursed at the end of every sentence. "Yes," he admitted. He looked quickly around the ale house, lowered his voice, and added, "not that I am displeased. On the contrary. I am flattered. No—mystified. Why this trial? Why me?"

Auriana raised a corner of her mouth into a half smile. "I came here recently from Amsterdam. My father sent for me. He wants to enter the politics here in Cape Town—run for Council. I will be managing the ale house while he does. And … shall we say … advising him."

"Well, that is news," Robert remarked, pulling out his notebook, "How would you like me to describe your role? Confidant? Aide?"

Auriana shook her head. "Neither. He is not quite ready to announce his candidacy. You might say I am his antennae. I sense the civic alchemy of the place. Your paper is one of the finer, enlightened elements. Also courageous. You've refused to submit to government censorship. You've published accusations of abuse of power against Governor Somerset. He's banned your paper twice. I thought I should become acquainted with its editor. What better venue than this trial. Treachery in love. Perfidy among lovers."

"Indeed," Robert said, somewhat disquieted. "I hope you are not speaking from experience."

Auriana burst into laughter. It was loud enough to draw stares from the other tables, from three women in handsome frocks accompanied by men in suits. Robert thought he recognized them from the courtroom. If they were discussing the trial it was in tones too low to overhear.

"You may learn those privacies in time," Auriana intimated, touching his hand again, then raised her glass in a toast. She motioned him to do likewise.

"Here's to my father's election. I will tell you this. He raised a daughter who excelled in literature, the zoological sciences, and mathematics—three talents not expected of women in Dutch society. Rembrandt portrayed few women. Those he did are not performing anatomical dissections or analytical calculations."

Robert laughed. "Consider me forewarned. What about your mother?"

Auriana pursed her lips. "She died in childbirth—my brother. I was four years old. My tanta—my aunt, her older sister—moved in with us. She cared for the household." Auriana paused. "But my father raised me," she repeated, firmly.

Robert sat back. "Of course, I know your father. He is an important figure here in the Cape. His views are valued. So is this ale house. It is more than a drinking establishment. It is a social house. Cape society does not have many places to gather and dispute the issues of the day. This is one of the few. A few pints loosen the tongue. Polite banter becomes impolite, honest, almost brutally so. Difficult change is coming to the Cape."

"Beginning with the Council's Slave Punishment Law," Auriana declared. "It's bare human decency to require slave owners to keep a record of a slave's misdeed, the penalty, and how it was meted out. What opponents really fear is that the Council and the Colony are creeping toward abolishing slavery."

Robert nodded. "Precisely. It will happen in stages. You have sensed much in your short time here. The *Commercial Advertiser*, of course, is for abolition. As is England. Our rival paper, *De Zuid-Afrikaan*, is against it. Did you know that it is owned by Advocate de Wet?"

"No!" Auriana exclaimed, surprised. "But I did hear that its editorials have spurred slave owners to riot in Stellenbosch and Koeberg."

"Yes, it's true. They resent the slave punishment law. It's taken away their absolute rights over their property—their slaves."

Auriana raised her arms, angrily. "It's taken away absolute rights over indiscriminate beatings and rape. Mr. de Villiers and Roosje come to mind."

Robert leaned forward. "Is that why you think she disappeared before the trial?"

Auriana shook her head. "No, Robert." She slowly sipped her ale, as if she needed time to contemplate her words. "I suspect otherwise. Roosje did not abscond out of shame. She absconded out of fear. De Villiers may have shamed her. But it was something else that frightened her into fleeing."

"What do you mean?" Robert asked, raising his brows, puzzled. He pushed his glass aside, grabbed his notebook and began flipping the pages. "Did I miss a revelation from the witness stand?"

"Remember Cloete's cross-examination of Sarah Bishop this morning? The midwife? Elisabeth Greef dispatched her to tell Verreaux of the birth of his child. Roosje led her there. During her testimony, Verreaux sketched a swaddled infant—one that he had refused to see! Why?"

"He's cocky. And a scoundrel, as de Wet said. He likes to taunt."

"Perhaps," Auriana agreed. "But as soon as Cloete spotted it, he swiftly turned the sketch over so no one would see it. Later I saw him slide it into his case. What are they hiding? There is a business here that remains unanswered. I think it is this business that scared Roosje away from the courtroom."

Robert scratched his head. "You are a suspicious one. Is that the legacy of mixing literature, zoology and mathematics?"

Auriana frowned at him. "Don't patronize me, Robert. There are legitimate questions here. As with John Wylde, our esteemed Chief Justice of the Cape Supreme Court. The rumors in my circles in Cape society are too salacious for the *Advertiser*. But surely you have heard them."

Robert signaled the bartender for two more ales. "Auriana, newspaper editors are barraged by rumors. Many are anonymous. Others are whispered to me as offerings, much as in church. They want to purchase a piece of heaven or revenge." He leaned back in his chair. "What have you heard?"

"Nothing meant for heaven or revenge. Perhaps for hell."

The bartender brought two ales to the table and nodded at Auriana. She waited for him to leave.

"Robert, what do you know about Wylde and his family?"

"He used to be a Judge-Advocate in Australia, in New South Wales. He left for England in 1820 to attain a better position. His wife stayed behind. Four years ago he was posted here. He has a large house a few streets away."

"It has to be large!" Auriana exclaimed. "He lives with his mother-in-law, his five eldest sons, and his daughter, Jane."

"You are well informed," Robert acknowledged.

"Did you know that his wife arrived here a week ago?"

Robert shook his head.

"No, you wouldn't. She has a six year-old daughter in tow."

Robert raised his eyebrows. "Is that meaningful?"

Auriana looked at him, incredulous. "Robert! For God's sake! When did Wylde leave Australia? Nine years ago! How old is the child? Six. My mathematical training tells me he is not the father! Unless he returned to Australia for an intimate visit with his wife six years ago. Or," she added, sarcastically, "he sent her a packet of his seed to deposit. We know he did neither."

Robert reddened. He quickly checked the other tables. Her fusillade hadn't been overheard. "So, the child is not his."

"Quite. He is suing for divorce."

"The paper will carry it. When the divorce is registered." He took a long gulp of ale and shrugged. "Wylde is not the first man to be cuckolded. Nor the last."

"He may be more than cuckolded by his wife. She may expose what Cape society has only whispered. Their daughter, Jane, seems to have been with child until a few weeks ago. Wylde kept her from public view during the fall and winter of last year and the spring of this year. Remember what de Vages said. Jane Wylde was the young woman who Verreaux was squiring at the Saturday dances last summer after he abandoned Elisabeth Greef."

Robert rubbed his face. "Yes, I remember. Are you thinking he impregnated her as well?" he suggested quietly.

Auriana pursed her lips. "Perhaps. But the whispers are much more vile."

"What do you mean?" He knew the rumors. He wondered how intimately Auriana had managed to penetrate Cape society.

"Incest!" She spewed the word. "Wylde bedding his daughter. By all accounts it has been ongoing. Some say forced. Some say consensual. But I don't believe it. The difference may be moot, as Jane is weak-minded. If she birthed the child, no one has seen it. And if she did not …" Auriana leaned forward and hissed "… Wylde took care of it! The child is likely his, not Verreaux's. He should be removed from the bench, thrashed a thousand times, and deported to a prison in England." Auriana sat back, the fury lingering before it slowly drained from her face.

"I understand, Auriana," Robert said, his tone sincere yet cautious. "But as with your suspicions about the whereabouts of the Greef child, there is no evidence. Such scandal could ruin Wylde. It would be tragic if it were false."

Auriana took a sip of ale, licked her lips, and leaned toward him, her eyes narrowed, secretive, about to reveal a conspiracy. "Cape Town society is particularly insular. Little goes unnoticed. Last November, at his home, Wylde consulted the family physician, Dr. Murray, about Jane. He wanted a remedy for what he said was her "female indisposition." According to the servants, that was polite language for an enlarged midriff, indigestion, headaches, and a sudden absence of the monthlies. When Murray allegedly surmised that Jane was with child, Wylde dismissed him. Sir John was then seen in the Cape library perusing books on midwifery and gynecology."

"Curious and suspicious," Robert admitted, "but hardly definitive."

Auriana held up her hand. "There's more. At the end of April, a doctor named Stevenson arrived in Cape Town on a ship on his way to Australia. He was subsequently seen paying three visits to the Wylde house. Shortly afterward, Jane began her monthlies again! Wylde abruptly moved the family to an inn on the south road to Simonstown. Jane has since been secluded from all visitors. The servants remain in the house in Cape Town. Ostensibly it is to save costs. More likely, it is suspected, to conceal Jane's recovery."

"From what?" Robert asked.

"The birth of a child." Auriana paused. "Or an abortion." She paused again and pursed her lips. "Perhaps infanticide."

"Has anyone seen such a child? Or know of it?"

Auriana pointed a finger at him. "No! But the damaging speculation has reached the highest levels. The Cape governor, Sir Lowry Cole, is no fool. My sources tell me he has written the Secretary of State for War and the Colonies, Viscount Goderich, in England, about the Wylde affair."

"If true, that is significant," Robert conceded, and scribbled in his notebook. "For Cole, such embarrassment could be disastrous. He must deal with the Wylde court on the laws governing the slave question."

"Exactly."

Robert downed the rest of his ale. "Well, I can tell you now that I have heard similar stories. Without the details, mind you. But what if Verreaux, not Wylde, is the father. Is that the swaddled child he drew in the courtroom? To taunt Wylde, not Elisabeth? Perhaps that is why Cloete hid it so quickly. He is undoubtedly aware of the rumors of … uh … incest. And he may well know of Sir Coles' letter. I suspect he would cite both the rumors and the letter in his motion to have Wylde recused from the trial."

"Yes, it is possible," Auriana agreed, sounding fatalistic. "Both Wylde and Verreaux could have taken advantage of Jane last summer. Wylde regularly. Verreaux after the Saturday dances." She shook her head, pushed her glass aside, then abruptly rose from the table. "I'm sickened by it all."

They left the ale house and turned up Waale Street. They covered their mouths as he steered her between the smoldering piles of dead locusts.

"I will see you home."

"I expect no less." She took his arm, and glanced up at him, pain and amity sparring across her face.

It was then he knew he would let himself be enamored.

24

Cape Town
Wednesday, January 27

Harry had missed the one-page document when he'd first leafed through the court record. He found it bound in the ledger immediately following the transcript of the first day of the trial, Friday, March 20, 1829. Cloete had filed a motion to the court to have Chief Justice Wylde recused from the trial.

In the Supreme Court of the Colony at the Cape of Good Hope

**To His Honor Sir John Wylde, Knight,
Chief Justice
and the Judges of the Supreme Court of the
Cape of Good Hope**

**Elisabeth Helena Henrietta Greef,
assisted by her father, Hendrik Greef, Plaintiff**

vs

Jules Verreaux, defendant

DEFENDANT'S MOTION

Jules Verreaux, the Defendant in the case, by his Attorney at Law, H. Cloete, petitions the court and states: that the honourable Chief Justice, Sir John Wylde, be recused from these proceedings for reason apparent from the testimony on cross examination of a witness for the plaintiff, Mr. Jan de Vages; that the defendant, Jules Verreaux, has been associated with Jane Wylde, daughter of the honourable Chief Justice Wylde, in a manner that may not be beneficial to the defendant; that serious matters arising concerning the honourable Chief Justice and said daughter, Jane Wylde, have been reported to the honourable governor of Cape Colony, Sir Lowry Cole; and that the honourable Sir Lowry Cole has seen it his duty to report said serious matters in the previous year to the honourable Viscount Goderich, Secretary of State for War and the Colonies.

For which reasons the Defendant prays that recusal of the honourable Chief Justice Wylde from these proceedings be granted.

Filed March 20, 1829
Henry Cloete
Advocate for the defendant.

Harry wondered whether the archives had Sir Lowry Cole's correspondence for "the previous year," 1828. Cole's letter to Goderich could be important. Harry filled out the request slip and handed it to the woman with the licorice hair and soft, melodic voice. After three days in the Cape Town Archives, he realized how often he'd been drawn to look up at her, to listen to the sound of her words, each one smoothed and polished, as if the raw letters had been through a tumbler or rounded by the waves at Cape Point.

She returned after ten minutes with a flip-top, gray, archival pamphlet box, its seams reinforced with black metal stitching. Her white ID tag read 'Dikeledi Abrahamse'. He asked her what it meant. Instinctively, she glanced down at her badge and back at Harry, intrigued by his interest.

"'Dikeledi,'" she sang out quietly, each syllable a half tone. "It is traditional Tswana. It means 'tears.'" She paused, then smiled, briefly. "My mother wept when I was not stillborn. Her first two died."

She glanced down at her ID tag again. "'Abrahamse' means we once were the property—slaves—of the family Abraham." She fingered her hair. "And your name?"

Harry handed her his card. "Przewalski. Harry. It's not as melodic."

She grinned. "Ah, a detective. You have curiosities about old trials, old letters, and old names. She examined Harry's card again. "Przewalski. Polish. Also the wild horse. From the steppes of Eurasia. But you are from Pittsburgh in America?"

"Blame it on emigration. My father."

"Yes, like the Dutch and English here. Abraham was a Dutch land owner. He bought slaves at auction at the Slave House. Have you seen it?"

"Just the outside," Harry answered.

"You should go inside. The Slave House became overcrowded. The slaves were moved out. The building was converted into government offices—and the Cape Supreme Court. Now it is a museum. I was taken there first as a schoolchild. Now I think that when the British installed the court there it was an architectural attempt at repentance and burial. Justice built over top of enslavement. Only the British would think of that."

She handed Harry the box of correspondence. "He was tried in that court, you know," she said nonchalantly, "your Mr. Verreaux—the case you are reading. I know about him."

It was the second time she had mentioned Verreaux. Before Harry could ask, a group of students burst noisily into the Archives on a class assignment and crowded around the counter. Dikeledi welcomed them, and quickly mouthed "later" to Harry. He retreated to his reading table, intrigued by her interest in Verreaux.

In the box of Sir Lowery Cole's correspondence Harry found a letter dated March 11, 1828, to Lord Goderich, the British Secretary of State for War and the Colonies. Two paragraphs pertained to the Verreaux trial, to Wylde, and to Cloete's motion for Wylde's recusal.

Late in the year 1827 the reports respecting Miss Wylde's being pregnant were in circulation, originating, I believe, from her appearance, which was such as to create suspicion and to

*attract observation from every one. There are also suspicions
of a base depravity respecting Sir John in this matter.*

*So long as those charges regarding his Daughter remain un-
explained there must & will attach a strong suspicion against
himself & I have no hesitation in stating as my opinion that
under these circumstances he ought not to retain the Situation
he holds.*

Harry wondered how Cloete, in his motion for Wylde's recusal,
had learned the gist of the letter from Governor Cole to Goderich.
The gossip about Wylde and his daughter must have permeated
every niche of Cape society. Certainly its legal circles. Had the
newspapers carried accounts of the rumors? Or records of Wylde
births and christenings?

It was too late in the day to ask Dikeledi for the archived records of the *South African Commercial Advertiser* and *De Zuid-Afrikaan*. But it was not too late to accept her silent offer and propose
a drink and dinner.

25

Cape Town
Wednesday, January 27

Dikeledi owned a cartoon Fiat, a green, miniature two-seat-er with tiny wheels that might have come off a lawn mower. Harry slumped forward to keep his head from scraping the roof. He noticed a pile of books on the rear jump seat and a workout bag squashed into the tiny hatchback trunk.

Dikeledi headed north on Adderley Street. After four lights it turned into Heerengracht Street. She pointed at the street sign.

"It's Dutch. Means 'gentleman's canal.' It carried water from Table Mountain down into the city. It ran between the Slave Lodge and the East Indies Company Gardens."

"Like the River Styx," Harry said, dryly, "separating the slaves in the underworld from the owners on earth."

She glinted at him, a quick register of surprise. "I didn't think detectives came metaphorical. Or up on Greek myth."

"I'm in the business of myth," Harry quipped. "Find a crime, I'll give you the myth."

Dikeledi laughed. At the next light, she swung the Fiat up Marine Drive, a narrow sinuous road that hugged the edge of the northwestern coastline. A black ink washed the horizon. In the dark, Harry couldn't tell whether it was sea or sky.

About ten kilometers up the road, she abruptly swung off and parked at a two-story wooden shack with a wide veranda. Faded letters spelled out 'Mollie's Fish Tavern.' Dikeledi let him to a table outside under a camouflage of fish netting.

"This is a shebeen," she explained, "an informal tavern owned by women—shebeen queens. They've brewed the traditional beer for generations, while the men were away at the mines. They were taught by a Dutch brewer. Do you trust me to order?"

"Please," Harry said. She went into the shack and returned with two beers, cloudy, unfiltered, barely cold. The mugs were labeled 'Brouwers Vintage Cask.' It tasted like a fine mead.

"Nice choice," Harry said. Suddenly, he was desperate for a cigarette. The Zig-Zag papers were sitting on his desk in Pittsburgh in the office on the fourth floor of the extinct steel mill. The can of Drum was rolling around on the south bank of the Monongahela River. He scanned the veranda of the shebeen, hoping to mooch a smoke. No luck.

"You mentioned Verreaux at the archives," he said to Dikeledi. "I'm suspicious of coincidence."

Dikeledi twisted her mouth. "History attracts coincidence. Do you know about El Negro, Harry?"

"Yes." He remembered Liza's brief. "Verreaux and his brother Édouard dug up a Botswanan chief around 1830, taxidermied him, shipped him back to Paris, put him in a display case, and shopped him around as El Negro."

"Right!" Dikeledi pointed her finger at him. "They stole the body the night after his burial in an old Tswana town, Kgatlane. It's about 900 kilometers north of here, near the junction of the Vaal and Orange rivers. The town is gone, a rubble heap. I was born near there, in Douglas, a few kilometers up the Vaal river. Now I'm here, at Cape Town University, doing a doctoral dissertation on El Negro. In history. There's your coincidence."

Harry nodded. "The body was eventually repatriated."

"Yes, in 2000. But he was re-buried in Gabarone, the capital of Botswana, not in his original gravesite in Kgatlane. It's not a pretty story. El Negro is a map of European racism."

The food came, large steaming bowls of fish stew in a hot red sauce, with a basket of flat bread and a white bean paste. Dikeledi ordered two more of the vintage ales.

"The Verreaux brothers brought the Tswana's body back to Cape Town," she recounted, her voice far off, as if she'd been a witness to the event. "There they prepared him, like they did an antelope or ostrich." She paused to eat some stew. "You know about taxidermy, Harry?"

He contemplated what to tell her about his past. He'd become impatient with having to explain his life. The bonehunting. Then the war. Now the greasy anatomy of human affairs. Each a separate era. They'd become curated in his mind as three discrete stratigraphic strata, each burying his previous physical and emotional deposits, each separated from the other by a thin, violent seam of blood. The bonehunting ended with Nicole's body parts in a barrel. The war ended with limbs and torsos strewn across the desert. It was a grotesque taxonomy of his life, but one that somehow produced sanity.

"I once worked amid taxidermy," he finally answered. "At a natural history museum in Pittsburgh. The Carnegie. They have a famous diorama, lions attacking a Berber courier astride a camel in the Tunisian desert. One of the Verreaux brothers, Jules, put it together for the 1867 Paris Exposition. Long after El Negro. Or the Greef trial. The diorama was vandalized a month ago."

"Hmmm. Did Verreaux also rob a Tunisian grave for the Berber?"

Harry grabbed a piece of flatbread and dipped it into the stew. "I don't know, but I wouldn't be surprised." He decided not to tell Dikeledi about the bundle in the belly of the camel. "Anyway, someone might have had it in for Verreaux."

"For robbing graves?"

"Perhaps."

"Or abandoning a woman with child?"

He nodded, trying hard not to look surprised that she knew about Elisabeth Greef. "I don't know. I'm just tracking Verreaux down the grubby alleys of taxidermy. That's how the Greef business came up."

"For me too. I dug through the Cape archives for any mention of Verreaux prior to El Negro."

Harry shrugged. "Maybe a relative of El Negro decided to take revenge. Or some zealot stoked by the reburial—you know, poetic justice, one diorama for another. Maybe even a Greef descendant."

"It's a long shot, Harry."

"Yeah, but vendettas are irrational. And petrified in time. What did you make of the Greef affair?"

Dikeledi held up a finger while she finished swallowing a mouthful of stew. "From what I remember of the case, Elisabeth was a strong-headed woman. Too bad she lost her head over that ... bastard. But her kind of woman does. It's the fate of being brazen ... you know ... seduced by independence, recklessness. Now, we women can do that. We have birth control. She didn't. She ended up being another Verreaux specimen, a trophy from the veldt. Like I said—bastard!"

Even when she swore she said it melodically, Harry thought. "What do you think happened to Elisabeth? To the child?"

Dikeledi hunched her shoulders, questioningly. "I don't know. Well-to-do family, the Greefs. If the child didn't die early on, it was likely sent away. That would have unburdened Elisabeth. Made it easier to attract a man. There were lots of men in Cape Town then. Widowers who'd lost their wives to consumption or childbirth. Men passing through from England. Or from the other colonies. Maybe even de Vages—is that his name? The poor sod who courted her, unknowingly, while she was pregnant?"

Harry nodded. "Jan de Vages. Maybe there's a record of a Greef marriage."

Dikeledi shook her head. "Save it. I checked. Nothing in the church or legal registers. Course, she could have gone elsewhere to get married. There were two Cape papers at the time. Neither had any notice of a Greef marriage. Doesn't mean much. The Greefs would not have advertised the christening of bastard child. Or the marriage of a daughter considered deflowered and despoiled."

"What happened to El Negro after Paris?" Harry asked.

Dikeledi wiped her bowl out with the last of the bread. "Like I said, El Negro is a tour of European racism. He reflects the pathologies of the time. And into the 1990s. He was created with forethought. He fulfilled the prejudices of the creator and the audience. The wild man-ape, half human, half beast."

"It's blessed by the Good Book, Dikeledi," Harry declared, leaning back. "Christ, you've brought out the preacher in me."

"What do you mean?"

"Genesis. It's the book that tells western civilization to take dominion over every living thing that moves upon the Earth—including other people. It gave us El Negro, the poor Berber, and countless other stuffed humans. Not to mention slavery."

Dikeledi raised her eyebrows. "Whew! Does this preacher have a religion?"

Harry grimaced, pushed his bowl away, and downed the rest of the beer. "Nope. Sorry. God is fiction. Religion is our very first psychological diorama—fear of death seeking solace in the absurd. It's no coincidence that every faith has a promise of an afterlife."

She put her fork down. "And a story of origins. African legend relates the story of Qamata, born from the union of the sun-god, Tixo, and earth goddess, Djobela. Qamata, appropriately enough, created the world, but was crippled in a titanic struggle with the great dragon of the sea, Nganyaba, and could not protect the dry land. The earth goddess, Djobela, intervened. She created four giants to help keep the sea from inundating the land. The giants asked to be turned into four guardian mountains—on the east, west, north and south—to hold back the sea after their death. Djobela did so. Table Mountain, here in the Cape, is the Watcher of the South."

"I like it," Harry said. "Full of fury and tempest and magic and warring gods. Just like all creation myths. Anthropology counts about a hundred and thirty of them—other peoples, other cultures, other fables. It's okay as long as fable remains fable. But when it becomes a professed ideology, watch out. No mountain will keep the irrational sea at bay."

Dikeledi looked at him intently, reached over, and momentarily brushed the sleeve of his shirt. "Yes, here is the irrational. El Negro ended up in Spain. A naturalist from Catalonia, Francesc Darder, bought him for his private collection around 1880. El Negro entertained thousands at the Barcelona Universal Exposition in 1888. He was the noble savage, a shade below human—"

"Yeah, a black shade," Harry murmured.

"Yes. They rubbed the body with boot black to make El Negro even darker."

Harry frowned. "Let me guess. The arsenic from the taxidermy was bleaching sections of his skin."

Dikeledi nodded. "You do know taxidermy, Harry. El Negro spent the next hundred years on exhibit in Banyoles, north of Barcelona, in a municipal museum named in Darder's honor. Then, in the 1980s, the editor of the local newspaper raised hell. He called it shameful racism and demanded that El Negro be removed from exhibit and repatriated to Botswana. The museum was a backwater, but the publicity instantly attracted 70,000 visitors. The town council refused to take down the exhibit and send El Negro back. One of the members declared, 'The talk of racism is absurd. Anyway, human rights only apply to living people, not dead.' This councilman also happened to be a curator at the Museo Darder."

"Keepers of the past," Harry uttered. "Museums can breed myopia—object focused, issue deprived. Too many have an immune reaction to change."

"It gets worse!" Dikeledi exclaimed. "Townspeople wore T-shirts that proclaimed 'Banyoles loves you El Negro, don't go!' They celebrated Easter with miniature El Negro chocolates." She sipped the last of her beer, fingering the label on the mug, and looked out across the blackness beyond the edge of the continent. "In the end, the Spanish government intervened to avoid international embarrassment. The 1992 Olympics were coming to Barcelona. So it forced repatriation of the Tswana."

"Did they do any forensics on his body before burial?"

"Yes. It was CAT-scanned and autopsied. On the outside, what remained of him was skin, pubic hair and penis. Inside, were his leg and arm bones, and his skull. He was short, about five-foot five in life. Judging from his teeth, he was about twenty-seven when he died in Kgatlane. Probably from pneumonia—his nails were clubbed. His toes were splayed from having walked long distances.

There was a long scar on the left side, from hip to armpit, where Verreaux had sewn up the skin with a basting stitch. And the foreskin was missing—he'd been circumcised."

It began to rain, heavy drops from a dark sky. In the car, heading to the lights of the city, Harry asked her, "Did the forensic team conduct any DNA tests on the body?"

She nodded. "Yes, from a bit of the Tswana's pubic hair. But, they never released the genetic information. It's buried, metaphorically, in a safe in the town hall of Girona, south of Banyoles. I've filed a request to see it, but haven't yet received an answer."

Dikeledi drummed her long fingers on the steering wheel, keeping time with the swish of the windshield wipers. "I had my own DNA sequenced at the university ... to compare it to his. El Negro had come from Kgatlane. So, originally, did I. My Tswana great-great grandparents were displaced upriver from Kgatlane to what is now Douglas town, where I was born. Perhaps he and I are kin."

She turned to Harry with a sardonic laugh and patted his arm. "Don't worry, Harry, I'm not the one who vandalized Verreaux's Carnegie exhibit to revenge El Negro."

26

Cape Supreme Court Saturday, March 21, 1829

At ten o'clock in the morning, Chief Justice Wylde opened the second day of the trial of Elisabeth Greef vs. Jules Verreaux. People from Cape Town had begun crowding into the courtroom gallery two hours earlier. They were anxious to hear how the justices would rule on defense counselor Cloete's request that Wylde be recused from the proceedings. His daughter, Jane Wylde, had been identified by Mr. Jan de Vages on the witness stand yesterday as having been on the arm of Verreaux at the Saturday dances after June, 1927.

Wylde's announcement was short and anticlimactic. After consulting with the other two justices, Menzies and Burton, he had decided he would not withdraw from the bench. He said the naming in testimony of his daughter, Jane, was peripheral and would not constitute a conflict of interest. Neither Cloete nor plaintiff's counselor de Wet objected.

Robert Fairbairn, editor of the *South African Commercial Advertiser*, had also arrived early. He looked for Auriana Brouwer to enter the gallery, then placed his jacket, notebook and pencil on the seat beside him. He couldn't imagine that she would miss the summaries.

Wylde hit the gavel, looked out at the gallery and intoned, "Both the plaintiff and the defense have called their witnesses. Advocate de Wet will present his closing argument, followed by Advocate Cloete.

De Wet stood up at the plaintiff's table and bowed slightly to the bench. Beside him, Elisabeth Greef had returned composed, almost prim, wearing a pink floral dress with flat blue shoes. Two matching blue ribbons again imprisoned her wild tangle of blond hair. Fairbairn noted that Verreaux had brought fresh sheets of sketching paper and sticks of lead.

"Your Lordships," de Wet began, pacing slowly in front of the defendant's table, "it is instructive to remind the court of the defendant's four original pleas. First, that he was minor when he pledged betrothal to Miss Greef. Second, that he did not receive parental consent to marry. Third, that Miss Greef willingly accepted his letter withdrawing his marriage offer. And fourth, his ignorance of Dutch. As your Lordships heard yesterday, Mr. Verreaux has wisely retracted this last plea, admitting that it was false. Nevertheless, it demonstrates the defendant's unprincipled and duplicitous nature in his treatment of Miss Greef, and his desperation to absolve himself of responsibility to her and his contract with her."

De Wet paused to walk over to the bailiff's table and pick up Verreaux's French passport and certificate of birth. Auriana Brouwer chose that moment to noiselessly make her way along the first row of chairs in the gallery and slip into her seat beside Fairbairn. She squeezed his arm and mouthed "thank you."

"It is also instructive, your Lordships," de Wet continued, "to compare the defendant's three remaining pleas with the evidence before the Court. His excuse of being a minor rests on these two documents. His advocate, Mr. Cloete, seems to be convinced of this being the case, and has accordingly endeavored to prove it so, but has failed. What do I mean by that?"

De Wet waved the birth certificate unceremoniously at the bench. "Mr. Verreaux's alleged *Acte de Naissance* is, at best, merely an informal record. It is not legally certified by any proper French authority, as is the custom with all official French documents, and as is required by Code Napoleon, title 10, articles 203 and 211. The defendant could have provided the reason for the lack of this official sanction, but has neglected to do so."

De Wet took a handkerchief out of his pocket, wiped his spectacles, and pointed at the defense table. Verreaux smirked, picked up his lead, and began sketching a rotund caricature.

"Mr. Verreaux is not a minor. He has lived in Cape Town for four years since his arrival from France in 1825. He had already domiciled and worked here for two years prior to engaging Miss Greef in his nefarious clutches. During this period, he has carried out his extensive labors alone, collecting—no, stealing—the animals and plants of our land for shipment to his father's emporium in Paris."

Abruptly, de Wet turned and pointed to the Union Jack hanging above the three justices. "And he has done this on behalf of his Catholic Majesty, King Charles X of France, and his national museum." Murmurs rose in the gallery.

Auriana nudged Robert. "He's insinuating treason," she whispered, "Verreaux's pillaging of wildlife for a foreign interest."

"Moreover," de Wet raised his voice, "now, in this courtroom, in this legal matter of most weighty import, Mr. Verreaux appears on his own. He is unassisted by guardian or representative. Indeed, the defendant has conducted this case as if he were of age ... a major!" De Wet turned to face the bench. "Which your Lordships should consider as Mr. Verreaux's full admission of that fact."

De Wet clasped his hands behind his back and began pacing slowly across the courtroom, as if he were lecturing to a class in law.

"Therefore the defendant has not come to this country under any kind of legal guardianship. No, he has come as an agent of the French monarchy for the express purpose of setting up business here on his own account. There is ample precedent in the law of this land for this circumstance. A minor was permitted by his parents to go and reside in a foreign country—this country—for purposes other than those of travel and study. He was sent here to transact all manner of business. The law here is clear: in such a case, the minor is considered tacitly emancipated, and therefore, to all purposes, a major."

Justice Menzies cleared his throat, and held up a thick leather-bound tome. "Yes, Mr. de Wet, we are familiar with Grotius' *Manual of Dutch Law*. If a parent permits his son to live separately, and to carry on a trade, it is a tacit act of emancipation. But, if the son runs away or absconds from his parents, it is otherwise—he is only considered emancipated after a year and a day. But in either case, Mr. de Wet, the emancipation may not necessarily apply to marriage without the consent of his parents."

De Wet nodded. "Yes, your Lordship, a fine point for deliberation, and one related to the defendant's second plea—the absence of parental consent." De Wet returned the passport and birth certificate to the bailiff's table and picked up a handwritten letter.

"In Mr. Verreaux's correspondence of June 4 to Miss Greef, in which the defendant withdraws his pledge of betrothal, he claims that 'everything has gone against him' with respect to marriage: he is too poor, and his parents have not given their consent. But, your Lordships, did Mr. Verreaux use his best endeavors to obtain such consent? Absolutely no evidence has been brought forward by the defense to prove that the consent of Mr. Verreaux's parents was ever sought or denied. No letter—either from parents or guardians—has been produced demonstrating their refusal. Undoubtedly, had Mr. Verreaux such a letter in his possession, Advocate Cloete would have offered it in evidence."

De Wet held up his arms in a show of incredulity. "Your Lordships, I contend that Mr. Verreaux never asked his parents for consent. If he did, it must have been by way of astrology!" The gallery burst into laughter. Wylde hit the gavel, but could not contain a grin.

Verreaux, clearly shaken, looked at Elisabeth. For a moment she broke her frozen posture, showing a devilish smile and a slight, impulsive tilt of her head. It made him remember how she would sit naked in the chair in his room, impishly erotic, posing for a sketch, before her sudden ferocious animal embrace, imprisoning him with her legs, consuming him until she was sated. He remembered rinsing the heated sweat from the undulations of her body, her angular frame still quivering, the long arc of her back under the damp blond curls, the glistening outward swell of her breasts. He told her of her wild similitudes—the springbok, that limber, quick-tempered antelope with gossamer legs and sinuous neck that bounded across the African veldt; and the araignee, the female spider that lured her lover, enmeshed him, drained him of his procreative packets, then devoured him.

When the laughter in the gallery subsided, de Wet waved the June 4 letter in front of Verreaux. "And likewise, his plea of poverty as an excuse for his dereliction is insufficient. Rather, it is no plea at all. It is a notorious fact that his French Majesty pays most liberally those gentlemen whom he employs for scientific purposes, as he has the defendant."

Fairbairn turned to Auriana. "I must ask Verreaux about the sums he is being paid." She nodded.

De Wet's voice turned solemn. "Defendant's third and last plea is that Miss Greef responded to his letter of June 4 by acceding to his retraction of the promise of marriage. No such conclusion is warranted. Your Lordships can only imagine Miss Greef's injured, distracted, even temporarily deranged, state of mind under which she wrote her response. And if her mental state is not sufficient, remember her legal state. She is a true minor, living at home with her parents. Therefore, no letter by Miss Greef, without the sanction and consent of her parents, was in any way binding. The law of our land—Grotius's Manual that Justice Menzies previously cited—declares that whatever she might have been competent to do with respect to herself, individually, she had no legal competency with regard to the interests of her offspring or her parents."

De Wet marched over to the defendant's table, grabbed Verreaux's sketch of him, looked at it, crumpled it up, and threw it on the courtroom floor. He leaned forward, put his knuckles on the edge of the table, and thrust his face across until it was inches from Verreaux. Cloete started to stand up to object, hesitated, then sat down. Verreaux, clearly discomfited, refused to look at de Wet. He fidgeted with his lead stick, then quickly pushed his chair back from the table until it wedged against the wooden railing that separated the gallery from court.

"Your Lordships," de Wet thundered, "Mr. Verreaux has no scruples. We accuse him of attempting to throw his guilt on an innocent young gentleman, Mr. Jan de Vages. This gentleman could not in point of time have been the father of Miss Greef's child, for his acquaintance with her had only commenced in July, 1827, when she was already advanced in her pregnancy. Mr. Verreaux laid a snare for young Mr. de Vages. Under pretense of employing him as an interpreter, he sent de Vages to the dark entryway of his lodging at the very moment that Miss Greef was expected. The young lady, supposing de Vages to be Verreaux, very naturally advanced to embrace him. However, the second that she discovered her error, she hastily retreated. This attempt by Verreaux to fix a stain on the character of Miss Greef, whom he had previously so deeply injured, happily failed. But it is indisputable evidence of the vile, calculating character of defendant."

De Wet walked back to the plaintiff's table, put his hand on the shoulder of Elisabeth, and addressed the three justices.

"Your Lordships, the character of this young lady had stood unimpeached and spotless as the sun. Until the ill-fated moment when she had suffered herself to be deceived and seduced by the solemn promises and asseverations of the defendant. The evidence presented—including the solemn oath of Miss Greef tendered to this Court—demonstrates most clearly that neither previous to, nor after, the illicit intercourse with Mr. Verreaux did Miss Greef have any such intercourse with any other suitor. This was an oath that Mr. Verreaux could not take. Indeed, I could not find a single bona fide act in his conduct throughout the whole circumstance of this case."

De Wet turned and motioned to Hendrik Greef seated in the first row in the gallery, and to Elisabeth's sister, Margaretha de Villiers. Her husband, Jan, had not reappeared.

"In summary, your Lordships, the circumstances of this case are of a profoundly aggravated complexion. This calamity did not alone affect Miss Greef. But it also fell most heavily on her father and mother, her sister, and her friends. Miss Greef did not institute the present action under vindictive motives. All that the young lady wishes and hopes for at your Lordship's hands is contractual justice. The injury Miss Greef has sustained is of a nature which can only be alleviated by a matrimonial union with the defendant."

27

Cape Supreme Court
March 21, 1829

At two o'clock in the afternoon, with temperatures cooled by a sudden thunderstorm and rain, Advocate Cloete rose for the defense. Robert leaned over to Auriana. "De Wet appealed to moral sentiment, to emotional sympathy for Elisabeth. Cloete, I predict, will appeal to reason based in law."

Cloete pushed his chair back, put his hands on the defendant's table, and leaned slightly forward. "Your Lordships, I choose to stand here alongside Mr. Verreaux. I will forgo the dramatic antics performed by my learned colleague, Advocate de Wet. The straightforward weight of law will decide this case, not theater. The facts are clear. They are supported by the evidence presented yesterday."

He put his hands in the pockets of his trousers and walked around to the front of the table, as if he were having a casual conversation with the three justices. "Mr. Verreaux was brought to this country by his uncle in 1825 who left him behind for the purpose of collecting a few natural curiosities. He is not in the service of the French Monarch, as asserted without evidence by the plaintiff's counsel. He is employed by his father's emporium, Maison Verreaux, situated on Rue Montmartre in Paris. In fact, the defendant is here on his travels and studies. He is actively employed in improving his intellects by the study of Natural History in particular, and making collections from Nature for the benefit of his father."

Cloete paused, took his hands out of his pocket and folded his arms across his chest. He seemed to be waiting for the justices to offer an objection or interruption. Getting neither, he continued.

"Mr. Verreaux became acquainted with Miss Greef in March, 1827. His passions seem to have been warmly excited. He certainly wrote her amatory letters—three within the first week, and two more within a month. They indicate that all these effusions of passion took place within a short period of time. The motives for his letter of June 4, 1827 to Mr. Greef retracting discussion of marriage to his daughter, Elisabeth, were sincere and remain so. He wrote very honestly of want of subsistence and non-consent of his parents. Without such consent, Mr. Verreaux could not inherit, according to the Napoleonic Code. In her letter of reply to Mr. Verreaux, Miss Greef formally accepted his retraction of promise. She asked him to think no more of her. She only desired to retain possession of a dagger, and a pistol bullet, to which she seemed to have taken a fancy."

Cloete abruptly stepped back around the table, grabbed Verreaux's right wrist and held it up. "As Mr. de Villiers testified, it was this hand that fired the pistol bullet in the Greef parlor one evening in April, 1827. Admittedly, it was a theatrical declaration of his commitment to betrothal to Miss Greef. But it was a sincere declaration, nonetheless." He let Verreaux's hand drop.

"Lastly, your Lordships, Mr. Verreaux was and remains a minor in the laws of this colony and in France, his country of origin. His passport and birth certificate, held in trust by his landlord, Mr. Linage, have been attested to as authentic by the Consul of France. Being abroad, Mr. Verreaux has no access to better proof of his minority than this evidence. Furthermore, Mr. Verreaux was known and considered by Miss Greef and her family as a minor. The argument of tacit emancipation so relied on by plaintiff's counsel is, at best, only an exception to a general rule. Therefore, the law ought to be interpreted and enforced strictly. Mr. Verreaux is a minor. It is a serious thing to tear asunder the ties of parental authority."

Cloete sat down and motioned to Verreaux to sit up in his chair. Chief Justice Wylde signaled the bailiff, who asked the court to rise.

"Gentlemen," Wylde nodded at de Wet and Cloete, "this case has been argued admirably on both sides. Judgment will occur at a future sitting of the court, of which you will be notified."

As the gallery filed out of the courtroom, Auriana turned to Robert.

"Mr. Fairbairn. I ask again, what has happened to the poor child—Miss Greef's son or daughter. Unseen in this courtroom. Perhaps this is understandable, given the testimony about her ... origins. She should be a year old now, by my reckoning. Yet, no mention is made of her, either inside or outside the court. What is more, I have checked the archives of your faithful paper. One would expect a record of a christening of a baby Greef after February 24, 1828."

She grabbed his left sleeve and tugged. "But there is none. Write that down," she ordered, "*there is none.*" She let go of his sleeve.

28

Cape Town Colony, March 21, 1829

On Saturday afternoon, at the end of the trial they walked hurriedly to Fairbairn's house and fell into immediate intimacy. His small parlor was as disheveled as his clothes. Auriana thought it was quaint. Newspapers littered the two overstuffed red chairs and the handsome cushioned sofa. The writing table in the center of the room held a scatter of open notebooks and sheets of paper on which he was summarizing the Greef trial.

Robert hurriedly scattered the newspapers off the sofa onto the floor, pulled Auriana to him, cupped her face, and kissed her deeply on the lips. She let him, then began to kiss back, opening her mouth, darting her tongue against his.

"During the trial I began to itch for this," he murmured teasingly against her cheek.

"Now we can scratch it," she whispered, seductively, "slowly, and often." She began unbuttoning her blouse and pulled him down onto the sofa.

Afterward, in the fading light of dusk, she lay on his chest, both breathing heavily, both wet from the heat. In her mind she knew that they were both too well known, that Cape society would be all the more harsh and judge them amoral. She didn't care. They had met through a trial, a singularity of fate. It had made them desperate and wise not to forfeit the present. They would sustain their private desire of this moment, and then the next, and the next, until time was done with them.

"I remember a promise of wine, Robert," Auriana said. "And to listen to me about the Greef child."

"Yes, I did. And I see that I best get used to this new order of things ... the cognitive succeeding the carnal."

"Only a newspaper editor would say that," she said, poking him in the chest.

He kissed her quickly on the mouth, fetched two white robes from a closet, tossed one to her, put the other on, and disappeared into his small kitchen.

Auriana sank into a corner of the sofa, her knees pulled up against her chest. She realized she was sitting in the deep haunch of a long-bodied lion. The two arms and front legs of the sofa, each a polished, naked mahogany, ended in immense carved paws. It triggered the image of Verreaux on the veldt, rifle raised, a shot fired, a massive maned beast crumpling to the ground, and the bronze skin-hide and skull of a male lion being loaded onto a ship bound for Marseilles and Maison Verreaux in Paris.

Robert came back with two glasses and an open bottle of red wine.

"Perfect," Auriana said, taking a long sip. "Here is my second itch, Robert. The Greef child. I believe it was murdered."

"Hmmm," Robert frowned. "Why this theme of mortem, Auriana, this business with murder. What brings it to mind?"

"Conspiracy. Perhaps obsession. The Greef family. No one will discuss the child's death. Neither will Sarah Bishop, the midwife who testified at the trial. She and the slave girl, Roosje, delivered Elisabeth's message of the birth to Verreaux that afternoon."

"Yes," Robert reached out and brushed a strand of her gray blond hair away from her face. "I remember. Elisabeth's last act of desperation. She hoped the arrival of the child might re-awaken Verreaux's instincts of fatherhood."

Auriana leaned forward. "No! I don't think so. Elisabeth Greef is not a woman given to desperation. Her last act was murder. She took the life of Verreaux's child after she received his answer. And it was calculated, not desperate."

Robert shook his head. "What's desperate, Auriana, is your conjecture. I don't believe it. What made you imagine that?"

"Remember Elisabeth's letter to Verreaux? How she reacted to his retraction of betrothal? She flaunts her ethics against his duplicity. She thanks him for revealing himself to be a 'dishonorable man without character.' She does not plead with him to reconsider. She does not ask him to pity her or their imminent child. No! Instead, she avows she is well rid of him. And she gives him her first warning—vengeance 'is the consequence of such a deed.' She has already begun to plan her acts of vengeance."

Robert wrinkled his brow. "I'm not sure. She and her family are church goers. Her letter echoed Christian retribution. Wasn't there something about God and punishment?"

"Exactly. It is her second warning in the letter. And almost prophetic: 'God cannot leave the author of such grief unpunished.' The grief is hers. She will be the one to exact punishment. She will be God's instrument."

Robert leaned over, dipped his finger in the wine, brushed her lips, and kissed her. "You perform autopsies on events before they are dead."

Auriana narrowed her eyes at him. "Here is the autopsy. The child was born at the Greef home during the morning of February 14, 1828. That afternoon, Elisabeth sent Sarah Bishop and Roosje to inform Verreaux that he had become a father. He sent them back with the message that he wanted nothing to do with Elisabeth or the child. The next day, Elisabeth smothered his baby. That was her first act of vengeance—the vengeance of God she threatened in her letter. But it was not sufficient. Nine months later, in November, she began her next act of revenge. She sued Verreaux for breach of contract. She would make him face his future in court. Do you know what will happen if she wins?"

Robert nodded, grabbed the bottle of wine, and refilled their glasses. "Verreaux will lose his passport. The authorities will confiscate it. He will then have a choice: either obey the court and marry Elisabeth, or go to prison."

"Exactly!" Auriana exclaimed. "Either choice would sentence him to a forced incarceration. And either would be loveless, save for daily sodomy by the men in prison."

Robert groaned. "You're right. Verreaux is a pretty boy. Fair-haired. Attractive. I know the prisons here. He's what the other prisoners will call 'fresh meat.'"

Auriana shuddered, reached out, and stroked his chin. "He's a younger you, Robert. Stay out of the penitentiary."

Robert raised his palm in a mock vow. "I plan to, at least until the *Advertiser* has a serious skirmish with the wrong people in the Cape."

Auriana's face darkened. "The Greefs are the wrong people. They are powerful. They will keep Verreaux in poverty. Married to Elisabeth, he will suffer the daily vengeance of a woman betrayed. She will cuckold him. And, perhaps worse, he will not even have the child for succor. He will not have the son—perhaps the daughter—he surely must have imagined he would take into the veldt to teach his arcane taxidermy, as his father had taught him."

"But what if Elisabeth loses in court?" Robert asked. "Surely, she would have considered that possibility before killing her own child—if she did indeed kill it."

Auriana shook her head. "I surmise she was certain she would win. And surely she still does. But even if she loses, her act of vengeance becomes a personal salvation. There would be no child to imprison her in her past. No child to remind her of Verreaux. No child to keep her from a new life. She is still a young, attractive woman—if a deflowered one. Without another man's child, men might woo her. Even Jan de Vages might return to court her again."

Robert sipped the rest of his wine and scratched his head. "All possible, Auriana. But the editor in me says that a story without proof is merely anecdote. It is just as likely the child died a natural death. Colic. Unsanitary conditions. Infant mortality in the Cape is unspeakably common."

"Yes," Auriana sighed, "the proof is circumstantial. Listen, Robert. Elisabeth's slave girl, Roosje, likely witnessed the smothering. Or surmised what had occurred when the child stopped breathing.

That is the reason, I think, she fled from appearing at the trial. Not because she had been shamed by de Villiers. But because she did not want to implicate her mistress. Or, worse, be blamed for the death of the baby."

Robert shook his head. "Flagrant conjecture, Miss Brouwer."

"Perhaps," Auriana agreed, "but there is something else that did not surface at the trial—or in your *Advertiser* account. Sarah Bishop would not speak with me about the child's death. She says she was not there. But she was willing to recount the birth. The delivery was a difficult one, which is not unusual for a first child. What was unusual was the inordinate size of the child—its head. Bishop said the labor was proceeding too slowly for the health of the infant. And Elisabeth was approaching exhaustion. Bishop was forced to use her obstetric forceps to help pull the baby forward through the birth canal."

Robert nodded. "Yes, I know the procedure. The pressure of the forceps clamps can deform a baby's head. The skull bones are soft and not yet fused to one another. William Smellie's *Treatise On the Theory and Practice of Midwifery.*"

Auriana eyes widened, momentarily astonished.

"It's research I did a number of years ago, "Robert explained, "for a case in England. The newborn, delivered with forceps, died at birth. Apparently the brain had been damaged. The mother sued the doctor. She lost."

Auriana shook her head, still shocked. "So. You know about forceps. The head emerges misshapen, somewhat compressed side-to-side. And the forehead will protrude."

"Yes," Robert agreed, "but the head resumes its normal shape in time."

"Usually so. But Bishop implied that the deformation of the child's head was not typical—more so than would be caused by the forceps. It was inordinately elongated, with a larger face than she had ever seen."

"Was the infant otherwise normal? It's breathing, for example?"

"Yes. But the weight was not—thirteen pounds, ten ounces. From Bishop's manner, it seemed she thought the newborn's physiognomy was somewhat grotesque. Imagine, Robert. For Elisabeth, it must have seemed like a sign of the devil, a divine damnation, everlasting punishment for her sinful behavior."

Robert grimaced. "You think the child became the personification of Verreaux's betrayal? An evil seed from an evil man? So she killed it?"

"Precisely! A cleansing, a catharsis, an act of purification. For her it is salvation. And she makes it into an offering. She wraps the corpse in a cloth, ties a ribbon around the bundle, and has her slave girl, Roosje, deliver it to Verreaux. Remember, it is the exact picture he sketched at the trial!

"Yes, I remember. But that is too grave an act to conclude from a sketch. Even if you are right, what would Verreaux then do with his dead child?"

A look of frozen horror crossed her face. "I don't dare think. Perhaps he sent it back to Elisabeth. Or buried it in the veldt during one of his expeditions. Or, God help us, pickled the child in a giant jar of alcohol, as he does the baby baboons he crates and ships to his father's emporium in Paris?"

Suddenly, they both realized the heinousness of what they had surmised. Finally, Robert spoke.

"Was Bishop, the nurse, there the next day, when you think the infant died or was smothered?"

"No," Auriana whispered hoarsely. "Bishop said Elisabeth sent for her, but she did not arrive in time to see the child."

Auriana held out her arms. He led her from the parlor to his bed. They held one other, breathing in the melancholy light as autumn's low sun dimmed through the curtains and the dark hues of night enveloped their sleep.

29

Three months later
Cape Supreme Court
July 6, 1829

The morning was damp and overcast. A wind laden with cold, rheumatic mist blustered off the ice blue sea caps into Cape Town. Robert Fairbairn and Auriana Brouwer shivered through the dark, wet streets to the courthouse. It was the first day of the new term of the Cape Supreme Court. First on the docket was the ruling on Greef vs. Verreaux. In the three months since the end of the trial, Auriana had failed to determine the whereabouts of the child. Was it alive or dead? Was it residing in the Greef home, or in the ground, or in a jar of alcohol in a storeroom in Paris at Maison Verreaux?

The courtroom was full. Two of the three justices, Menzies and Burton, were seated behind the dais. Elisabeth arrived on the arm of her father. They walked slowly, deliberately, down the middle aisle of the gallery between the rows of benches.

"Looks like a wedding procession to a forced matrimony," Auriana whispered to Robert. "The father giving away the bride. All that's missing is the organ, the bouquets and the minister."

"And a willing groom," he added. "Elisabeth is playing this for the justices. Menzies and Burton are watching."

Jules Verreaux stood beside Advocate Cloete at the defendant's table, fidgeting, not finding a place for his hands. He watched Hendrik Greef hand his daughter to Advocate de Wet, who escorted her to the plaintiff's table. Elisabeth turned slowly, deliberately, toward Jules, gave him an acidic smile, then nodded at the two justices on the bench, as if the verdict were foretold. Verreaux looked at her blond tresses straining to explode outward from her hair pin. She was as wild as the veldt, he thought. I caught her, like a gazelle in mid-flight. I tamed her as I do them in a piece of taxidermy, a still life behind glass made immobile by that child.

Wylde appeared on the dais, mumbled something to Menzies and Burton, and sat down between them in his special, raised, high-backed chair. He looked sickly, his face grayish against the black robes.

Auriana leaned over to Robert. "The rumors about his daughter are clearly preying on him."

Wylde surveyed the audience, waiting for quiet in the courtroom. "Good morning. Greef vs. Verreaux was an action to compel the performance of a promise of marriage. I will introduce the ruling. Justice Menzies will complete it. This is a case involving high and serious principles, one that has called into exercise all the zeal and ability of both advocates, and invoked the earnest and anxious consideration of the Court."

He paused, turned to face Elisabeth, and spoke directly to her. "The Court holds that, by the evidence, the defendant, Mr. Jules Verreaux, made absolute and unconditional promises of marriage to the plaintiff, Miss Elisabeth Greef. He made those promises in writing at the time alleged by her. By means of those promises he seduced her and became the father of her child."

A few murmurs arose in the gallery. Wylde started to reach for the gavel, stopped, and turned to Verreaux at the defense table.

"With regard to the defendant's plea, and its four averments. The defendant wisely withdrew the first, that he was misled by unfamiliarity with the plaintiff's language in composing his letters. The second and third averments were clearly false and unfounded. The plaintiff, Ms. Greef, never, either in writing or conduct, accepted or acted upon the defendant's retraction of his promise. Neither did she receive the addresses of any other man, as the defendant averred."

Wylde paused, scanned the courtroom, spotted Fairbairn, and acknowledged him with a slight nod. Auriana thought she detected a slight scowl mixed with fear.

"Therefore," Wylde intoned, "of the defendant's four averments, the Court holds that only one remains to be decided: whether the defendant has proved his minority. And, if he has, what effect the defendant's minority ought to have in the judgment of this case."

Elisabeth leaned over and whispered something in de Wet's ear. She had allowed herself a quick smile, perhaps a foretaste of victory. He placed his hand on hers, reassuringly.

Wylde picked up the gavel, gave it to Menzies, and sat back. Menzies adjusted his robes, cleared his throat, and pointed at Verreaux.

"The defendant, Jules Verreaux, produced a birth certificate from France, an *Acte de Naissance*, from the year 1807. The certificate sets forth that on August 24, 1807, Jacques Philippe Verreaux, naturalist, presented before the *adjoint du maire* of the Twelfth Arrondissement in Paris, a male infant, the child of himself and his wife, born on the preceding day, to whom he declared to give the name of Pierre Jules."

Menzies cleared his throat again, poured a glass of water from a large, silver decanter, drank it slowly, and licked his lips.

"The defendant also gave as evidence a French passport dated April 4, 1826, in the name of 'Mr. Verreaux (Pierre Jules)', a naturalist, granted to proceed to Toulon, and thence to the Cape of Good Hope, in which it was stated that Mr. Verreaux was 18 years of age. The *Acte de Naissance* and the passport are exactly in the form prescribed by the Code Napoleon. In addition, the French Consul in Cape Town swore in this court that both documents were genuine and authentic in every respect."

In the gallery, people began coughing and shuffling their feet. Auriana poked Robert with her elbow. "They're restless, impatient for a verdict. Everyone knows he was a minor in 1827. He turned twenty in August of that year. So was Elisabeth. Why are they dragging it out?"

"It's reputation, Auriana," Robert cautioned. "And case law. The Cape Supreme Court is only four years into its existence. Wylde became Chief Justice then. He, Menzies and Burton are appointees. They are vagabonds from overseas. They must demonstrate that the law in the colonies is as thorough and professional as the law in England. Menzies will take his time."

"The Court," Menzies continued, "therefore holds that defendant's documents are prima facie proof of his being under the majority age of twenty-five years in March 1827, when the promise of marriage was made, and also when plaintiff brought this action in November, 1828. The law of majority age changed to twenty-one years on June 24, 1829, shortly after the end of this trial.

Therefore, by the law of this colony and the Code Napoleon of France, defendant would normally have required parental consent to marry, and the law cannot compel the defendant to marry without such consent. Such a marriage would be *ipso jure* null and void."

Auriana noticed Elisabeth momentarily shaking her head, then turning to glance at her father in the first row in the gallery. He sat impassive, his mouth curled down at the edges, staring stonily at Wylde. Jules Verreaux tapped Cloete on the shoulder and grinned, suddenly confident. Cloete rebuked him instantly in a stern whisper.

"However," Menzies continued, "Dutch law provides a relaxation of this point in certain cases. When a young man, such as the defendant, under a promise of marriage, has effected the defloration of a young woman, the law does not allow the mere absence of parental permission necessarily to prevent marriage. The logic is clear: the absence of parental permission could be due to the young man's malicious motive. The law cannot inadvertently assist a minor in such duplicity, a minor such as the defendant, who was the seducer. Indeed, the evidence produced at this trial shows that the unfortunate girl, Miss Greef, was most artfully seduced, and that Mr. Verreaux likely never intended to seek the permission of his parents to marry. Further, morally speaking, Mr. Verreaux's defense that Miss Greef was a light-mannered woman, disgraces this Court. It is impossible to look without horror at the diabolical plan of seduction that the defendant pursued. In this country, public manners are remarkably simple. And they are very different indeed from those of defendant's own country."

The gallery exploded in agreement with Menzies' denunciation of French morals. He allowed the commotion to subside on its own.

"Nevertheless ..." Menzies paused to tug on the collar of his shirt, take a drink of water and clear his throat.

Auriana whispered to Robert, "Not a good sign. He's about to choke on his own words."

"Nevertheless," Menzies began again, "the Court must hold paramount in this case the lack of parental consent to a minor, vide Code Napoleon and the law of this colony. Had Mr. Verreaux been of majority age at the time this case was brought, he would be unhesitatingly condemned."

Menzies looked down at his notes, then directly at Elisabeth. "It is therefore the ruling of this Court that the defendant, Mr. Jules Verreaux, is absolved, but only because the trial was brought too soon."

A slow, angry roar spread across the gallery as the crowd rose almost in unison.

Menzies pounded the gavel and raised his voice, trying to be heard above the tumult. "Silence! The Court therefore advises the plaintiff, Miss Greef, of her right to institute a new action against the defendant, Mr. Verreaux, to compel him to perform his promise of marriage now that he has reached the age of majority, twenty-one years."

The crowd, not mollified, became a mob. It stormed out of the gallery toward the bench, shouting insults and shaking their fists at Wylde, Menzies and Burton. The justices hurriedly retreated from the dais and the courtroom. The bailiff tried to position himself between the crowd and Verreaux. Jules smiled weakly at Cloete, seemingly stupefied by the uproar. He craned his neck to find Elisabeth.

In the frantic melee, she made her way unnoticed through the crowd toward the defendant's table. Jules scrambled to this feet. The crowd parted and grew silent, transfixed by the former lovers facing one another. Elisabeth cocked her head, smiled invitingly at Jules, and flung her arms out toward him.

He stepped forward to embrace her. At the last moment he saw the poniard. He remembered that he had left it with her as a memento, along with the bullet.

Elisabeth slipped the blade into her hand from under her long sleeve, swung her arm back, and plunged it into his groin. She kept her hand clenched around the knife, pinning his eyes with hers as his face gradually registered what she had done to him. Slowly, he crumpled to the floor of the courtroom.

Only then did she let go.

30

Cape Supreme Court July 6, 1829

Case tried March 20, 1829

Elisabeth Helena Henrietta Greef

v

Jules Verreaux

Mr. Advocate de Wet, counsel for plaintiff
Mr. Advocate Cloete, counsel for defendant

Witnesses for plaintiff
Petrus Johannes de Villiers
Reverend Mr. Wagener
Sara Bishop

Witness for the defendant
Christoffer Linage
Francois de Lettre
Jan de Vages
Charles Boniface

JUDGMENT

Defendant absolved of the instance without costs.

By the Court
J. Wylde
Witnessed 6th July, 1829

BOOK THREE

THE CAMEL DRIVER

31

Paris, Friday
January 29

The Air France flight to Paris left Cape Town a few minutes after midnight. Harry downed a couple of scotches and fell asleep. He dreamt he was standing naked in a tall exhibit case, a giant glass test tube in the middle of a museum gallery. He was cold and huddled over. Embarrassed, he covered his genitals from the onlookers. They were standing in rows, pointing at him, whispering. Was it the Carnegie? He couldn't tell. Suddenly, he spotted Nicole in the crowd. Three rows back. Her face was contorted, the tendons in her throat rigid with terror. She was screaming! But he couldn't hear her screams inside the tube. Neither did anyone else in the gallery. Why not? Desperate, he wanted to pound on the glass to alert them. But he froze, unable to move his hands away from his privates and expose them.

He woke over the Sahara. The low dawn light flung long shadows to the west, a thousand dune sun dials telling time in the desert. He watched Tunisia creep toward the Mediterranean, and wondered where in the sands below Verreaux had shot two Barbary lions and stolen the body of a Berber tribesman from his grave. At the coastline, over Tunis, awakened by the morning summons to prayer, the coral sky ceased refracting the sun.

At Charles de Gaulle, Harry negotiated the maze of hallways to baggage pickup and immigration control. The signs were in French, English, Chinese, German and Arabic, an urban landscape painted in stylized, mannered hieroglyphics. In the crowd of faces, he felt himself dive into the uncertainty of space, of who is me and who is they and who is us. On the train to Gare de Nord, he understood why his father refused to fly. He'd reminisce that trains were a forgotten civility, that train stations were the stately parlors of the past. Planes, in comparison, were cattle cars. And airports were the concrete stockyards for branding and processing.

At the Gare de Nord, Harry bought a pack of Drum, then took a cab through the gray, cold mist to the Muséum Nationale d'Histoire Naturelle on Rue de Buffon. Even in the rain, the row of neoclassical buildings was majestic, architecture imposing the weight of knowledge. He made his way to the Gallerie de Paleontologie where Liza had arranged for him to meet the zooarchaeology curator at noon. Harry had been here years earlier as a student. Nothing had changed. Emmanuel Frémiet's immense bronze sculpture was still standing guard at the entrance, "Ourang-Outang Strangling a Borneo Savage." The "Savage" was a young woman. And the orangutan wasn't "strangling"—he was raping.

Harry peeked into the Gallerie. He'd worked in the fossil collections in the floor below: long rows of ornate wooden cabinets; drawers with brass handles; bony bits of extinct life unearthed from a distant geologic past, from a Europe without form or name, a drifting piece of continent choked with rain forests, primitive lizards, snakes, lemurs, shrews, and opossums. It was ironic, Harry thought. He had returned here to unearth Jules Pierre Verreaux, who had shot, trapped, collected and stuffed their modern evolutionary descendants.

"Monsieur Przewalski?"

Harry turned to see a woman in a white smock. Late thirties, short, black, spiky hair with a faint tinge of purple at some of the ends. She smiled at him, full lips, no lipstick, green eyes behind wire-rimmed glasses, inquisitive, intelligent.

"Yes."

She smiled again and stuck out her hand. *"Bon.* Christine Dumoulin. Welcome to the museum. Ms. Kole from the Carnegie … she described you quite well!" Christine's English was perfect, Harry thought, with a hint of a French accent begging to be accompanied by an accordion.

"You've been to our museum before?"

"Many years ago." Harry decided to explain, then regretted it. "In the paleontology collections."

Christine, puzzled, tried to make a connection. "Monsieur Verreaux … you've asked to see his correspondence. He was not a paleontologist."

"Yes, I know. Neither am I any longer."

She furrowed her brow but chose not to investigate. She led him around the building into an old stairwell with a circular iron staircase. It smelled of cigarettes and urine. Four flights up they reached a small enclosed landing with a table and chair. A hinged dormer window overlooked a flat rooftop and a graveled alley. Harry was winded. Christine wasn't, despite her high heels.

She pointed to four large archival boxes on the table. "Here are the papers Monsieur Verreaux left the museum. And, of course, he left many specimens of plants and birds. I apologize for this space. Normally, we would be in the library of the Laboratoire de Zoologie. But it's closed for renovation … a water leak."

"No problem. This is better," Harry said. "I can smoke."

"Ah! The roof, please." Christine motioned to the window and gave him a matronly look that wavered between rebuke and sympathy. "My office is off the zoology laboratory on the second floor, below here. Also the toilet. The museum closes at four-thirty. I will come remind you." She looked at her watch, turned, and clanked down the circular iron stairs."

The archival boxes were marked "Verreaux, JP 1807-1873." Harry quickly checked their contents: field records, correspondence, and a few scientific articles. A notebook in the first box listed the plants and animals Verreaux and his uncle, Delalande, had collected in Cape Province from 1818 to 1821. Jules was eleven years old when he'd embarked. It was his first expedition.

His uncle must have trained him to record each of the specimens they collected, the species names, the date, and the locality. The columns were neat, orderly, vertically meticulous. Jules's script was precise. The notebook paper, a grayish white and almost parchment-like, was unblemished by age. A few pages had small ink stains. One page, with a list of antelope, an ostrich, and a whale, had a blood smear. Harry wondered if the DNA could still be recovered and sequenced. The animal was now either stuffed in an exhibit, preserved in a museum, hanging in a private chateau, or decomposing to organic dust. Delalande had recorded the length of the whale. Seventy-five feet. It had washed up on the beach at False Bay. Harry remembered cycling past its long arcing stretch of sand to the east of the highway, imagining an eleven-year old boy and his uncle coming upon the carcass of a leviathan.

The last page in the notebook listed the expedition's totals: 131,405 specimens; 22 were human skeletons, African tribesmen unearthed from the Grahamstown battlefield of 1819. Harry put the notebook back in the archival box. Nothing there about a bundled child destined for a taxidermied camel.

He rolled a cigarette, swung open the dormer window, and clambered out onto the roof. In the distance, beyond the alley, he could just make out the Jardin des Plantes, Louis XIII's original gardens and zoo. It was where Verreaux had learned the anatomy of exotic beasts for taxidermy, as had Frémiet for sculpting.

The human skulls that Verreaux had brought back from the Cape Province were still stored somewhere under this roof. Harry knew that anthropologists in the laboratories below had studied and measured the bony curvatures and angles and brain cavities until they got the racial calculus they wanted. The African was more ape than human, they would conclude—in body, in evolution, in intelligence, in animal instinct.

Then they commissioned Frémiet to sculpt this narrative in bronze, this ferment of fear and erotic threat, an ape, a savage orangutan, raping a woman under the crazed eye of the orangutan's young son.

32

Paris, Friday
January 29

Christine Dumoulin gave Harry a ride to his hotel off Place d'Italie. The worn wipers on her little red Citroen smeared the mist over the fading Parisian light. She pointed to a brasserie just off the traffic circle. He tried to bury the fatigue from the long flight and lost. They'd have dinner there tomorrow evening.

A couple with two massive suitcases was checking in ahead of him. The man had a big mustache and slicked back hair. She had a broad, mournful mouth and oblong black glasses. The hotel elevator was a cramped box with a glass door and a sliding iron lattice gate. Without a word, the man dragged the two suitcases onto the elevator, closed the door and the gate, and left the woman standing in the lobby for the next run. She glanced at Harry and shrugged, almost imperceptibly, as if long ago she had gotten used to this order of things. It seemed to him, at this moment, that she secretly yearned for this stranger in the lobby to attempt to walk off with her, that if left alone outside the elevator, she was a more desirable item of theft than a suitcase.

The concierge handed Harry an envelope with a message from Liza. Mazeroski had received an Interpol alert. Over a three month period last fall, vandals had struck museum exhibits in Holland and Belgium. They'd stolen a chunk of elephant ivory in Brussels, sawed off the horn of a rhino in Leiden, walked off with some archaeological artifacts in Liège, and lifted a painting by Franz Hals in Maastricht.

The hotel room was spare: a single bed, a narrow table against the wall, a couple of wire hangers, and an old Sylvania television. The bathroom had a tiny sink, toilet, bidet, and a shower head above a rusted metal drain in the tile floor. Harry would have traded the bidet for a few more cubic centimeters of shower space. The water draining down his body was tepid. He remembered his father telling him about the decrepit hotel rooms. Each night, after each stage, they would drain the romance from riding the Tour de France.

Harry slept poorly. The bed was too short for his six-foot-one frame. At three in the morning the couple in the next room began a vicious domestic quarrel and woke him. The wall was semi-permeable, too thin to muffle the shouting, too thick to let through what the shouting was about. Harry wondered if it was the man with the slicked-back hair and the woman with the oblong black glasses. When the shouting stopped, Harry heard the room door slam, then a television at full volume.

He lay awake trying to connect an embalmed child in Pittsburgh with the museum vandalism in Europe. No luck. The Hals painting was likely a commissioned theft, headed for a private collection in Europe or Japan. The archaeological artifacts likely had angered sensibilities about disrespecting the past. The ivory and rhino horn likely were by now ground to powder, cut with baking soda, and headed to Asian market stalls as a male erector. Elephants and rhinos were harder to poach than old museum specimens.

It was ironic, Harry thought, organs of species on the verge of extinction being harvested for procreative prowess.

33

Paris
Saturday, January 30

At eight-thirty in the morning the sun was out, bouncing light off the hard white limestone buildings into the stiff, cold air. Harry grabbed a triple espresso at a corner patisserie, asked the barista to put it in a big cup and fill it with regular dark roast. She looked puzzled. He told her in the best French he could muster that it was called a "depth charge" in Pittsburgh.

He walked the thirteen blocks to the museum and took the circular iron stairs two at a time to the landing. Mistake, he thought, wheezing and coughing up a brown phlegm. The Drum, the sweet Dutch tobacco, was dyeing his fingers and lungs the same shade of nicotine. He opened the window, stepped out onto the roof, rolled a cigarette, sipped his coffee, and watched the hoar frost rise in the distance from the grass on the Jardin des Plantes. He thought he could make out a bridge across the Seine. He was hungry. He should have bought a roll at the patisserie. He lit the Drum.

Yesterday, he'd returned the first box of Verreaux's notebooks to Christine and left the other three on the table. If she minded, she didn't indicate. The second box covered 1825 to 1831, Verreaux's second expedition to the Cape, this one with his brother, Édouard. Two of the notebooks were field ledgers of the animals and plants they'd collected. Jules' neat, precise script was squeezed into each column and row, recording, as he had for his uncle in 1818, the species name, locality, date, and number of specimens.

On the opening page of the third notebook, Verreaux's handwriting changed, his cursive script swelling and swirling across the page.

> Cape Town. 13 Mai, 1827
>
> I looked at her, the African moon rising across her skin, the last beautiful woman I would see in the tawny light of morning, seeping into the nocturnal blood.
>
> I knew the end had begun. I knew she had conceived in the night, that hours after our uncontrollable pleasure the milky seed would plow it's inexorable route, intent on consummating the act. I knew it when we became unentwined, when the mind was no longer the fevered prisoner of abandon. So did she.
>
> Now I see Elisabeth dreams of it, her face in tortured pilgrimage to a life lost through a life begun. She knows I will leave her with child alone.
>
> Édouard tells me I will not marry. It is a disease in my psyche, he says, the one that slowly constricts my throat, suffocating the permanent breaths I might share with another. Édouard has avoided infection. He is already married, his wife with child in Paris, in the rooms upstairs above Maison Verreaux, above the tableaux, the displays, in which nature is now illusion, safe not to threaten or move, but free to pretend it could at any moment. He says I inhabit a series of tableaux of my own making, capturing passion, making it a still life, then proceeding to the next.

There was a pencil sketch of Elisabeth on the bed, her mouth contorted in troubled sleep. Harry stared at the portrait, mesmerized by her presence. She was on her side, naked, a bed sheet clutched over her breasts, rising and falling with every silent breath.

This is the woman. The woman Verreaux had wronged, the woman at the plaintiff's table in the courtroom in Cape Town in 1829, the woman who had bedded Verreaux in passion and promise, borne him a child, and sued him for betrayal. For a moment, Harry was lost in the damp heat of her bed, that angular face fierce in love or revenge, the full lips primed to kiss or slay, the wild hair on the pillow exploding in fervor or fury, the bare back arched in rapture or revolt, the long legs in ecstasy or constriction. She was the duality of desire.

Harry rolled a Drum, opened the dormer window, climbed outside with the notebook, lit the cigarette, and let the cold air kill his melancholia. He looked at Elisabeth again, now the woman on the page, not the bed. He grimaced. He'd allowed himself to lose his head in a romance unconsummated by time. Cheap to imagine. An emotional swindle. Verreaux had done it too.

He turned to the next page in the notebook. Nine months later: 18 Fevrier, 1828. A drawing of a swaddled bundle. It hung on a ribbon from the beak of an African Yellow-billed Stork. Verreaux the collector, the taxidermist, the ornithologist, could not resist displaying the anatomical pigments of the bird: the brilliant red band collaring the face; the long, yellow beak; the mottled red diffusing to pink down the thin, spindly legs. The stork's neck, a curved, slender white, was wrung.

Harry remembered the date from the trial transcript. It was the day Elisabeth had given birth to their child, when in the afternoon Sarah Bishop, the midwife, and Elisabeth's servant girl, Roosje, had brought the bundle to Verreaux's lodging.

34

Paris
Saturday, January 30

A large feather lay compressed between the next two pages of Verreaux's journal. The vane, an opaque gray, was sewn to the manila paper with black, taxidermic thread. The feather was faded, except for faint yellow and green tinges at the tip. The natural oil had stained the pages into an ancient inked lithograph. It reminded Harry of science's first notion of *Archaeopteryx* in 1861, a solitary feather of a Jurassic bird imprinted in the black limestone of Solenhofen, Germany. On the opposite page, Verreaux had sketched the nude body of an African male, prone, face up, dead, not yet skinned.

Harry recognized the face of El Negro. Verreaux had trained as a painter in the Paris morgue, dissecting corpses, drawing the muscles of the face, the torso, the limbs. He'd learned well. There were two inscriptions. The first said the feather had come from the headdress buried in the grave. The second said that the Betchuanan was the last specimen he and his brother had collected in the Cape.

Kgatlane, Vaal and Orange rivers. 14 Aout, 1831.

It was Édouard's idea to skin the Betchuana. It was no matter to steal a fresh body from a graveyard, or earlier an old skeleton picked clean in the earth. The Boers did not object. Betchuanas, they held, were slightly below human, and far below the white man.

This too I was taught, this Great Chain of Being of Aristotle. Lowest on the chain are rocks. Then come plants, which are mortal, but, like the rocks, are prisoners of the ground and immobile. Then come the animals, which are both mortal and capable of motion. Above the animals reigns Man, who to mortal flesh adds an immortal soul. Above Man sit the angels and archangels, and then the Creator, the Dieu.

Each kind in the chain has subkinds. Among plants, trees are at the top. Among animals, wild ones, such as lions, are higher than domesticated ones. Thus, eagles rank above pigeons, and aurochs above cattle. Among insects, the attractive butterflies and useful bees rest at the top; the irksome flies are at the bottom.

In their religious zeal, the ancients made snakes the lowest of the animals, allowing scripture and the serpent's role in Eden a greater voice than anatomy. Snakes are lizards, merely limbless. They belong, as Linnaeus held, with the crocodile and the turtle, above the fish, and below the bird and the mammal.

Among Man, we were taught at the Paris Museum, there are five ranks, each with many subranks. The Mediterranean European is supreme, followed by the Mongoloid Asian, the Negroid African, the Hottentot African and the Pygmy African. Boers believe the African is barely Man. They call them "four handed-apes." They claim that Africans have the same strong, moveable toes that apes use to clasp the branches for their life in the trees.

Hottentots are placed below Man because of their language of clicks, not words. Cuvier concluded likewise, based on anatomy. He published his famous autopsy of the Khoikhoi woman from the Eastern Cape, the 'Hottentot Venus', Sarah Baartman. Hottentots, he said, were an intermediate stage, closer to the great apes than humans. This he deduced from the inordinate size of Baartman's genitalia, which he said would make the Khoikhoi more sexually barbaric and less civilized.

It was strange that even as a student I suspected otherwise. But it was not my place to question Cuvier's writings. Now, from my years here in the Cape, I know this physical feature, the enlarged pudenda, to be typical of Khoikhoi women and not of apes. I also know that the Khoikhoi near the Cape are highly intelligent, speak fluent Dutch, have a superb memory, and can play musical instruments.

It has come out that Cuvier tried to have carnal knowledge of Sarah, but she refused. He did not record whether her anatomy excited his senses. Or whether he was conducting a scientific experiment on the mating between the Dieu's higher and lower kinds of Man.

When I prepared the Betchuana, I held his skin and organs and skull in my hands. I could find no difference between him and the noble cadavers in the morgue that Frémiet and I beautified before their embalming. Or the peasant cadavers that we dissected and sketched. Or the ones preserved in the Paris Museum that I studied with St. Hillaire.

The Betchuana's toes are no different from mine in spread or girth. They are no closer to those of an ape than the toes of a Dutchman or Englishman in the Cape. I measured the external dimensions of his cranium and found them not to be distinguishable from any Mediterranean in the museum.

And when I removed his brain I calculated the inside volume of his skull using Cuvier's method. To my surprise, it was 1451 cubic centimeters, slightly larger than the normal Caucasian. His brain had all the lobes in the right place, and all the folds and fissures of the French or German brain in the same proportions. The Betchuana was not inferior by any measure that I could find, against what I have been taught and what has been written.

My brother, Édouard, put the Betchuana in a glass case, with an orange brown antelope cloth about his loins, a spread of bird feathers from the grave behind his head, a barbed spear in his right hand, an orange shield in his left, and a bush-pig bag with beads, bones and seeds slung around his neck.

I insisted that he be mounted with his own skull and limb bones so people would later know his anatomy was not different from ours.

35

Paris
Saturday, January 30

Christine came up the stairs carrying a sandwich and a tall coffee. She was wearing jeans, a white blouse, and high-top yellow trail shoes.

"I'm guessing you like French bread, camembert, and mustard. I'm also guessing you're hungry."

Harry put Verreaux's notebook down and looked at his watch. One o'clock. "You guessed right. Both counts. French bread, cheese, and mustard were a staple in our house."

"Really? Unusual for Americans. How come?"

"My father. Trying to recreate the meals from the Tour de France." Harry didn't know why he was volunteering his history.

Christine looked puzzled. "I'm sorry, I don't understand."

"My father was a bike racer. On the professional circuit ... the peloton. He rode as a domestique. For Eddy Merckx and others."

"Really? I've been on the Champs Elysée for the last stage of the tour. Not at the finish line, but where they come whizzing around the Place de la Concorde."

Christine pushed Verreaux's notebooks aside and put the sandwich and coffee down on the table. "It's just a snack ... an early appetizer. This evening we'll have Italian at the brasserie I pointed out yesterday. You remember? Le Foumaillon. Around the corner from your hotel, off the traffic circle at Place d'Italie."

"I'll be there."

"Good," she stated, and walked down the stairs, her footfalls softly strumming the ironwork.

Harry took off his while gloves, wolfed down the food, rolled a Drum, and decided to break the rules. He climbed out on the balcony with the coffee, the cigarette, and Verreaux's third box of journals.

Paris. 17 Novembre, 1831

Édouard and I came back from the Cape to great acclaim. Dignitaries from Versailles greeted us in Paris. *Le Constitutionnel* published a long article extolling our bravery, and the exotic riches of Nature that we brought back to Maison Verreaux and exhibited in the salon of Monsieur Delessert.

Two young people, Messieurs the Verreaux brothers, Jules and Édouard, have recently arrived from a voyage to the ends of Africa, to the land of the Cape of Good-Hope. They have been in the wild country north of the land of the Hottentots, between the latitudes of Natal and the top of St. Helena Bay. How can one possibly imagine what deprivations they had to endure? Our young compatriots had to face the dangers of living in the midst of the natives of this zone of Africa, who are ferocious as well as black, and among the fawn-coloured wild animals about which we do not need to tell.

We want to speak only about the triumphs of their collecting, and do not know which to admire more, their intrepidness or their perseverance. Humans, quadrupeds, birds, fish, plants, minerals, shells—all of these they have studied. Their hunting has given them tigers, lions, hyenas, an admirable lubal, a crimson antelope of rare elegance, a host of other small members of the same family, two giraffes, monkeys, long pitchforks, very-curious rats, ostriches, birds of prey which have never been described before, and a great quantity of other birds of all sizes, colours and species. They also have

*a collection of nests, which could be the object of a charm-
ing descriptive essay. There are plants with roots like onions,
and others of remarkable shape and extraordinary size. Also
snakes, a cachalot, and a crocodile of a type previously unknown.*

*But their greatest curiosity is an individual of the na-
tion of the Betjouanas. This man is preserved by the means
by which naturalists prepare their specimens and reconstitute
their form, and, so to speak, their inert life. He is of small
stature, black of skin, his head covered by short woolly and
curly hair, armed with arrows and a lance, clothed in antelope skin. He has a small bag made of bush-pig, full of small
glass-beads, seeds, and small bones. Another thing that we
are rather embarrassed to find a suitable term to characterize,
is the very special accessory of modest clothing worn by the
Betjouanas, which we find most striking.*

*How most fortunate for France that Messieurs Verreaux
have used their time, talent, energy and skills to go out to
Africa to catch Nature in the act.*

It is fortunate that the stories of Elisabeth, our child,
and the trial did not follow me to these shores from the
Cape. Édouard will not speak of them. He assures me
that he has stitched his lips with taxidermic thread. I believe and trust him.

His silence about the affair of Mademoiselle Wylde
and her child is also assured, as he knows nothing of it.
He also did not see me pack the bundle in with the other specimens from the Cape. And he did not see it in
the boxes unloaded in Paris. It is now safe in alcohol in
the underground cellar of the museum, amid the jars of
vipers and toads and gar and the deformed babies that
Cuvier and Frémiet collected from the morgue. It is not
entered in the catalogue. There will be no entry. No specimen number, no name, no locality, no date, no collector.

36

Paris
Saturday, January 30

Le Foumaillon Brasserie looked out onto Place d'Italie. Harry got there early, bought a draft beer, rolled a cigarette, and took a table that faced the current of cars honking in and out of the traffic circle. The brasserie was an all-purpose shop: food, beer, tobacco, lotto tickets, stamps.

Christine arrived in a purple sweater, jeans and low pumps. In the night light, Harry couldn't see the green eyes behind the glasses, or whether she had put on lipstick. She sat down, told him not to bother looking at the menu, shoved his draft beer aside, and motioned to the bar. A guy in a white apron showed up with a couple of stem glasses and two bottles of beer called Trois Monts. The label pictured three mountains in the background, four skinny trees in the foreground, and a windmill to the side.

"This is bière de garde," Christine said, holding up a bottle, "literally, beer for keeping. It's made in the winter. Then we wait ... to drink it later."

She turned to the waiter and ordered in rapid fire French. Harry could make out a couple of pizzas with extra garlic and oregano. The waiter left, nodding, as if he'd heard it from her before.

"I live close by," she added. "I bring my son here. He likes it better than my cuisine." She hesitated. "I agree with him."

She wasn't wearing a ring. Harry wondered whether there was a man at home with the kid. Or whether early on he'd fled both her kitchen and her bed.

"I'm admiring your English. Can't follow your French, though. Too fast."

Christine laughed. "American father, French mother. He was a diplomat posted in Paris. I was born here, went to the American school."

"University?" Harry asked.

"Michigan for archaeology. Kansas for zoology. And you?"

Harry felt the reticence rise and clamp a vise around his past. He was in the business of excavating other people's histories, not his own. He'd sealed off his private life from public inspection. He turned down invitations to introspection, where people made their narcissism into drama. It's why he avoided current fashionable fiction, every minor psychosis pimped as literature.

"It's a short story, Christine. Boring plot. Paleontology at the University of Pittsburgh and the Carnegie Museum. Fossil mammals. I couldn't sustain the interest. One day it just didn't matter."

It had become his standard line, his personal diorama, an inanimate rendering behind glass. He'd compressed and hardened his actuality into a neat, protective stratum overlying the past. It kept him from resurrecting Nicole from his own psychosis—her rape, torture, and dismemberment, her body parts found in a sealed drum. Then, with his life anaesthetized, his flight to a desert war.

"And your work now?" Christine asked as she poured the beer. "Ms. Kole said you were a private detective."

"Yeah." Harry shrugged. "Events that matter."

Christine raised her eyebrows. Harry could tell she didn't believe him. "Like Jules Verreaux? What brings a detective from Pittsburgh to a French museum ... to a naturalist who died more than a century ago?"

Harry wasn't sure how much to tell her. "It's another short story. An exhibit at the Carnegie was vandalized. Verreaux's."

"*Merde!*" Christine exclaimed. "Like Liège. They—" She stopped abruptly, as if she had already revealed too much. "Wait! Not Verreaux's exhibit from the Paris Exposition?"

Harry let Liège go. "Yes, the diorama, *Arab Courier Attacked by Lions.* You know it?"

She raised her eyebrows. "Of course we know it! What could the thieves possibly take?"

"Good question." Harry wondered why Christine had assumed theft, not vandalism. "The police want to find out who did it. The Carnegie wants to find out why. Maybe there's something in his notebooks here. It's a long shot."

She scrunched up her mouth, skeptical. "But Verreaux's field notes from North Africa are 150 years old. What could be in them?"

Harry shrugged, opened his pouch of Drum, and rolled a cigarette. "Like I said, it's a long shot. Do you mind if I smoke?"

"No," she shook her head, grabbed his tobacco, pulled out a packet of extra-long papers from her pocket, and rolled a thin cheroot. She had long fingers, short nails, no polish. "You're not telling me everything, Harry."

"There isn't much to tell. Except, possibly, revenge. Verreaux was part of two expeditions to South Africa, the Cape area. The first was with his uncle, when he was eleven, the second with his brother, when he was nineteen. He seduced a Dutch woman … promised to marry her. When she became pregnant, he reneged. After she had the child, she sued him for breach of contract. There was a trial. She lost. I'd like to know what happened to the child."

Christine nodded, drank some of the Trois Monts, and wiped her mouth. "Go on."

"There's also El Negro, the body of a chieftain that he and his brother stole from a grave in Botswana and displayed around Europe. Maybe there's a relative, a descendant—Dutch, Botswanan—who decided to take revenge on all that's left of Verreaux—his exhibit. There might be something in his notebooks from the Cape or Tunisia. The affair with the Dutch woman isn't mentioned in your museum's official biography of Verreaux."

She tilted her head up and exhaled a few circles of smoke. Harry liked the way her lips curled.

"No, it's not. You must mean the museum's collection of 516 biographies of its scientists, *Du Jardin Au Muséum*, published last year. Verreaux's entry is short. He learned anatomy from Baron Cuvier here in the museum. You know about his expeditions for Maison Verreaux to South Africa, Indochina, Australia, Tasmania and North Africa. Mostly he studied the birds he brought back. Lots of new species, many papers. He helped Prince Bonaparte, Charles Lucien, the nephew of Emperor Napoleon, prepare a catalog of the birds of the world based on the museum's collections."

"The Arab Courier exhibit. Why didn't it stay here … in the museum?"

Before she could answer, the waiter returned with the food and two more bottles of Trois Monts. She put out her cheroot, drank some beer, and ripped off a hunk of pizza with her fingers. Harry watched her, her movements delicate yet deliberate.

Christine held up a finger while she finished chewing. "Too theatrical. The museum wanted academic exhibits … you know … the zoology of the world. It was sold to the American Museum in New York. They too thought it was too dramatic. So they sold it to the Carnegie."

"El Negro, the travelling anthropological freak show, didn't make it into Verreaux's bio either."

"No, it did not," she said. "We know about El Negro, Harry. And many other terrible things from those days. Biographies are our written exhibits of people. They're like the exhibits in our museums. We remove the reality that disturbs. We exhibit only what we want to show. And perhaps only what we want to know."

Harry nodded. "There is nothing in Verreaux's biography about his personal life. Did he marry? Any children?"

"No … there is no record … we don't know. The photos of him … a sad man."

Harry thought of Verreaux slowly collapsing to the floor, bewildered by the knife embedded in his groin, Elisabeth finally letting go of the handle.

"What happened in Liège, Christine? I'm guessing an exhibit was vandalized. Pittsburgh police received a notice from Interpol."

She looked at him closely, assaying the depth of trust beneath the skin. "I have been asked to keep it confidential."

"I understand. But it might be related to the Carnegie incident."

"No!" she stated, emphatically. "It involves archaeology, not zoology, not animal mounts."

"Still. I'm leery of coincidences. When did this happen?"

Christine looked down, ambivalent, as if whether to break a confidence could be divined from the wooden knots in the table. She reached for his tobacco, rolled another cheroot, sat back, curled her lips around a smoke ring, and nodded.

"Bien, okay. A few months ago, late October, someone smashed an exhibit case at the Université de Liège. In the gallery of the Laboratoire de Paleontologie Animale, the little museum associated with the research collections. I have a friend—" she quickly caught herself, then continued. "A curator ... a colleague there. The university, the museum, and the police do not want any publicity. They're keeping it quiet—Belgian police ... and Interpol."

"What was taken? Projectile points? Hand axes?"

She shook her head. "No. A skull. Of a Neanderthal. It will sell for much on the black market."

Harry tried to kick in his archaeological memory about specimens of Neanderthals, and failed. "More so than other fossils?"

"More so than many. It's famous," Christine asserted. "It's the first Neanderthal material found... in 1829 in the Engis-2 Cave near Liège. But no one recognized it as Neanderthal for more than a hundred years. Not until 1936!"

"How come?" Harry asked.

"Because it is the cranium of a child ... a Neanderthal child."

Before they left the brasserie, Harry bought a bottle of port. Christine took his arm as she walked him back to the hotel, both shivering. He asked her to go with him to Liège on Sunday. She hesitated, then said maybe. She needed to make arrangements for her son to stay with his father. Harry held out the bottle of port and invited her for a drink. She hesitated again, looked at her watch, mumbled something about her son, then quickly bussed him on the cheek, smiled, stamped her feet for warmth, told him she'd see him tomorrow, and left.

Harry sat in the dark drinking the port much too quickly. He debated calling Liza, and lost. The beer and port and scent of a woman had let sentimentality cloud his skull. He wondered whether the Neanderthal parents of the child who died so young in Engis-2 cave had ever mourned, reminisced and gotten sentimental. Or Verreaux over his daughter, who might not have lived more than one day.

37

Paris
Sunday, January 31

Harry overslept. He'd lain awake in the middle of the night, listening to the dogs bark in the street, wondering what creature had set them off. Pittsburgh had the odd coyote or opossum wander into a neighborhood from Schenley Park or the Homewood Cemetery. In Paris it was likely rats.

He fell back asleep and dreamt of black sewer rats crawling on the museum rooftop outside the landing, scratching madly at the dormer window, hurling their bodies against the latch, until the window suddenly swung open and the dark-whiskered horde poured in across the sill, crawled onto the table, sniffed Verreaux's notebooks, and began devouring them, as if they could taste the blood and flesh in the list of African animals.

He woke with a start. Light from a blue sky suffused the room. He looked at his watch. Nine-twenty. Shit, he thought, he'd kept Christine waiting for an hour and a half. Then he remembered. She'd meet him at noon. He went into the bathroom, checked for rats, showered quickly, and was on the street by ten. At a boulangerie around the corner he grabbed a baguette and a coffee, and ripped off hunks while he walked. It reminded him of the ravenous rats. The streets were deserted, except for a homeless man bundled against a heating grate at the edge of the sidewalk. Harry gave him what was left of the bread, kept the coffee, and handed him three euros so he could get his own.

The guard was pushing back the metal gate to the Gallerie de Paleontologie. It screeched along the floor, deepening the well-worn groove in the marble slabs. Harry had consciously avoided the exhibit hall on the way to the stairwell. He was leery of mingling with the hundreds of fossil skeletons, the guilt of having abandoned them and himself. He'd learned about descents into nostalgia from his father who was still trapped in the peloton, the former pro cyclist racing his Bianchi across the flatlands and up the mountains of post-war Europe.

Instead, Harry deliberately dodged the past. Sequestering it, he thought, was as effective as facing it. Psychologists would scorn it as escapism, but what the fuck did they know, shilling the public, making up a living off the least understood organ of the body. The human brain was adept at bricking-off recall, no doubt ever since a *Homo erectus* killed his brother at Lake Turkana, or a Cain killed Abel somewhere in the biblical Middle East. Quarantines were preventive medicine—against viral disease, or viral memory.

The paleontology gallery hadn't changed since Harry had been here years earlier. It was like strolling into the 1890s, when it first opened. Hundreds of fossil skeletons of extinct beasts were still mounted in neat rows: giant armadillos and tortoises, plesiosaurs, mosasaurs, mastodons, mammoths, saber-toothed cats. All were headed toward the entrance to the gallery, as if trying to reverse extinction, the death sentence of geologic time. Museums, Harry thought, were bastions of stasis in a world hurtling pell-mell to somewhere else.

At the front of the gallery, the magnificent skeleton leading the procession also hadn't changed: the gigantic pitch-black bones of *Diplodocus carnegii*, eighty-four feet long, thirteen feet high. Beside it, a framed, black-and-white photograph from 1907 showed Andrew Carnegie in a tux formally presenting an exact replica of his dinosaur to President Fallières. Carnegie is beaming, even smirking. Here he was, the son of a thread-poor Scottish weaver, barred as a kid from the parks and bathhouses and libraries in Dunfermline, now lording it over European royalty—Fallières, King Edward VII, Czar Nicholas, Emperor Franz Josef, Kaiser Wilhelm. He was presenting each one with a plaster replica of *Diplodocus* for their respective national museum. The real skeleton, petrified in a muddy Jurassic graveyard in Wyoming, was the centerpiece of his new, opulent museum in Pittsburgh. Carnegie's revenge wasn't subtle, Harry thought. The dinosaur embodied the manifest destiny of the New World, the armature forged from steel and sweat and smoke, the bones unearthed from the rough, raw badlands of the American West.

On the landing at the top of the stairwell, there was no sign that rats had ripped up and devoured Verreaux's notebooks. The dormer window was closed. The archival boxes were still neatly stacked on the table. Harry cursed the demonic deceit of dreams. They were like prions, infecting the cinematographer of the night with mad-man disease.

38

Paris
Sunday, January 31

Harry turned the page to Verreaux's next entry. Drawings of bones from a human skull. Also of part of an upper jaw with four teeth, the sockets for two missing teeth, and six individual cheek teeth. On the opposite page, there were six sketches of the partial cranium pieced together from the bony fragments. Verreaux, ever the anatomist, had drawn six views of the skull: from right and left sides, front and back ends, and from top and bottom. The skull was missing a good part of its left side. It looked to Harry to be the skull of a young child. It fit with the teeth. They were milk teeth, except for the single lower molar, which was permanent.

22 Avril,1832

A man came to the museum in the morning with pieces of a skull. He needed an anatomist to unite the bones into the natural shape of the cranium. His name is Philippe-Charles Schmerling, a paleontologist and geologist from Liège in the Walloon. He told me he found the bones in a nearby cave called Engis-2 three years ago, when I was still in the Cape.

It is clear to me that the osseous remains are human. Although fragmentary, the bones have the correct osteological landmarks. The frontal bone extends to form the upper borders of eye sockets. The occipital has the foramen magnum, the telltale opening for the passage of the spinal cord into the skull and connection to the brain. On the underside of the skull bones, blood vessels of the brain have left a faint pattern of grooves distinctive to humans.

The front part of the upper jaw is present. Four teeth are in place: two incisors and both canines. The two missing incisors fell out, either in life or after death, leaving two empty sockets. There are also six loose cheek teeth, three from the upper jaw and three from the lower.

Schmerling is convinced that the skull bones are very old. He is right. They are discolored to a whitish brown, no doubt from lying buried in the cave mud. Also it seems they have begun to fossilize. They are heavier, and impregnated with minerals, like the petrified bones of fossil saurians found in the Paris Basin, as described by Lyell, and as we have examples in the museum. I told Schmerling he had found the skull remains of an ancient human who lived and died in the Engis-2 cave a thousand years ago or more.

Then I showed him something even more astonishing. The incisors and canines are milk teeth, not permanent ones. So are four of the six cheek teeth. The other two, the first upper and lower molars, are permanent but had only just begun to erupt. Their roots are barely formed. And some of the sutures at the edge of the skull bones are still not fused. The conclusion was inescapable. Lying in front of me were the remains of a very young child, perhaps no more than two or three years old. Schmerling was stunned.

A greater shock awaited us. On a plaster form, I fitted the skull bones to one another until each arc, each aspect, fore and aft and from side to side, conformed to the curvature that nature had endowed to the cranium of this child. The upper jaw with the incisors and canines could not be attached to the front of the skull, because the facial bones, the maxillaries and malars, were missing.

The shape of the skullcap was one I had never seen before. We compared the Engis-2 child to crania of children in the museum's collection from the Cape, from Australia, from the Orient. It was radically different—human, yes, but unlike us and unlike a human from any continent. The outline of the skull from above resembles a teardrop, narrower across the front and broadening toward the rear. From the side, the cranium appears flat and elongated, rather than rounded and high. The forehead is steeply receding, not vertical. The occiput shows an unusual rear protuberance. Viewed from behind, the skull is almost circular—the sides are not parallel, but bulge outward. Compared to normal humans, the foramen magnum is noticeably larger; the eye sockets are more rounded than square, and placed far apart. Strangely, the upper rim of each eye socket appears to be thickened, as if each was in the process of developing a bony prominence.

The skull from Engis-2 has begun to drive me to madness. It violates all that we know of God and life and Creation, which Nature has forced me to discard. It belonged to a child of a human species that does not exist on Earth today. How can this be? Was there once another, different variety of Man? People of a foreign kind who lived at an earlier time, before *Homo sapiens*? Why did they vanish? We know that other varieties have vanished, such as certain shells and mammoths and plesiosaurs. Most think these are the beasts of scripture drowned by the deluge.

I cannot hold this view. I am with Hooke and Steno. They say the Earth is ancient. Over the ages, its surface has been constantly transformed by Nature, upheaved, eroded and deposited by wind, water, volcanoes, and earthquakes. These transformations have allowed different varieties of animals and plants to arise since Creation, such as the myriad birds and insects and plants I collected in the Cape and reside in the museum's cabinets. The transformations also caused many varieties, unsuited to their new surroundings, to perish. They are now forever gone from the face of the Earth. Fortuitously, their hard remains—their shells, bones and teeth—were buried by soil, sands and volcanic ash, and became petrified. When we find them, we behold the fossil remnants of a lost world of beasts and trees from an era of time prior to man.

This is the meaning of fossils that produces the madness of the mind. It is an inescapable truth that there are too many varieties of plants and animals on Earth for Creation to have been instantaneous or final. And too many varieties have vanished in the past, such as this human-like child, for Creation to have been perfect. For how could Creation have been perfect if some of its products did not survive the ages of geologic time?

Before Schmerling departed, I made faithful plaster copies of the child's skullcap, its partial upper jaw with its four milk teeth, and the six loose cheek teeth. I dutifully entered the information in the museum ledger.

Collector: Philippe-Charles Schmerling
Date: 1829
Locality: Engis-2 Cave near Liège
Material: Skull bones and teeth of a child
Genus and species: Unknown human, extinct.

My colleagues at the museum think I am deranged. So does Édouard. They say it is a child malformed by disease, such as is common among the peasants. Or malformed by incestuous mating of siblings and cousins, as we have among royalty.

But I have seen those unfortunates in the morgue, those infant monstrosities presented to us during anatomical classes. Frémiet, the morgue artist, has seen them too. A few of these infants lie pickled in jars in the cellar of the museum below me, grotesques floating in brine, eyes open, staring out at me through the glass.

The Engis-2 child is not a such a monster. It is a heresy. I behold this skull, an ancient, alien form of man, petrified, alive once in a time unknown, now vanished from the Earth.

On the next page, Verreaux had sketched a life reconstruction of the face of the child. A girl, perhaps three years old, perhaps younger. Vibrant red-ochre hair. A longish head, almost flat. A strongly sloping forehead. The hint of a ridge above each eyebrow. Bluish, quizzical eyes. A delicate nose. Slight cheek bones. A somewhat prognathous mouth. A large chin. A tiny hand.

Harry took the notebook onto the roof, rolled a cigarette, and studied the face of the girl. Verreaux had drawn the first portrait of a Neanderthal without knowing it. It would be thirty-four years before a human-like skull, limb bones, ribs, and bones of the shoulder and hip were found in the Neander Valley near Dusseldorf, Germany. Science recognized the skeleton in 1856 as a new, archaic, extinct form of human. The biologist Ernst Haeckel tried to name it *Homo stupidus*, because of its low, flattened skull, but *Homo neanderthalensis* won out. It took eighty more years for science to stumble onto the bones in a drawer in a museum in Liège, and finally place the girl from Engis-2 Cave that Verreaux had sketched among her Neanderthal kin.

Verreaux had guessed wrong on the parts of her face that had not been preserved. Her nose should have been larger and somewhat bulbous. And her chin a bit smaller and weak. How did he know the color of the hair? Or about her hand?

Harry almost didn't see it. A page from the notebook was missing—the page between Verreaux's description of the Neanderthal girl's cranium and his sketched reconstruction of her face. An expert razor job.

39

Paris
Sunday, January 31

There were two more entries in the journal. Both concerned Schmerling and the Neanderthal child. The first was written a year and a half after Schmerling's visit.

13 Novembre, 1833

Yesterday, the Museum received a publication authored by Schmerling on the ossements fossile of humans found in three caves at Engis: two skulls of adults from the caves he has numbered Engis-1 and Engis-3, and the cranium and teeth of the child he recovered from Engis-2.

I am dismayed that he does not acknowledge my work during his visit to the Museum in April of last year. I presume it is because he does not concur with my anatomical reconstruction and analysis of the child's skull bones as belonging to a vanished race of *Homo* that lived prior to modern humans. Instead, he identifies the adult and child skulls as being of the Negroid "Ethiopian type", one of the human "types" on the *Scala Naturae*, the Great Chain of Being.

From my dissections in the morgue, and of the Betchwanas and others in Africa, this "type" and these races have no foundation in anatomy—they simply do not exist. It is also evident to me that Schmerling's drawings in the publication of the two adult human skulls from Engis-1 and Engis-3 caves place them as indistinguishable from modern *Homo sapiens*, unlike the skull of the child from Engis-2.

Schmerling's publication provided a troubled sleep, from which I was startled by screams from the Rue Montmartre. I ran from my bed onto the street, where I witnessed a magnificent spectacle, a storm of fire and light falling through the sky such as had never been seen before. Luminescences streaked across the darkness in such multitude and density that it etched every piece of the sky in slashes of silver and white, and lit every corner of the night into day. For a moment it struck me as a celestial bombardment, an unceasing fusillade from the cannons of heaven, but in which the silence of the cannons is frightening.

It is not a wonder that people knelt in the street, exclaiming "the second coming of Christ." I tried to tell the ones who would listen that they were seeing a massive shower of rocks descending from stellar space, meteorites burning up in the air above the Earth.

What Verreaux had seen, Harry realized, was the famous Leonid meteor shower of the night of November 12-13, 1833, one of the most intense ever recorded.

Harry turned to Verreaux's next entry. It was the last one in this notebook, also about Schmerling, dated three years later.

13 Novembre, 1836

Today I received word of the death of Schmerling in Liège a week ago. I am saddened that he has gone to his grave not realizing how momentous is the discovery he made of the child in Engis-2 Cave. It will forever change the accepted view of Man and place and purpose in Creation.

Harry re-read both entries. He'd hoped to find some pointer to the contents of the missing page that someone had razored out of the notebook. He pulled out a Zig-Zag paper, rolled another cigarette, and remembered when he'd spent weeks prospecting barren terrain.

40

Paris
Sunday, January 31

At noon, Harry met Christine outside the Gallerie de Paleontologie in front of the Frémiet sculpture. The bronze made him feel like a voyeur, riveted by its horror. The male orangutan has trapped a young woman under his massive torso, about to rape her. She is on her back, pinned down, her arms spread-eagled, her wrists apparently bound. His huge hands are clamped around her throat. His mouth is open, teeth bared, panting. Her eyes are clamped shut, but she smells him, hears him, his quickening roars of sexual frenzy. Her face is contorted in terror. She looks European. Scandinavian. High cheek bones. Large eyes. Hair pulled back. But Frémiet labelled her a "savage from Borneo," where the only ape is the orangutan. The ape's son sits beside him, screeching, spurring his father on, intoxicated by the savagery, an apprentice learning how to ravish a human.

"What do you know about Frémiet?" Harry asked

"What they taught us," Christine said. "An eminent sculptor, mostly of animals. He's famous for his equestrian statues of Napoleon I. And a bronze of Jeanne d'Arc—it's standing in the Place des Pyramides. He's less famous—actually infamous—for his wild animals. Like this one, 'Ourang-Outang.' Originally, critics called it repulsive."

"Let me guess," Harry said. "Too graphic for refined tastes. Too wanton."

"Right. Even though, as the label here says, the Muséum commissioned it in 1895. That's twenty-four years after Darwin's *Descent of Man* … from the ape … came out."

Harry pointed at the orangutan astride the woman. "Could Frémiet be depicting the ape's revenge for the European rape of the colonies?"

Christine arched an eyebrow. "Interesting thought. Some French art historians think the sculpture expresses our angst about that … a savage progenitor siring a civilized heir. They called it our "existential ambivalence."

"A useful catchall," Harry quipped, "French existentialism. It goes well with pernod, garlic, and berets, but no one knows what it means."

Christine laughed, looked around, and whispered, "it's simple—it means ennui, malaise and self-pity. Anyway, deep down, I think the orang and woman are all about the threat of raw, primal sex. Look at him." She knelt down and patted the orangutan's muscled thigh. "Frémiet made him wild, barbaric. It's through the eyes of European gentility. They look at the orang, they see the 'dark-skinned savage,' untamed, barely up from the apes. They're terrified he might awaken primitive, carnal desires in their cultured women."

Christine stood up, stuck her hands into her jeans, and curled her lower lip into a pretense of innocent sensuality. At that moment, she looked to Harry like a rakish urchin, punky hair, her lean body arched into an insouciant object of desire.

Harry broke himself away from the image. "Frémiet did another piece like this. Same theme. A gorilla abducting a young woman, carrying her off on his hip … presumably also to rape her. Hollywood made it into *King Kong*."

Christine raised her eyebrows and nodded. "I'm impressed, Harry!"

"Don't be. Just osmosis. My mother was an art historian. Italian and French Renaissance. You know, lots of picture books. A few things stuck."

"Hmmm," she gave him a skeptical look. "I bet a good deal stuck. So, you know that Hollywood turned *King Kong* from a monster into an anti-hero, an ape with human emotions. Remember, the woman … I forget her name."

"Ann," Harry interjected. "She was offered to the gorilla as a sacrifice. Maybe they were hinting that the gorilla had read the Bible. About sacrifices to the gods."

Christine laughed. "Seriously, I thought it was actually a subtle blow against racism. Whatever the gorilla stands for, it wasn't untamed savagery. He climbed the Empire State Building to rescue her, not to rape her."

Christine led Harry outside onto Rue de Buffon and around the corner to the entrance to the new Grande Gallerie d'Evolution.

"You probably know that Verreaux and Frémiet were colleagues."

"Really? No, I didn't."

"Yeah, it's in Verreaux's notebooks. They both studied at the Paris morgue, dissecting cadavers, learning anatomy … sketching the form beneath the skin."

She eyed him quizzically. "There is a hint of the poet in you, Harry. I did know that Frémiet was the official painter to the morgue. His job was to mask the blemishes on bodies of aristocrats before they were embalmed."

"Right," Harry acknowledged. "He and Verreaux overlapped for a time at your museum's Jardin des Plantes. Frémiet likely used Verreaux's taxidermied mounts as models for his animal sculptures." Harry didn't tell her that Frémiet could also have provided Verreaux with the bundled child in the camel—a child from the Paris morgue.

They lingered for a smoke in the cold outside the Grande Gallerie. Tour buses lined Rue Geoffroy St. Hillaire near the entrance to the evolution gallery, idling, crystallizing their diesel exhaust onto the cold pavement.

Inside, the crowds milled about carrying their coats and scarves. The exhibit hall was the size of an airplane hangar. A thousand black canister spotlights illuminated a long line of African wildlife snaking toward them from the far corner of the gallery: elephants, cheetahs, hippos, hyenas, zebras, baboons, giraffes, rhinoceroses, topi, kudu, gerenuk, water buffalo, pelicans, wildebeest, bush pigs, males and females, some with young, strolling two by two, as if to an invisible ark.

"Those two are Verreaux animals." Christine pointed to a pair of African oryx, male and female, standing in line behind two chimpanzees.

"Hell of a showpiece for Genesis," Harry remarked. "I guess Noah must have docked at the Serengeti. And here I was rooting for New Jersey."

Christine didn't laugh. She waved derisively at the exhibit, her face grim, almost despondent. "*Merde,*" she scowled, "no evolution for the public. We protested … the scientists at the Muséum. But politics won." She shrugged. "Harry, our exhibits are the face of culture after cosmetic surgery. I'm sure it's the same at the Carnegie."

Harry nodded. "Yeah, the dioramas, those pretty fictions about the natural world, pretending Nature is pristine, untouched by humans. They're the first fairy tale, Christine. There's not a human in any of them. All those exhibits of elk and moose and lions and rhinos. No humans. The book says we were created separately. Even on a separate day. A breed apart."

They drove to the Gare de Nord in Christine's red Citroen and boarded the 5:58 train to Liège. The "5:58" was the mark of civilization in steel and smoke, Harry thought, a train schedule set to the minute and expecting it to be so. Christine said her friend would pick them up in Liège. Harry pointed to the French national motto engraved across the concrete arch of the station: *Liberté, Egalité, Fraternité*—freedom, equality, brotherhood.

"Idealistic," Harry declared. "And impossible."

She looked at him oddly. "Who says?"

"History. Philosophy. An *egalité* society means all are truly equal. Trouble is, it takes coercion to enforce it—not freedom. That's why communist equality means no freedom. And capitalist freedom means no equality."

She furrowed her forehead. "Hmmm. I'd like to read that philosopher. Who is it?"

Harry shrugged. "My father. He had long hours in the saddle on the bike to cogitate the philosophies of life."

"Okay, what about brotherhood according to Przewalski the elder?"

"Yeah, well, that's the most fundamental contradiction. Sure, there's brotherhood. As long the brothers are in your tribe. Watch out if they're not. Then it's tribe bashing tribe. Tribalism rules human behavior. Religion. Politics. Sports. Nationalism. Ethnicity. The tendency is hard-wired, genetic. Inherited from our social ape ancestors. Otherwise, why do humans seek the slightest excuse to form a tribe?"

"Wait!" Christine objected. "All the anthropology I know says its culture, not genes. Social groups form around a common heritage …you know … a common language, a common cause, a common belief."

"Yeah, well," Harry said, dismissively. "Feel-good euphemisms. Like 'ethnic pride'. At any one time, anthropology obligingly blesses whatever belief happens to be trendy in society. A hundred years ago it was Africans and non-Europeans as sub-humans. Anthropology obliged with phrenology, measuring skulls and cultures to quantify racism. Today, perhaps in atonement, it heralds indigenous exceptionalism."

Christine raised her arms in protest. "Harry, you can't just indict all of anthropology. That's pretty cynical."

"Yeah, well, look at history. It'll make you cynical. The line between ethnic pride and ethnic cleansing is thin and drawn in blood. Serbians and Croatians. Hutus and Tutsis. It's about genes. The cleansing is genetic—kill the men, rape the women, impregnate them. No *fraternité* there. Like Frémiet's Orang-Outang. One way or another, it's about tribe."

The train inched silently out of the Gare de Nord, gathered speed and emerged from a tunnel into the fading, colorless dusk, whizzing through a monotone of gray apartment buildings and warehouses. Harry looked at his watch—5:58.

Christine reclined her seat and slumped back. "I don't like it," she uttered with despair. "If you're right, Harry, how the hell do we stop it?"

"I don't know. Education maybe. Travel. Spend time with tribes other than one's own. It's what changed Verreaux during his expedition to the Cape. He's your 1830s poster boy for *egalité* and *fraternité*."

"What do you mean?" Christine asked.

"It's in his notebooks. Ironically enough, it was the human taxidermy. He skins the Botswanan chief in Cape Town for the El Negro exhibit. And he can't help but see that an African is no different from the European cadavers he's dissected in the Paris morgue. Not the skull or brain or internal organs. The Botswanan could pass for a Frenchman, except for the hair and skin. The Africans he dealt with were also intelligent, articulate, and creative. He cites Sarah Baartman, Cuvier's 'Hottentot Venus'. He realizes that everything he believed, everything's he's been taught is bullshit: creation, the Great Chain of Being, the races of humans with Africans at the bottom and Europeans on top."

Christine had closed her eyes. Harry thought she'd dozed off to the rhythmic hum and sway of the rails. Without opening her eyes, she put her hand on his arm.

"Ironic is right, Harry," she half mumbled. "He discovered humanity through his own inhumane acts."

A minute later she was asleep. Her head lolled onto Harry's shoulder. She continued to hold his arm, as if she'd always slept that way with him on trains. He managed not to wake her when the conductor came through for the tickets. A couple across the aisle had begun devouring a baguette lined with tomatoes, cheese and ham, washing it down with a couple of cans of Kronenbourg 1664. Harry thought of the Trois Monts bière de garde and was suddenly famished. An attendant came by pushing a dinner cart of sandwiches. Harry passed, then wondered why he was unwilling to disturb Christine and the sudden comfort of her closeness.

The train whistled through Bastogne. Harry remembered his father telling him about the annual bike race, his finger slowly tracing the route of Liège-Bastogne-Liège on the map of Belgium that hung in his bike shop in East Liberty. Beside it his father had framed a copy of an article from a British cycling magazine. The headline read, "L-B-L: the oldest and hardest of the one-day classics." The race was usually held on the last Sunday in April, invariably in the cold rain and snow of the Ardennes, 173 miles across the most bitter terrain of World War II, over twisting farm roads, nasty cobblestones, and wickedly steep climbs, 14,000 feet in all. His father had underlined one sentence near the end: "Nicholas Przewalski, a domestique for the Ford France-Hutchison team, helped Jacques Anquetil win the race in 1966." A year later his father would crash on the rough-hewn cobblestones of Paris-Roubaix, break his pelvis, and hang up his race bike.

Christine woke as they were pulling into Liège. She sat up, gave Harry an embarrassed smile, fiddled with her spiky hair, and gathered her coat and bag. The station was a modern, high-tech cocoon. A series of glass and steel arches formed a vaulted roof over the main concourse. Christine explained that striking coal and steel workers had damaged much of the original structure in a battle with the army during the winter of 1960-61.

Her colleague was late. They went outside, breathing vapor into the damp cold air. Harry rolled a Drum, and Christine a long cheroot in brown paper. There was a strange sensuality to how she rolled the tobacco between her long, slim fingers. The smokes lasted until a tall woman, wrapped in a long parka, boots and a faux fur hat, leapt out of a blue Peugeot that had rolled up, blinkers flashing.

Christine tossed the cheroot as they embraced and bussed one another. It seemed more intimate to Harry than the polite greeting between friends. The man in Christine's bed had been replaced by her colleague, Marie LeBoeuf, curator and professor of archaeology at the University of Liège. She was middle-aged, buxom, with a curiously warm face despite a perpetual frown and a sharp chin. Thick brown hair stuck out from under the fake fur hat.

They ate at a brasserie that served fresh mussels. The waiter said they were especially recommended in months with an "r". Harry asked him for a scientific explanation, but didn't get one. Perhaps marine parasites increased from May through August.

Marie confided that she was having nightmares ever since the theft of the Engis-2 skull of the Neanderthal child from the Liège museum. She felt responsible, despite assurances from the police and university rector. Nothing like this had ever happened in her more than ten years there. Yes, once, someone had accidentally knocked over a case with fossil ammonites.

But she did not want to talk about the theft over dinner. It would spoil the occasion. Tomorrow, at the museum, they'd see the vandalized exhibit case. She placed her hand over Christine's. Harry noticed the thin gold band on her index finger.

Marie offered Harry the futon couch in her flat. She didn't register too much disappointment when Harry declined. He'd seen a Best Western hotel a block from the train station.

41

Liège
Monday, February 1

In the morning, Harry grabbed a coffee in the hotel lobby, went outside, and rolled a cigarette. Last night, he'd told Christine and Marie that he would walk to the university. They'd looked skeptical. So did the hotel receptionist, who handed Harry a schematic map. It was five miles, over bridges, under rail yards, and through an extensive, forested park.

From a block away the new train station looked as if three, huge alien ships, steel-and-glass saucers, had landed one on top of the other, tilted over at crazy angles, and fused. Harry crossed a rusting bridge over the Meuse River. A barge loaded with brown pipes disturbed the early-morning steam rising from the water. Beyond the Meuse, dirty industries had blackened the bricks of the city, then succumbed to obsolescence and death. A dank pedestrian tunnel led under the rail yard. Harry emerged into a series of blue-collar neighborhoods of two-story flats. For a dizzying moment he felt he was in Pittsburgh, standing in front of his row house on Orkney Street, below him the defunct steel mills and smoke stacks eroding along the banks of the Monongahela River.

The walkway to the university wound through the thick-treed forest. Harry was relieved it was winter. The trees were denuded. The canopy was pulled back. Light could penetrate and drive his ogres back into the dirt. As a child, his father had given him a book of Polish fairy tales. Forests were the devil's earth. Every horrific evil lurked in the blackness of the woods. It was why, years later in Wyoming, that his first sight of the badlands had seduced him into paleontology. He remembered losing his mind to the freedom of an untrammeled terrain, a raw earth running naked to the horizon under an unbuttoned sky. The fossils were the sideshow, entertaining, intellectual, asking ultimate questions about origins and extinctions. It was convenient that the badlands preserved what paleontology dug up, the myriad contingencies of life through time.

Harry found Christine having a smoke outside the Natural Sciences Building on the Allée du Six Aout. He asked her what piece of history on the sixth of August had earned a street name. She told him that on August 6, 1914, 320,000 German soldiers crossed the Belgian border and attacked Liège. It was the opening battle of World War I. A garrison of 35,000 men, vastly outnumbered, held out against the siege of the city for eleven days. Most were killed or executed. But they delayed the German advance long enough for the British and French armies to set their defenses and win the battle at the Marne. Yet another war, Harry thought, gruesome and bloody, the remnants and casualties preserved here under crosses and tilled fields.

The science building was a long, low, prefab affair. Large, square windows looked out on a wooded area. Christine led Harry through a maze of doors and hallways into the exhibit gallery, a plain, oval room adjacent to the Laboratoire de Paleontologie. It was ringed with cases displaying the usual assortment of fossils and artifacts: trilobites from the Devonian; pearled ammonites and plesiosaur paddles from the Cretaceous; a mammoth tusk and fluted quartz projectile points from the Pleistocene. The labels were typewritten. Most were yellowed and curled at the edges. They matched the antique exhibit cases, handsome walnut boxes with hinged, glass-framed tops that sloped down to the front.

Marie LeBoeuf was leaning on the Engis-2 case in a corner of the gallery. She looked despondent, elbows on the glass, face propped up in her hands, staring blankly at the bare, black, velvet cloth lining the case, as if she were trying to will the skull and teeth of the Neanderthal child back into the empty space. There were scrape marks around the simple latch at the front. Someone with a plain knife or screwdriver had jimmied it open in seconds.

"After three months, no progress. Belgian police, Interpol—nothing," she raised her hands in frustration. "You know how valuable these remains are? On the black market? The first Neanderthal found—a Neanderthal child?"

"Christine told me."

She raised her hands again, her face a mixture of anger and disbelief. "Like art thieves! Clients give them a list. Steal this Van Gogh. Or that Vermeer. Or these Neanderthals. I warned the museum. Put replicas on display. No, they want to be like art museums. Show the real thing. *Stupide.* We don't have the security of art museums. No guards. No alarm systems."

"When were they taken?" Harry asked.

"At the end of October. I put them back here myself! On a Friday. On Saturday morning, pffffft!" She waved her hand to the outside. "An *étudiant* ... a student intern ... opened the gallery. Gone."

"You said you put them back? Were they out?"

"Yes," Marie nodded. "In a study area in the research collections. We had a meeting here that week. An international Neanderthal conference. Archaeologists. They wanted to see the Engis-2 cranium."

"The skull ... there's a controversy," Christine interjected. "It has cross scratches on the bone in the temporal area." She tapped the side of her head above her ear. "European archaeologists think it was cannibalism, the girl's muscles being scraped off the bone for food after she died. But the archaeologist at Berkeley disagrees. He thinks the scratches were made after 1936, when the Engis-2 bones and teeth were rediscovered here in the collection and identified as a Neanderthal child. Whoever pieced the cranium together filled in the gaps with plaster and carelessly smoothed over the joints with sandpaper."

"Who would have done that?" Harry asked.

Marie shrugged. "Back then? We don't know. There are no records."

Verreaux never mentioned scratches on the cranium in his notebook entry of April 22, 1832, when Schmerling brought him the Engis-2 skull bones. Verreaux would have noticed. His plaster casts of the skull bones would also show the scratches. Harry wondered whether anyone knew that Verreaux had made copies of the Engis-2 remains before Schmerling left that day with the originals? Or that the casts were lying in a drawer somewhere in the Paris museum? Likely not. Were they still around? Verreaux recorded that he catalogued them, but left the species name blank. He just called it an extinct form of human. Did he make the connection to Neanderthals twenty-four years later, in 1856, when their adult bones were discovered in Germany and officially recognized as an archaic human? Lousy odds, Harry thought. Likely, Verreaux's cast specimens of the Engis-2 child's skull were lying nameless and mute in one of thousands of drawers among hundreds of cabinets. He doubted Christine knew.

Harry turned to Marie. "What did you do with the Engis-2 material every evening during the conference? Put them back in the case?"

"No," Marie answered. "It was too much trouble. I locked them in a cabinet in the collection room. On Friday, at the end of the conference, I put them back in the gallery. We had an evening reception—wine, some food. We left the gallery open. For the conference participants. Also for their spouses … and partners." Inadvertently, she gave Christine a quick glance. Christine blushed. "No one said anything about the Engis-2 material. If it was missing, no one noticed." She shrugged. "I do not know. I did not go into the gallery during the reception."

Harry frowned. "People might have noticed, but no one would think the empty case was strange. They'd assume the specimens were still in the cabinet in the laboratory. Like they were all week."

Marie's face turned pale. "So, the cranium was stolen during the reception?"

"Could be. Could be later. Are both doors to this gallery locked?"

"No," Marie answered. "Only the door to the hallway. Not this one." She pointed to the door that led to the laboratory and collection cabinets. "It is open for people to work in the evenings and weekends—scientists, students."

"I can't believe one of the archaeologists took it?" Christine declared.

Harry grimaced. "Believe it. Or one of the spouses. Or partners."

"*Non!*" Marie stated, incredulous. "*C'nest pas possible.* It is not possible. You are saying what the police also say. Why? It makes no sense! What can they do with the skull somewhere else that they cannot do here? In this museum? In our laboratory?"

"They can own it," Harry said, drily.

He walked around the small gallery and mulled the odds. Carnegie Museum had hosted an anthropology conference the same week the camel in the exhibit was sliced open. Ditto here in the Liège museum. Two continents, two museums, two exhibits, two acts of vandalism, each preceded by an archaeological symposium. What the hell was the connection? A mummified kid stuffed into an 1867 French exhibit. The cranium of a Neanderthal kid found in a Belgian cave. Coincidence isn't proof, Harry thought, but it's good enough to watch your back.

42

Paris
Monday, February 1

On the train back to Paris, Harry pulled out Verreaux's notebook that he'd quickly stashed in his backpack before leaving with Christine on Sunday. He knew it violated every protocol of the museum's archives. Christine wasn't there to object. She'd stayed behind with Marie. Just a day or two, she'd said, to finish some research.

The notebook was from the fourth and last archival box, 1859-1867. Verreaux's first entry skipped ahead thirty-four years since he'd confronted the meaning of the Neanderthal girl with the auburn hair from Engis-2 Cave and drawn her portrait. It also skipped across a continent from the Paris museum to the outskirts of an Arab village in North Africa.

18 Juin, 1859, El Kef, Afrique de Nord.

It wasn't until my brother and I arrived here, to hunt the Barbary lions in the North African desert, that the Arab Courier was again born in my mind. The seed was planted many years earlier, when I was 10 years old. My father took me to the grand building in the Jardin des Plantes to see the riches that Napoleon had brought back from his adventures in Bavaria. Crowds of women dressed in hoop skirts, and men in black frock coats and top hats, milled past the stuffed bestiaries of mammals and birds and crocodiles and snakes from foreign lands. Many of the animals were misshapen and in a state of decay. Their skins were rotting and split, spilling out their straw stuffing. King Maximillian's taxidermists were amateurs. And they lacked the arsenical soap of Maison Verreaux, the elixir of immortal death.

There were many fossils laid out on tables: fish skeletons from a place called Messel, lying in shale, perfectly preserved, as if they had just been caught, broiled and defleshed; monstrous marine saurians with long necks and paddle limbs that did not resemble any living creature in the world's oceans; gigantic coiled shells called ammonites, with shiny, pinkish pearled surfaces; and strange, segmented black animals that looked like obese stone beetles. My father told me they were trilobites, so named because of the three large lobes that made up their bodies.

There were paintings that Napoleon had stolen from the King of Bavaria's art collection. One of them, a huge canvas in a gilded frame, rooted my body to that spot and made me let go of my father's hand. He strolled on, oblivious to his son transfixed by a ferocious battle between man and beast such as I had never imagined. Later I discovered it was Peter Paul Rubens' Lion Hunt. Maximillian had commissioned it in 1616. Rubens knew lions. He had seen them illustrated in the zoological tomes of Aldrovandi, then sketched them from life in the private zoos of royalty.

Under a deep, turbulent sky, six Moors on horses have chased down two lions for the kill. But the lions, a female and male, have turned the battle. Three of the Moors have been wrestled to the ground, their turbans and shirts ripped from their bodies. One of them still grasps his knife in death. The second Moor tries to rise from the ground and re-enter the battle. The third, pinned by the lioness, is moments from being disemboweled. Her mate has dragged the fourth Moor from his horse till he hangs upside down, his turban unfurled, brushing the ground. The last two Moors, still mounted, have thrust their lances into the powerful male. But it is to no avail. One of them turns his horse to flee the battle. The lions are moments from victory.

Then, without warning an English knight, sheathed in black armor and black-plumed helmet, thunders in from the rear, his red cape fluttering high in the air. With his right arm he plunges his long lance into the lion.

I waited for the outcome. Who would prevail, lion or hunter? But time had stopped. The battle hung suspended, the end forever in suspense.

As a child I thought nothing strange of the knight's intrusion. Later, in my years in Africa, I grew to resent it. Rubens had given us the comforting lesson of scripture—Man and Nature, created apart, the pitting of biblical foes. In Ecclesiasticus it is said that God put the fear of man upon all flesh, giving him dominion over beast and fowl. Rubens complied. Here was Nature—savage, animalistic. Here was Man—civilized, exalted in the hierarchy of creation. And here was the Knight, exalted in the hierarchy of civilized Man, elevated above the native Moors. The Knight, Rubens was telling us, was as superior to the Moors as they were to Nature. All with God's sanction.

The writer of The Book was mistaken. So was Rubens. He had painted our ignorance and conceit. I learned this later when I captured the lion in the veldt. I learned it when I exhumed the bodies of the two Africans—the Betchuanan chief in the south, the Berber tribesman in the north. I learned it when I skinned them, when I examined their hearts and brains and bones.

I told my brother, Édouard, that we were all bred as one through the ages, animal and Man. We could not shed Nature from our being, nor could we shed ourselves from her. Except in divine delusion. My brother shook his head. He told me I had lost all sense of the ordained order of the world.

The Rubens stayed with me, a Saharan tick under the skin gorging on my blood. He had breathed dabs of red, yellow, brown and blue into a primitive, violent theatre playing out before our senses. It was theatre stained bloody without the blood, in motion without movement. It hung there, a still life horrifically alive, like the mute, macabre beasts standing in our glassed-in showcase on Rue Montmartre. It was of the flesh, arousing men and women to illicit desire by the writhing of feral animals and natives in deadly battle. Yet it kept the public safe, behind paint, as Maison Verreaux did behind the taxidermal art.

Now I will transform the Rubens into a shocking tableau such as no one has yet accomplished. I imagine a lone Arab courier on his camel crossing the hot yellow sand of the North African desert. Suddenly, two lions spring on them from behind a dune. The courier shoots the lioness, but not before the male lion has leapt on them from the side, burying his claws into the large fleshy hump of the camel. Terrified, the Arab courier pulls out his curved-bladed knife, his jambiya, and plunges it at the lion's chest. In that instant, the lion lunges at the courier, his jaws ready to sever the courier's arm from his body.

As in the Rubens, there will be no winner. The duel will continue to be fought in each of our minds, alternating victor and vanquished the longer we linger and look. Eventually we will begin to see the pulse of the beast in Man, and the beating of the soul in the beast. The diorama will disrupt our sense of kind, our reckoning of the place of Man and beast among beings on Earth. It will be as Creation itself. In this one moment in the desert, time will be immobile, yet hurtle forward. The battle will rage, yet be in rigor mortis. In this one moment, Nature and Man will become one flesh.

Only when we look away will there be relief.

43

Paris
Monday, February 1

The train slowed and pulled into Bastogne. An unscheduled stop, the announcement came over the speakers. The French was too rapid-fire for Harry to catch how long it would be or why. The conductor on the platform merely shrugged his shoulders. Harry rolled a cigarette, noticed the conductor's stare, and handed him the Drum and Zig-Zag papers.

Verreaux's notebooks had not yet unzipped the camel's belly. If there had been a kid in there, all the candidates were long shots. Verreaux's and Elisabeth's child, preserved and pickled since 1828. Jane Wylde's child, conceived in incest with her father. Or with Verreaux after a dance one Saturday evening in Cape Town in 1829. What if it had nothing to do with Verreaux's escapades in Cape Town? Maybe a stillborn from the Paris morgue, a grotesque prank played by Frémiet on Verreaux. It would be in character, this sculptor who could imagine an orangutan raping a woman. Verreaux likely invited him to the museum workshop to see his masterpiece, his variation on a Rubens, his entry into the 1867 Paris Exposition. All Frémiet would need is 30 minutes alone in the museum workshop. Unstitch the camel's belly, stuff in the bundle, sew it back up.

The conductor motioned Harry back onto the train. He stubbed out his cigarette in the iron ashtray by the station entrance. Above it a bronze bas relief was bolted to the wall: a cyclist, body thrust forward, back parallel to the ground, hands in the drops, head arched up, going full gas. The inscription read "Liège-Bastogne-Liège." Harry wondered whether his father had ever seen it.

21 Decembre, 1859. El Kef, Afrique de Nord

The Berber was two days into death. He was short, as is usual of his kind in the Levant. And rather lean, with a hooked, protruding nose, almost like a beak. Before we dug him up, I was afraid he would be hirsute, which would make his skin more difficult to preserve. Baboons and bears are most troublesome. Luckily, he proved to be almost hairless, like the elephant.

My brother, Édouard, and I traversed the villages west of Tunis until we found the Berber and the Barbary Lion in the desert near El Kef. The village was built into a flat-top summit, the highest we saw in Tunisia. Its graveyard was distant from the walled medina at the edge of the desert, where the sand begins to encroach on the soil above the wadi.

We encountered the male and female lion prowling near the sheep and goats of the Berber encampment in the far desert, and shot them. They are much hunted, as the Barbary is larger and heavier than the other breed of lions from below the Sahara. There are none to be found to the west in Tripoli, and soon they will be gone from here. The Romans took many to fight the gladiators in the Coliseum.

We waited outside El Kef for the Berber funerals. There were two in one day, then one the next. They rode in on their camels from their black tents in the far desert to bury their dead, stayed for a day, then left. We watched them disappear, dots floating in the miraged heat above the sand.

We disinterred him during a night with no moon. It took longer than we had planned. The first two graves held women, whom we quickly reburied. They had been left adorned with their amber beads and cowrie shells, which they believed would protect them from the evil-eye. Even in the dark I noticed the tattoos on their bronze skin, hidden in life under their embroidered, colorful caftans and head scarves. I thought it sensual that they exposed these intricate swirling shapes only during the night to a lover. And now, after death, to me, a grave robber.

The third mound held the Berber man. His body was fresh, with no putrefaction, wrapped in an oiled linen cloth that smelled of goats.

I sat with him on the cart, holding him down as we bounced over the rocks of the desert plane. Édouard guided the mule to the whitewashed stone hut at the foot of El Kef, near a wild growth of elephant cactus. I could smell the charcoal burning on the night wind, an intoxicating smoke from inside the medina.

We carried the Berber into the house, laid him face down on the table in the middle of the room, and hung a kerosene lamp above the body. I made the first incision at the top of the neck, then slit the skin down the midline of the back to the tail bone. The scalpel bounced gently over the vertebrae, first the seven cervicals, then the twelve thoracic, then the five lumbar.

This count of bones was a common feature of all Mammalia, as Cuvier taught us, whether human, mouse or giraffe. He said it was given to us by a creator who appreciated mathematical symmetry. Now Darwin says it was bequeathed to us by our apish ancestors. I agree with Darwin. A creator would have been more merciful, not constraining Man with the vertebral calculus of other beasts.

My father must have thought so too. In the workshop at Maison Verreaux, he would point out the anatomical similarities among the different animals to me and my brothers. I think this why my mother went to church without him. She alone believed that the animals that stared out onto Rue Montmartre from our emporium were made one by one by the Dieu, the Creator, then rescued one by one by Noah in an ark.

Édouard helped me turn the Berber's body over. I began the second incision at the throat, skimmed down the midline of the chest, over the abdomen, around the genitals and across the inside of the buttocks. The scalpel met the first incision at the coccyx. With my third cut, I severed the head from the body.

There was no blood. It had already congealed in the arteries and veins. But there was a faint odor of death, despite the absence of rot of flesh or organs. Édouard said the smell was from the release of a moldering soul.

He asked me if I felt sin, or conscience, dismembering a dead Berber. No, I told him. We were rescuing him from an anonymous eternity in a grave near a Saharan wadi. We were arranging his resurrection in Paris, to be viewed in awe by multitudes, a star in a thrilling tableau in an Exposition du Monde. We were giving him his afterlife.

I spread the legs apart and made the last incisions along the inside, from the sole of the feet to the abdominal opening. Now the skin could be peeled from the body.

I worked from the abdomen toward the pelvis and back again, rolling the body from one side to the other, slowly pulling the skin back in small sheets, careful not to tear it. In an hour, the Berber was naked. Then I skinned his head.

When I stretched it out on the table, it was no longer skin. It was hide, epidermis, an animal's pelt, but almost hairless and easy to treat. I washed the inner and outer sides with salt and arsenical soap, then rubbed them smooth with a flat rock. The smell of the preservative brought back my childhood, the fifty red, brown and green birds falling through the quiet of the woods, their bodies warm in my hand, my father coating them with the chemical potions.

I rolled up the hide and locked it in a wooden drying box. Before light, before the distant call to prayer, we removed the Berber's limb bones, wrapped his skinned body in the linen cloth, carted the carcass back to the cemetery, and reburied him in his grave alongside the tattooed women.

Two days later, the last few pieces of the Berber's flesh still adhering to the skin had spawled off. I rubbed both sides of the hide again with arsenical soap. We let the skin cure for a week, then applied a thick coat of powdered alum and laid it carefully in the shade to dry.

Twenty days after the first incision, I shipped the Berber's hide, bones and skull to the Maison from Tunis. The skin alone weighed nine pounds and measured twenty-two square feet. I remembered Cuvier's lesson at the museum in Paris. Man's skin is the largest organ of the body. It is what meets the air first. It shields us from water, dirt, and sickness. It gives us our shape. It makes the man shrunken or heroic, the woman wrinkled or desirable. It makes me think of Elisabeth. The touch of her skin was molten in a time long lost.

In Paris, in the laboratory of the museum, I placed the hide in a relaxing bath, and the Berber's head in the beetle colony to strip away the muscle and tissue. Museum exhibit workers under my direction attached the Berber's leg bones to iron bars, each a centimeter thick, each bent to conform to a Berber riding a camel. We did the same with the arm bones, the left ones stretched forward to hold the camel's reins, the right ones bent downward to stab the lion with the jambiya. For the Berber's backbone we fashioned an iron bar a meter long and two centimeters thick, to which we bolted his ribs, pelvis, legs, scapulae, clavicles and arms. We wrapped his bone and iron skeleton with a plaster lattice and filled the cavity with straw, molded to recreate the Berber's lean torso.

For the head, I bolted the Berber's own skull to the front of the iron backbone. The muscles, brain and eyes were gone, eaten clean by the beetles. Still, he stared at me, as if he knew his fate.

At last, we removed the Berber's skin from the relaxing tank, smoothed it over the manikin, and sewed the suture down the front of the body and along the inside of the arms and legs. The seams would be covered by the Berber's clothing.

The face was last. For two days, I applied thin layers of dark clay to the contours of the Berber's skull, sculpting his panic into his old skin. I put the terror in his eyes and bared his mouth, screaming in fright yet silent, my courier astride his camel, set upon by two Barbary lions, confronting death in the blinding yellow heat of the desert.

44

Paris
Tuesday, February 2

Harry brought a couple of ham croissants and a large café Americain up to the alcove. There had been a dusting of snow overnight. The museum roof scattered a blinding light over the Jardin des Plantes. Harry cracked the window, lit a cigarette, and watched the snow begin to melt around the forked imprints of wrens and robins. He ate quickly and moved the coffee to the floor, away from Verreaux's open notebook.

23 Decembre, 1859. El Kef, Afrique de Nord

Today Édouard and I went to the village to purchase a dromedary for the exhibit. The Berber women do not look at me. On the street or in the souk, they avert their eyes until it seems they stare at a blankness. They are covered in black cloaks, as if in mourning for the light their skin will never see. It is Islam. It hides women from the sun. In the narrow alleys of the souk, the women shadow into one another, without shapes, without faces, nonexistent. Except the slit for their eyes, like a fortress with a narrow peephole. To live here is to become a sensitive reader of eyes.

Harry remembered the village market in Iraq. Women sheathed in black, his senses taut, at the edge, not knowing whether the shapely bulge underneath the hajib was a bosom, a gun or a bomb. He stared at their faces, trying to pierce the veils that hid the telltale contours of innocence or intent. He couldn't.

Schoolchildren began shrieking in the snow outside on the Jardin. It snapped Harry back to the museum alcove, relieved to be facing Verreaux's notebook.

I was told the women are concealed for their honor, for modesty before their God. But, as I told Édouard, unseen means undesired. Undesired means untouched. And untouched means assurance of chastity in the unmarried, and faithfulness in the married. It is our inbred animal nature, the certitude for men that they have sired the children they are raising. In Africa we witnessed the zebra stallion stomp to death a foal he did not sire. Then he mated with the mare, who had stood on the side, watching and waiting, seemingly knowing nature's merciless rule of paternity.

I find the black shrouds of the women devilishly alluring. Perhaps it is the mystery behind the mask. I want to know where the black, thick rebellious eyebrows lead, how the olive skin flows over cheek and forehead and breast and thigh. I want to touch their "ouchams", the tattoos applied to their bodies to ward off evil spirits in advance of life's thresholds—marriage, childbirth and death.

I saw the ouchams, shaped as round circles and stars, on the two Berber corpses in the graveyard. I was told a pregnant woman will paint a sharp dagger on her belly to stab the devil. They use henna, crush it to a powder, mix it with sandalwood oil to form an aromatic paste, and draw the dye directly on their skin. The tattoo can re-

main for weeks. Only the women are tattooists. I think it
is their private revolt, adorning the body they must hide.
The Quran, I am told, strictly forbids tattoos.

In a market stall near the outside wall of the village,
we purchased a suitable camel. We bargained a suitable
price, after we told them we would only take the skin and
bones, and leave the meat for them.

On the facing page, Verreaux had sketched an Arab women
looking directly at him. She resembled a tall black raven cooling in
the heat of the day under an archway in the souk. A ruffle in the
floor-length jilbaab hinted of a wind, or a leg suggestively angled
outward. He'd emphasized the eyes behind the jihab, penetrating
yet stealthy, like a periscope, secretly scanning a world framed by
the narrow slit in the veil.

That evening, Harry and Christine had dinner at the brasserie.
She'd returned from Liège in the late afternoon, met him at the
hotel, and took his arm as they walked through the cold drizzle to
Place d'Italie.

Harry asked her if she had ever read Verreaux's notebooks.

"No, I haven't. Why?" She eyed him, suspiciously. "Have you
found something?"

"Many things. How to disinter and skin a Berber in the 1850s
at the northern edge of the Sahara. How to bargain for a dromedary camel. How Verreaux recognized the skull cap and teeth of
the Neanderthal child from Engis-2 Cave as a different, archaic
type of human. And he did that thirty-four years before Neanderthals were formally discovered, recognized and named as a different
species. How—"

Christine bolted up. "What! That's impossible. The Neanderthal child? He never ..." She sat back and grinned, sheepishly.
"Okay, I get it, you're fooling with me."

Harry shook his head. "Not this time. Schmerling, the guy
who found the Engis-2 bones, brought them here from Liège in
1832 and showed them to Verreaux in the museum. Verreaux knew
his anatomy. Skinning humans and animals for exhibits will do
that. So will working in the Paris morgue. He pieced the cranium
together. He knew immediately that it wasn't recent—the bones

had begun to mineralize. And that it wasn't *Homo sapiens*. He even sketched a picture of the child, a reconstruction of the face. He got most of it right—low skull, sloping forehead, hint of eyebrow ridges and an occipital bun. Even the reddish hair."

Christine stared at him, wide-eyed, her face frozen in shock. "Verreaux? ... Engis-2?" she finally managed to burble. "I can't believe it. It's impossible. All that is in his notebook?"

Harry nodded. "Believe it. The entry for April 22, 1832."

She put her hands on her head and gaped at him, as if her entire sense of equilibrium had crashed. "Show me tomorrow morning." It sounded like a command. "Christ, if it's true, then it was Verreaux who was the first to discover Neanderthals, although he didn't know it at the time. And he should be the one to get the credit. Also us—the Paris Muséum. Neanderthals first identified here. That would make it a French discovery, not a German one."

"There you go, welcome back to tribalism," Harry quipped.

Christine groaned. "That's cruel, Harry." Then she managed a shy smile. "But I forgive you in the spirit of *fraternité*. Anyway, I'm stunned. No one knows that Verreaux did this."

Harry hesitated, prospecting for the right words. "Actually, at least one other person does."

"What? What do you mean?" She reached for Harry's tobacco and rolled a long brown cheroot.

"Someone else has read Verreaux's notebooks. Any chance you know who that was? Does the museum archive keep a sign-out ledger?"

She scrunched up her face and spit a piece of tobacco on the floor. "Well, maybe the professors who wrote Verreaux's biography for the museum's compilation. They might have consulted the notebooks. Otherwise, I don't know. But I will ask at the library tomorrow."

The food came, bowls of pasta, dressed with olive oil, garlic and mussels. Christine ordered a second round of Trois Monts, stubbed out her cheroot, and grabbed Harry's hand.

"How do you know someone else read them. Did they leave a note?"

"No." Harry shook his head. "No notes."

"*Merde*," she exclaimed, "I hope they didn't write anything in the margins!"

"Nope, nothing like that." Christine didn't need to know that the page after the April 22, 1932 Neanderthal entry had been razored out of the notebook. "Oh yeah, Verreaux also made a cast of the kid's cranium for your museum. Is it in the collection?"

Christine shook her head in disbelief. "What? Really? Is that also in his notebook?" She raised her arms in exasperation. "You want to know if it's in the collection? Who the hell knows it even exists? I've never seen a cast of that specimen here. No one else has ever mentioned it." She scowled. "Right now, I'm stupefied. I'll check the collection catalogue tomorrow. After you show me the journal entry."

She grabbed a mussel and chewed on it, eyeing him suspiciously, reading his face. "Harry, you are not telling me everything."

He nodded, drank some beer, pushed the bowl away, rolled a Drum, and lit it. "Yeah, well, information is like armor. Revealing everything peels off the protection. Only the deepest intimacies can afford that." He lit the cigarette and added, "and maybe not even those." He thought of Liza in Pittsburgh.

45

Paris
Wednesday, February 3

Early Wednesday morning Harry dropped off a coffee and a couple of chocolate croissants beside the homeless guy on the corner. Three blocks on, the massive iron doors to the museum were still closed. He sat alone on the marble steps on Rue de Buffon, downed a cheese baguette, and had the first cigarette of the morning with his coffee. A hundred years before Darwin, Georges-Louis Leclerc, Compte de Buffon, formed heretical evolutionary ideas from his studies of nature. His history of the Earth's animals and plants countered the biblical account—and Bishop Ussher's reckoning of 6 pm on October 22, 4004 BC for the time and date of creation. Theologians condemned Buffon.

The sun was trying to burn off a layer of gray mist that hovered low above the rooftops. Yellow buses began lining up along the curb, spilling out school kids smartly dressed in blue tunics and blazers. They scampered up the steps, across the smooth, concave depressions worn down by centuries of science, by footfalls that had dared to tread on scriptural canon.

Christine had not yet arrived by the time Harry climbed the three flights to the alcove. He leafed through Verreaux's last notebook. All but four of the entries were lists of specimens, mostly birds, that he and his brothers had brought back from expeditions in Asia and Australia.

12 Mars, 1865. Paris

My brother Alexis returned from Brno, Austria yesterday, from St. Thomas' Abbey. A local baron had shot an Ursus, a brown bear, on the grounds of the abbey. He wished to have it mounted for his baroness.

Alexis recounted that one of the friars named Gregor Mendel had planted a large garden of peas to conduct experiments on inheritance. In all he used 29,000 plants of seven different purebred varieties: peas with round skins or wrinkled ones, green pods or yellow ones, white seeds or gray ones, short stems or long ones, and so on. These he crossbred over many generations to see how their distinctive features were transmitted from parents to offspring. Just last week, Mendel presented his findings at a gathering of the Natural History Society of Brno. Alexis brought a newspaper account of the proceedings.

Mendel's results are astonishing. The distinguishing traits of the plants pass from one generation to the next independently. They do not blend or become diluted with one another as is commonly thought. Even more revolutionary is his mathematical conclusion that there are discrete hereditary particles inside the peas—indeed inside all animals and plants—that control the inheritance of specific traits. Mendel says these particles are permanent, immutable. They pass without alteration from one generation to the next. And they are invisible. He calls them "elementen".

If Mendel is right, he has deduced the first true principles of inheritance. He has also disproved our own Lamarck, who thought that an animal's or plant's use and disuse of its characteristics determined how strongly they were passed to the next generation.

I have spoken to my colleagues of this and shown them the newspaper account. As Frenchmen, they rally around Lamarck. What does an Augustinian monk in Brno know about the natural world, they scoff. His rightful place is scripture, not science. If these particles of inheritance, these elementen, are invisible, they ask, how can this monk vouch for their existence? How can we verify his claim? Mathematics alone, they say, does not make it so.

No matter. From my own observations of the species of birds from Africa and Asia and Europe, I sense that Mendel is correct. There is no blending of external traits in these avian kinds through the generations.

I am told by Alexis that Mendel will publish his paper. Perhaps Darwin in England will see it. I have read Darwin's volume on the Origin of Species by Means of Natural Selection. He makes no mention of discrete factors of inheritance, such as Mendel's elementen. But surely it is the natural selection of these elementen in each generation that produces the procession of species through time.

Harry barely heard Christine bound up the metal stairs into the alcove. She was wearing high top trail shoes, muddied by the slush on the street. Wordlessly, she pointed to the archival boxes on the table. He showed her the entry he had just read, in which Verreaux had anticipated the selection of genes as the major force in evolution. She looked at Harry, silent, stern, seemingly unimpressed. Either she didn't realize the implications or didn't care. Harry picked up the journal from the third box, paged to the entry of 22 Avril, 1832, and handed it to her.

She ran her finger along each line of Verraux's script, slowly, deliberately, as if to make sure she would not miss a word. He watched her read, the slight, silent movement of her lips. When she was done, she closed the hard covers and looked at Harry again, stone-faced. She grabbed his Drum tobacco from the table, climbed out onto the roof, rolled a cheroot, lit it, and sat mute, staring out at the first visitors tramping through the snow in the distance in the Jardin des Plantes. Harry sat beside her, took the cheroot from her fingers and helped her smoke it. Neither of them spoke. After a few moments, she crushed the lit end of the cheroot on the roof tile, eased back through the window into the alcove, and disappeared down the stairs.

She hadn't noticed that the next page in the journal had been razored out. At least, Harry didn't think so. If she had, she'd kept it to herself.

46

Paris
Wednesday, February 3

At one in the afternoon, Christine came up to the alcove, carrying lunch for the two of them: cheese, tomato, and basil sandwiches on demi baguettes, and a couple of beers.

She told him she'd done a quick search for Verreaux's plaster cast of the Neanderthal child's skull from Engis-2 Cave. No luck. It could be anywhere in the collections.

She'd also talked with the museum's archive librarian. Verreaux's notebooks had been checked out twice. First, a few years ago by the professors who were compiling the biographies of the museum's former naturalists for Du Jardin Au Muséum. Then, last year by the museum's ornithology department. They were preparing to database its vast bird collection. Verreaux had brought back and prepared thousands of them. The curators wanted to verify the geographic localities in the card catalog against what he'd recorded in his notebooks. They made a copy of the notebooks for their everyday reference."

Made sense, Harry thought. Most of Verreaux's notebook entries were long lists of specimens from his expeditions in South Africa, Australia, Asia and North Africa.

"No one else?"

"No. At least there is no record."

"Can anyone walk in and browse the archives?"

Christine held up a finger while she finished chewing. "Well, of course not anyone. But, yes, our scientists ... staff ... students."

"Visitors?"

"Researchers, yes." She looked at him, quizzically. "Harry, why—" she started to ask, then stopped, shrugged and handed him Marie's list of archaeologists who had attended the Neanderthal symposium in Liège. Harry scanned it quickly. About 45 participants from Europe, Israel, Canada and the US. He recognized four names: Christine Dumoulin; Marie LeBoeuf; Anna Storck from the Carnegie Museum; and Professor James Porter, an archaeologist from the University of Kansas. Harry grinned. He was still living off Porter's payments for the Fulbright case.

Harry pointed to the list. "Anna Storck. Did you—"

Christine grimaced. "Yes. Of course. You know that she ..."

"They told me. So, she was in Liège in October?"

"Yes," Christine said, haltingly, "with Gideon, her husband." A shudder seemed to well up through her body and into her face. "They came here first and stayed with me. Anna and I went to the conference in Liège. He worked here in the bird collection with the ornithologists. Until the last day of the conference. He came to Liège to be with Anna at the closing reception."

"Tell me about them."

She shrugged. "There's nothing to tell. The professional couple. She's famous. Her work on Neanderthal genomics. Lots of grants, publications. She has collaborators at the Max Planck Institute in Leipzig."

"What about Gould?"

"He ... he's not been as successful. He didn't get tenure at Carnegie last year. He's on probation now. It's difficult for him, Anna said ... the competition. She got tenure first shot."

Harry decided to probe Christine's earlier discomfort. "So, when did Gideon make a pass at you?"

Christine started choking on her food, then stared at him, shaking. "What ... how ... what do you mean?"

"You know what I mean. You have a readable face. That's a compliment."

Christine shoved her food side, knocking over her beer on the table. Harry rescued the notebooks ahead of the spreading brown puddle.

"Goddamn it, Harry," she snapped, "don't bullshit me. You sneak up on me from behind. You whack me across the head. And then you tell me the wound is a compliment. I have a rule not to swear in English, but ... fuck off!"

"Yeah, that was calculated. Sorry. Tell me about it."

She picked up the bottle, wiped off the table with the lunch napkins, grabbed the Drum tobacco and papers, and rolled a cigarette.

"It happened last summer. There was a meeting of the International Ornithological Union here at the museum. Anna asked if Gideon could stay with me. Of course, I said. She flew in with him, stayed a day, and went on to Leipzig to work with her colleagues at the Max Planck. Sequencing DNA from a finger bone found in a cave in Siberia. Gideon was ... well ... depressed. He kept saying how everyone at the meetings knew he didn't get tenure. At the last minute he pulled the paper he was supposed to give. Stage fright. No confidence. Paranoid that no one respected him any longer. It's all he would talk about. That ... and sex. He and Anna ... well ... weren't. He made comments ... suggestive."

She stood up and began pacing the alcove. "At first, I just ignored him, thinking he'd get the message. He didn't ... or wouldn't. Then I told him straight out. There's Anna. There's Marie. And most of all, there's me—I wasn't interested. He said he and Anna were on the outs. That he could make me be more interested in him than in Marie."

Christine opened the window overlooking the Jardin, lit the cigarette, and hugged her shoulders tightly with her hands. "One night ... I ... I woke. He was on top of me ... groping. I fought him off. It was horrible."

She turned and faced Harry. "Christ, my son was sleeping down the hall! Gideon didn't care."

Harry handed her what was left of his beer. "You didn't tell Anna."

She shook her head and drained the bottle. "I didn't. But it's likely she too could read my face. I don't think it was the first time Gideon had tried that with a woman."

"Okay, you saw them again here in October—the conference in Liège. Then at the archaeology meetings at the Carnegie in Pittsburgh in December."

"Yes. Marie and I stayed with her and Gideon. Reluctantly. I didn't want to. But Marie insisted ... to save money. That's when Anna ..." Christine's voice trailed off, then came back as a whisper. "We moved to a hotel."

Harry nodded. "Were you there when it happened?"

Christine narrowed her eyes. "Does every death attract you, Harry?"

"No, just ones that chase after me."

"What!" she exclaimed. "What does Anna's suicide have to do with Verreaux? You don't think ... that because she fell in front of—"

"No." Harry shook his head. "I guess you were there."

Christine sat down, tugged at her short hair, and stared out the window onto the grassy expanse of the Jardin des Plantes. "I can't forget it. It was a Wednesday morning. We went to her office ... early. Anna seemed upset ... stressed. She complained that Marie and I were in her way ... that she needed to get a ton of things ready for the presentations that day at the meeting. She kicked us out of her office. I went into her adjoining lab to work on my paper. Then I heard screams from the exhibit gallery outside her office. I ran out. I looked over the railing of the open atrium. She was down there, on the floor, crumpled up. I could see a dark pool spreading from her head. I realized it was blood."

Harry placed a hand on her arm. "I'm sorry, Christine. There is no art to prepare one for that."

She leaned over, kissed his cheek, held him for a moment, and wiped her eyes.

"Who screamed?"

Christine hesitated. "A cleaning lady ... sweeping the floor. Why?"

"Just wondering. Was Marie there?"

She shook her head. "No. She'd gone to the archaeology lab in the basement. She was lucky. She saw nothing. Except police carrying Anna away in a bag."

"What about Gould?"

"Gideon? No, he was in his office." She screwed up her forehead, puzzled. "Harry, what's going on? What aren't you telling me? First, you suspect someone might secretly have read Verreaux's notebooks. Now these questions about Anna's suicide."

Harry rolled a Drum. "Better you don't know, Christine. That way you have deniability."

Her face went to hurt, then anger. "You don't trust me, Harry." Her lips quivered as she spoke. "*Je suis très desolé.* No, that's too polite. Like I said before, fuck off." She stood up, gathered the paper wrappers and empty beer bottles, and retreated down the stairs.

Harry stopped himself from calling after her. He took the notebook onto the roof, lit the cigarette, and paged ahead. There were three more entries: 8 June, 1866; 1 November, 1867, about the Universal Exposition of Art and Industry in Paris, where Verreaux unveiled his *Arab Courier Attacked by Lions*; and 10 November, 1867.

47

Paris
Wednesday, February 3

8 Juin, 1866. Paris

Yesterday Alexis received a reprint from Gregor Mendel of his scientific paper. It is called "Experiments in Plant Hybridization", published in the Proceedings of the Natural History Society of Brno. There was an accompanying note from Mendel thanking Alexis for his interest and asking him to show the paper to as many naturalists as he could at the museum and universities.

All day I have studied Mendel's experiments and repeated the mathematical calculations. I cannot find any errors. And I have had a wonderful realization. Perhaps it is a premonition. It concerns Mendel's elementen, these immutable particles of inheritance that pass from one generation to the next unchanged in the expression of traits they control. Yes, they are invisible. But for how long?

We know too well the lessons of Van Leeuwenhoek. Until he built the microscope that magnified life 200 times, we knew nothing of single-celled organisms in the water, soil, and air. Until then, the bacterium and the amoeba were invisible. Just as the elementen are now.

In my estimation, someone in the future will invent a superior microscope that will make these elementen visible to the naturalist. Such a microscope will be capable of magnifying the ingredients of life 10,000 times or more. Then, if these elementen are truly immutable, we will know their individual anatomy. We will learn how they are transmitted and expressed in each generation in each animal and plant.

Most exciting will be the ability to identify these elementen in us, in the races of Man alive today, or in mummified peoples from the past, or in the fossil bones of archaic Man, such as the skeletons of Neanderthals found in Germany ten years ago. Surely the bones preserve the elementen of this primitive species.

Verreaux's biography in *Du Jardin Au Muséum* had paid him short shrift. Somehow, Harry thought, the professors had missed his anticipation of gene sequencing in living and fossil species, including Neanderthals. A hundred and fifty years later, Verreaux, in the new genomics lab of the Paris museum, would have prepared a pinch of ground bone from the skull of the Engis-2 child and tossed it into an Illumina Next Generation Sequencer. He would have discovered that he and she shared about four percent of their genes, that Europeans were hybrid descendants of Neanderthal-human romances.

Harry climbed back into the alcove, grabbed the earlier notebook from the table, and reread the entry with the missing page—22 April, 1832. Schmerling brings Verreaux the skull bones and teeth of the child. Verreaux reconstructs a portrait of the girl with the red hair. It gave him an idea.

48

Paris
Wednesday, February 3

1 Novembre 1867

The Exposition Universelle d'Art et d'Industrie ended yesterday here in Paris. It was magnificent, spread across hundreds of hectares on the Champs-de-Mars. There were 50,000 exhibitions from 42 countries, witnessed by more than seven million visitors.

The industrial section revealed many brilliant inventions, all of which were awarded prizes. They have convinced me that machinery is devised to derive answers, but it is through science and art that humans are needed to ask the questions.

A French engineer demonstrated a hydraulic elevator that lifts people from floor to floor without having to climb stairs. An Italian professor from Rome showed a large hydrochronometer, a tower with a clock driven by water, and visible from all four sides. The Americans displayed a number of wondrous machines: a telegraph that can transmit across the oceans; another that can print the messages; a mechanical reaper to harvest crops; and a fleet of special ambulances to rescue the wounded in war.

We will need the ambulances. Krupp ironworks of Prussia exhibited a new, 50-ton steel cannon capable of firing 500-kilogram projectiles. They say it is for protection of coastlines against iron-plated warships. But, in truth, it is meant for armies to kill from a far off distance. It will make us complacent to war, indifferent to the infliction of horrible deaths, merely because we cannot see it.

The art exhibitions were not as inventive. The Exposition committee refused to accept the paintings of Édouard Manet as too "slapdash" in execution, too avant garde. His critics decry him for employing a "strange new style". They object to his portraits of life, as much an impression as a precise, faultless rendering.

It was Frémiet who introduced me to Manet. I invited him to the museum laboratory to show him "Arab Courier Attacked by Lions." Manet recognized immediately that I had paid homage to Rubens, transforming his Lion Hunt into a dramatic theatre of suspense. In the end, my Arab Courier won the Prix d'Or.

Manet scorned the committee. He displayed his canvases in his own gallery, directly across the quay from the Exposition. Crowds flocked to see them: Luncheon on the Grass; Music in the Tuileries.

One of Manet's paintings has shocked the Paris salon: Olympia. She is a demi-mondaine, a courtesan, a nude reclining on the bed on an oriental shawl. But, it is the barest adornments on her alabaster skin that make her scandalous: the orchid in the hair; the pearl earrings; the thin black ribbon in a bow circling the neck; the gold bracelet on the wrist; and the slipper dangling from the left foot. The adornments advertise her naked allure, her scarlet contradictions, refined yet brazen, elegant yet erotic, arousing our carnal temptation.

I was forced to turn away. All I could see was Elisabeth, reclining on our bed in the Cape, naked, beckoning, the wildness of her hair betraying the seductive heat of her skin. I am forever accursed with her and our child.

Harry wondered which child Verreaux meant. The one that might be floating in formaldehyde in a 10-gallon glass vessel in the sub-basement of the museum? Or the one hidden in the belly of the camel for 150 years? Or the child who in 1867 would have been a grown woman of thirty-nine?

He turned the page to Verreaux's last journal entry. The odds weren't good that it would have the answer.

10 Novembre, 1867

The museum has deemed that the collections are to be purged of "unnecessary objects", as determined by a committee of the curators. Every collection is overcrowded with specimens of all kind, already more than a million skins, mounts, bodies in alcohol, skeletons of living and petrified species, and archaeological treasures. Every day more arrives from expeditions to all the continents and seas. There is no room for them.

I know the curators on this committee. They are wedded to custom. They will retain the traditional objects of study. They will empty the museum drawers of what they are calling "curiosities", specimens irrelevant to conventional science.

I have learned that two such curiosities are among the specimens I deposited in the museum. They are to be disposed. I tried to convince the committee that study of this material awaits a future Leeuwenhoek, a future Mendel, but failed.

Yesterday, in the evening hours, I secretly rescued the two specimens from their cabinet. For the moment they are hidden in my taxidermic laboratory. For the future I have devised the most devious means to safekeep them for study. The means came to me from observing the Arab women of El Kef, who hide their treasures for pleasurable study in the night.

The words ended on the bottom of the final page of the journal. Fitting, Harry thought. He began to close the notebook, then saw it. There used to be more words, but someone had razored out the page between this entry and the back cover. He or she had removed it carefully, almost flush with the spine, neatly enough to escape casual notice. Like the missing page before Verreaux's drawing of the Neanderthal girl with the reddish hair.

Harry put the notebook down, opened the window, rolled a cigarette, and lit it. Verreaux had rescued two specimens, "curiosities," from being tossed by the museum curators. What were they? The baby in alcohol from South Africa? The cast of the skull of the Engis-2 child? By "devious," did Verreaux mean hiding a bundle in the belly of the camel?

Someone in Paris had performed surgery on two pages of Verreaux's journal, entries written thirty-five and a half years apart: April 22, 1832, and November 10, 1867. They had the pages. Harry was willing to bet that they knew what Verreaux might have wrapped up in the bundle. And why a vandal in Pittsburgh had ripped it out of the camel's belly 150 years later.

BOOK FOUR

THE BUNDLE

49

Paris
Thursday, February 4

A noisy street sweeper woke him early in the morning. A warm wind had blown into Paris yesterday during the late afternoon and through the night. It melted the snow and left a grimy sludge along the edge of the boulevard. It had also left a sludge on the edge of his senses when he'd walked back from the museum to the hotel, the air trading its cold, crisp bite for the sensual tremors of Spring.

It hadn't helped that he'd called Liza yesterday to get him on a flight to Pittsburgh on Friday.

"So, detective, how well have you gotten to know our Monsieur Verreaux?" He liked hearing her voice again, playful. Harry could imagine her licking her lips.

"Well enough, Liza, to be looking for an admirer of Verreaux's who has a talent with a razor blade"

"I don't understand, Harry."

"Neither do I."

"Hmmm. Not like you to be confused. I better get you back here on Friday. All that French wine is pickling your brain."

Before she hung up she told him she was thinking of their last evening in Pittsburgh, how she would like to repeat it. It left him with that fine madness he'd hoped he would feel.

At Place d'Italie Harry flagged a cab to the Place de la Concorde. The Arc de Triomphe rose in the distance at the end of the broad, bricked boulevard, the Champs Élysées. He imagined the peloton whizzing by, eight circuits around the cobbled heart of Paris, the final furious minutes of Stage 21 of the Tour de France. The cyclists accelerate up the Champs, bank hard through the tight U-turn in front of the Arc de Triomphe, and explode into a full gas sprint for the finish line. He remembered his father bemoaning that he'd been cheated out of the romance of finishing the Tour de France on the Champs Élysées. In his day, the tour ended at a finish line in a soccer stadium on the southwest side of the city instead of on Paris' grandest boulevard.

Harry walked back along the Quai des Tuileries on the banks of the Seine past the stately expanse of the Louvre. With the Tour over, Nicholas Przewalski would park his race bike and let Emilia Cappa, his fiancé, romance him from art gallery to art gallery, through the landscapes impressioned by paint, not speed.

At the Pont d'Arcole, Harry crossed over the Seine to the Ile de la Cité. Hesitating, he entered the cavernous, arched nave of Notre Dame Cathedral, lured by a sonorous harpsichord and a soaring soprano invocation. A young boy in a white vestment was singing in front of the altar. An older one, also in white, was at the keyboard. A couple of priests magically appeared, as if they'd ghosted out of the tall stone columns that rose toward the arched rafters. They were armed with candles, chalice, and patens to prepare the altar for mass.

Harry retreated. He had no use for spiritual currency. Or a deity. Both, he'd long felt, were intellectually counterfeit. Spirituality was the collateral damage of having evolved consciousness—we learned we were mortal, then became desperate for an afterlife.

He pulled out his Drum tobacco and Zig-Zag papers and headed toward the door, sidestepping the people arriving for mass. Notre Dame, he thought, manifested one of the great tricks of irony played on us by evolution. Our brain, atop the first truly sapient species, had created a supernatural and became beholden to it.

Outside, on a bench beside the entrance, he rolled the cigarette and watched the smoke waft back into the vestibule. A believer would say it was sign that what he was missing was inside. "No," Verreaux would have written in his notebook—not a sign from above, just the physics of a purposeless wind. In the end, reason had forced Verreaux to overcome a canon of preconceived beliefs and bigotry. In his journals, he'd opted for art and science, for their subversive story-telling, their fluid cartography, the uncertain maps they made of reality.

On Rue Descartes, Harry bought coffee and a baguette for the homeless guy on the corner, but he was gone. Maybe he too had been driven mad by the sudden stirring of Spring. In the museum, on the way to the alcove, Harry patted Frémiet's orangutan on the head and winked at the skeleton of Carnegie's *Diplodocus*. They had both risen from an imaginative fervor. Like Verreaux's conversion of Rubens' The Lion Hunt into *Arab Courier Attacked by Lions*.

At the top of the iron stairs he had a momentary shock. Verreaux's notebooks were gone. There was note a on the table from Christine to come down to the archaeology collections on the second floor. He found her in one of the aisles between the rows of tall, white specimen cases. She was leaning against an open drawer labeled "Divers Ossements," studying a slip of paper.

He held out the coffee and baguette. She shook her head, like a disapproving school marm, and beckoned him with her finger to follow her to her office.

"Harry," Christine chided, "you should know better. No food in the collection area. It's bad enough you smoked near Verreaux's notebooks."

"Tell me you have them," Harry said. He handed her the coffee and half the baguette.

She gave him a mischievous grin. "I do. It's also bad enough I sneaked them home last evening. I re-read Verreaux's diary entries. *Incroyable*! The visit from Schmerling. The cast of the Engis-2 child's cranium. Deducing it had belonged to an archaic human a hundred years before it was re-discovered in Liège and identified as Neanderthal. Then he reads Mendel. Elementen, inheritance, genetics. Damn, he saw it coming. Remarkable!"

She drank some coffee and ripped off a piece of the baguette, littering her desk with crumbs from the crust. "Who was Elisabeth, Harry? She's haunted him. He seemed desperate in his love for her."

"Yeah, but not desperate enough to marry her. A Dutch girl in Cape Town. He was nineteen, on his second expedition there when he met her, romanced her, and promised to marry her. She allowed him into her bed."

"Always a mistake!" Christine laughed, shyly, and pulled on her spiky hair.

"It was for her. She got pregnant, he dumped her, she sued for breach of contract, and lost. He was underage. The court respected Napoleonic law. He couldn't be compelled to marry without the consent of his parents—which he'd never sought."

"Ah," Christine put her hand over her heart and tilted her head up in a mock dramatic pose, "but he sentenced himself to perpetual suffering, the pain of *amour perdu*. Love forever lost."

"Yeah, I know what it means," Harry said, pensively, then wished he hadn't.

She studied him closely for a moment and began sweeping the crumbs on her desk into a pile. She wet her forefinger, shot Harry a playful glance, and idly began dabbing the pile of bread crumbs and licking them off.

"Anyway," she said, pointedly, "I still don't know why you were being so mysterious about the notebooks. But I do know what Verreaux saved from the museum rubbish heap." She held up the slip of paper she'd been reading in the archaeology collection.

Harry played along. "Let me guess. His casts of the partial skull and teeth of the Engis-2 child. He left a note in the collection drawer. Ever the good curator."

"You are a detective!" she teased and handed him the note. Verreaux's handwriting.

9 Novembre, 1867. Ossements et dents humain du cave Engis-2, Liège. Hors site. Retiré—conservation.

"It means," Christine translated, "'human bones and teeth from Engis-2 Cave, Liège. Off site. Removed for conservation.' It can also mean 'for safekeeping.'"

"Come across any other notes? He mentioned two specimens."

Christine shook her head. "No. I think he counted the cranium and the teeth as separate specimens."

"Any idea where he put them for safekeeping?"

She raised her hands in protest. "You have to be joking. After all these years? Someone probably found where he'd stashed them in the exhibit preparation laboratory and tossed them out."

Not, Harry thought, if Verreaux bundled the cast of the child's partial skull and teeth in a linen cloth, unstitched the hide of the camel, carefully secured the bundle inside the rib cage, and sewed up the seam. He'd likely inserted a note. Ever the good curator. In re-reading Verreaux's notebooks, Christine had either missed the razor job again or wasn't going to mention it. There was time enough to tell her.

Harry asked her to take him to the museum's ornithology department. "I'd like to talk to the bird curators."

She looked at him oddly. "*Vraiment?* Really?"

"Yeah. Humor me."

50

Paris
Thursday, February 4

Christine led him up a floor and down a long hallway lined with white specimen cases. Harry detected the lingering smell of Vapona, an insecticide banned years ago as carcinogenic. It was chemistry's successor to Maison Verreaux's arsenical soap in the arms race against the beetles intent on devouring the skins, hair and feathers of dead birds and mammals in museum drawers.

In the ornithology office, portraits of the museum's past bird naturalists looked down on modern desks and computer stations. Harry checked the nameplate below each portrait. No Verreaux. Apparently, as collector and taxidermist, he didn't make the museum's ornithological hall of fame, despite publishing on hundreds of new species.

A couple of young women at computers were entering specimen data from hand-written ink records in old, leather-bound ledgers. An older man in a lab coat rose from behind a massive desk and greeted Christine. A museum ID card hung from his neck: Yves Fleury, Conservateur, Ornithologie, MNHN. He was slightly stooped over and wore a blue beret bearing an emblem of the fleurde-lis. A short pony tail of gray hair stuck out at the back of the beret. He shook Harry's hand and apologized in broken English that his English was broken. He preferred Christine to translate.

"Good," Harry began, "I'm interested in the notebooks of Jules Verreaux."

"Okay," Fleury answered, hesitatingly.

"I understand that a year or so ago the ornithology curators checked out Verreaux's notebooks from the museum archives."

His eyebrows rose, somewhat puzzled. "Yes, that is so."

"To database the information from his lists of specimens," Harry prompted, pointing to the two women clicking away on keyboards.

"Yes ... you are observant."

"Actually, Christine told me. Did you use the original note-books for the data entry?"

When Christine translated, Fleury seemed bewildered by the question. "No. The archivist insisted we make a paper copy of the notebooks. To reduce handling of the originals ... the risk of damage. But why is this important? I don't understand?"

"Neither do I," Christine added.

Harry nodded. "It's complicated. Did you copy all the pages, or just the ones with the lists of specimens?"

Fleury shrugged. "All the pages. It was simpler. We had to be careful not to crack the binding."

"Are you done with your copy? Are all the records captured?"

"Yes. Half a year ago."

"I would like to borrow your copy of the notebooks, if possible. Just for the afternoon. It won't leave the museum. Christine will be with me."

Still bewildered, Fleury looked at Christine for assurance. She said something in French. Harry understood the word *respons-abilité*. Fleury went over to a stack of ledgers on a corner cabinet, grabbed four piles of paper held together with black binder clips, and handed them to Christine.

"*Merci beaucoup,*" Christine said.

"Yes, thank you," Harry added.

They retreated to Christine's office down the Vapona-laced corridor

"Explain, Harry. Now!" It was an order.

"Okay. Here's a prediction. There are two diary entries in that copy that you and I haven't seen. They will explain themselves."

She looked at him, incredulous. "What? Show me."

Harry removed the clasp from the copy of the second notebook, found the April 22, 1832 entry on Schmerling and the skull cap and teeth of the Engis-2 child, and handed it to her.

"Right, I read this last night."

Harry pointed to a cabinet behind her desk. "I see a bottle of Merlot there. Open the wine. Pour us two glasses. Time to test my prediction. I'll let you do the honors, Christine. Turn the page to the next entry."

22 Avril,1832.

In the afternoon, Schmerling showed me an "oddity" he said he found in Engis-2 Cave near the child's skull bones and teeth. He had secured it in a soft cloth bag such as geologists use for the safekeeping of gemstones.

When I took it out, it appeared to be a lump of vegetation, perhaps a dried remnant of regurgitated cud from a ruminant. On closer inspection under a magnifying glass, it was revealed to be a piece of mat woven from vegetable fiber and animal hair. It was torn and frayed at the ends, as if something had eaten away at it. And I could discern that the mat was crumpled tightly around an object.

I asked Schmerling if he had tried to unwrap it. He said he lacked the skill. It is a humility that is rare in our academies.

Carefully, I used tweezers, a scalpel, and anatomical probes to find the edges of the tattered mat and dissect it open. The woven fibers were extremely dry and brittle to the touch, such that the layers refused to separate cleanly one from the other without breaking. In the end, despite my patience, it proved impossible to preserve the mat intact. When I finally peeled away the last fibers, to my shock, I observed the tiny hand of a child.

The skin was brownish red and shriveled around the little hand bones: five metacarpals, three phalanges in each finger, and two phalanges in the thumb. The bones were separated at the joints, but had been held together in articulation by the shrunken skin and the fibrous mat. I combed carefully through the fibers of the mat for any of the eight wrist bones, but there were none. The hand was all that remained of the child.

I asked Schmerling about the characteristics of the Engis-2 Cave. Was it dry or wet? Was it exposed to the elements? How far into the cave had he found these remains? He said the cave appeared to be without moisture, almost arid, and unusually cold, with a narrow, slit-like entrance that was protected from rain or snow or wind by an overhang of rock. He'd discovered the bones, teeth and this oddity scattered on a bed of stones about two hundred meters from the entrance.

I told him that his oddity was a mummified hand. It was all that remained of a child who had died. Its skin would have been painted with a red ochre, its body wrapped in a mat of fibrous vegetation and animal hair and placed deliberately in the cave. The dryness and the cold had kept the pestilence from attacking and decaying the flesh. Instead, it began to desiccate and become mummified, naturally, such as I had witnessed in a cave in the Western Cape. The Khoikhoi had coloured a naked body with red ochre and wrapped it with boophone leaves, which they knew to be poisonous to insects and other flesh-eating organisms. Then they placed the body deep in a dry cave on a platform of stones and closed the cave entrance with a large boulder.

Schmerling agreed to leave the mummified hand with me, to be returned upon completion of my study. I would attempt to identify the plants and the animal hair used to weave the mat, and determine whether they were gathered in the spring, summer or fall. The museum has excellent comparative collections of European

plants and mammals for this purpose, as well as knowledgeable curators.

He asked what I thought had happened to the rest of
the child's body—its torso and limbs and head. I told him
that wolves or cave bears or weasels or badgers likely
had entered the cave, rent the body apart, and feasted
on the parts or carried them off. A head has little flesh
and was left behind. The child's hand must have been
ripped from the forelimb and escaped predation. It remained sealed in the fibrous mat and became mummified.

The revelations of the cranium and teeth had fevered
Schmerling's imagination. When he departed, he vowed
to scour Engis-2 for more remains of this child and her
kin. He envisaged these ancient humans making their
shelter in the cave, living and hunting among the large
animals of the glacial epoch—the mammoths, the aurochs, and others now extinct. He said he should find the
meat-bearing bones the hunters dragged back to the
cave, roasted over a fire, feasted on, and discarded. The
bones would be charred and bear the marks of butcher-
ing.

I did not lose my heedfulness. Truly, I told him, it did
not seem fortuitous that the fossil skull bones and teeth
were found near the mummified hand. They almost assuredly belonged to the same child from a primitive race
of humans that had become extinct. But, I cautioned
him, it is not certain.

Wordlessly, Christine handed the copy back to Harry, grabbed
the original notebook from her desk, and leafed through the pages.

"My God!" she exclaimed. "The page isn't here! You knew, Harry. This is what you wouldn't tell me."

Harry finished reading the missing entry. "Look closely. It's
been razored out. The person with the razor didn't want anyone
else to learn about the mummified hand of a Neanderthal child."

"Who would do that? It's unbelievable!"

"Someone who realized the obvious. Find it, sequence it, shake up Neanderthal genomics, rewrite human evolution. Instant stardom. I can think of three candidates."

"Really?" she said, nervously pulling at her spiky hair. Who?"

"Anna Storck. It's—"

"You're crazy. I don't believe it. Anna? She would never do this."

"It's her territory. Neanderthal genes. She was here. She had access to the archives and the notebooks. Could also have been Gideon Gould. He was working here in the ornithology department in July and then in October. He sees them using the copy of Verreaux's notebooks to capture the bird specimen data. He skims it, finds the entry, and makes another copy for himself. We can check with Fleury. Then Gould shows all of it to Anna."

Christine shook her head. "But why? It makes no sense. The specimen was lost 140 years ago. I've searched the collections. All I found was Verreaux's note for his casts of the skull bones and teeth."

Harry picked up the copy of Verreaux's fourth notebook, removed the clasp, paged to the last entry, read it quickly, and handed it to Christine. "Here is your answer."

51

Paris
Thursday, February 4

Verreaux's journal

11 Novembre 1867

I have decided to save the two specimens for posterity, for discovering in the future what we cannot now know. It is in violation of the museum rules and in defiance of the orders from the curators. They are scouring the cabinets for material they judge to be scientifically suspect, without trial, without the opportunity of defense. My birds are safe. But they have dismissed the cranium and teeth from Engis-2 as a malformed infant, whose parents disposed of it in a cave, either dead or alive, to be rid of the deviant. They joked that such monsters are common to Belgium, to the lower forms that inhabit the low countries.

I failed to convince them that the child is ancient. They were unmoved by the plaster casts. Without the original cranium, I was not able to demonstrate to them the degree of petrification that had occurred in the child's bones, as we find in the fossils of mammoths and cave bears. They were unmoved by the departure of the anatomical features of the skull from those of a modern human, or by their resemblance to the shapes and protuberances of the adult skulls found many years later, in 1856, in the Neander Valley in Prussia. I now understand the sorrow of the investigator of nature whose audience becomes deafened and blinded by a still mind.

For these reasons I have refrained from showing the curators the mummified hand of the child from Engis-2 cave. I retrieved it from the cabinet before they could come upon it. I know that they would claim it to be not extraordinary, but the result of the primitive ways of those 'lower forms' from Belgium. I left a note in the cabinet for the curators: "Ossements et dents humain du cave Engis-2, Liège. Hors site. Retiré—conservation". But I did not leave a note about the hand.

Years ago in the Cape, Édouard and I prepared the Betchwana chief and dressed him as El Negro for a patron in Paris. He put it on exhibition and sold it for travel to other salons. It is now in a private museum in the east of Spain in a place called Banyoles. I deliberately included in the mount, under the skin, his shoulder and pelvic girdles, limb bones, and skull to preserve his natural form and stature for taxidermy.

But now I realize that it was prescient. In the future, when El Negro is eventually disassembled in a museum in Europe or abroad, anatomists will study the skin and bones and be forced to declare to the public that the African was never inferior in any respect to any other race. Not in the size of his brain, or in the detailed convolutions of the cortex impressed on the internal face of his cranium, or in the external contours and metrics of his skull. They will see that his limb bones are as ours in geometry and in articulation with the shoulder and hip. They will write that he is no closer to an ape than we.

Such are the true powers, I now realize, possessed

by the natural history tableaux in our museums: they preserve our cumulative understanding of things for a future time, when our beliefs, our ignorance, and our moralities will be examined and exposed. In depicting Nature, we have revealed our predeterminations about that Nature, for which the writers of the past used the term "bigoterie." Our dioramas will tell of Eden before Adam or Eve, and the sins we have wrought on it and each other. Our dioramas are the mirror of our civilization locked in time. The lock, I am convinced, is a stillness of the mind.

This is my desired fate for El Negro. And for my Arab Courier, in which I will plant the seeds of revelation. I will secure in the belly of the camel the remains of the Engis-2 child: the casts of its skull and teeth, and the mummified hand found nearby. I will leave with them the information about each specimen, and my description of their importance that cannot now be published. Eventually they will be uncovered to their rightful acclaim.

Christine sat back. Her face was chalky, her lips quivering. She picked up Verreaux's fourth notebook and examined the binding between the last page and the back cover.

"Hell! This page was also cut out." She looked up at Harry. "I get it. The Verreaux exhibit at the Carnegie Museum. The break-in. To get this specimen from the camel's belly. It's unbelievable."

Harry told her about the bundle, the bits of fiber and flesh, the briefing Mazeroski had given him, Samantha Mayer, and Preston Stewart, and the job he was doing for the Carnegie.

"And you think Anna is the criminal," Christine asserted. "Not a chance. You said you had three candidates. Who are the other two?"

"Gould." Harry paused, then looked directly at Christine. "And your friend—Marie."

Christine gasped and held her hand to her mouth. "Bbb ... but—"

"Hold on a second. Marie had access to Verreaux's journals here in the museum, and maybe even Gould's copy, if he left it lying around. I bet she's handy with a sharp blade at razoring pages or the underbelly of a camel. She was in Pittsburgh at the anthropology meetings when the exhibit was hit. The stakes were high enough to fuck scruples. For all three of them."

Pain crawled across her face with cruel slowness. She pushed Verreaux's notebooks away and stared at Harry with a dark disquiet. "What about me, Harry? Same opportunity. Same motive. And I can handle a scalpel."

Harry shrugged and shook his head. "No. I don't want to think so. So I won't."

Her laugh was laced with relief. "That's earned you more wine. But," she picked up the bottle, "you are wrong about Marie and Anna. One is my lover. One was my close friend and colleague. Gideon is the bastard among us. There, I swore in English again."

Harry knew he had let the personal shove aside his professional savvy. The stakes were just as high for Christine. The mummified hand was what remained of the blood and guts of Neanderthals in Europe fifty thousand years ago. They mated and warred with a new invader, *Homo sapiens*. Who raped whom? What genes did they implant in us? The bad ones, like the ones suspected in autism, would exact revenge in us long after we drove them to extinction. It was the moral of the history of life on Earth, Harry thought: evolution was unscrupulous in meting out genetic justice.

52

Pittsburgh
Friday, February 5

Liza got him on the earliest flight out of De Gaulle, 6:45 in the morning on Lufthansa via Munich and Newark. She made up for the two stops, and having to wrestle himself out of bed at three in the morning, by bumping him to business class.

A champagne breakfast doped him into sleep over the Atlantic. He dreamt he was being chased through woods thick with stunted trees and brambles by someone wielding a box-cutter. Suddenly, his way was blocked by a steep cliff of rocks and sand. Frantic, he scrambled up the slope, spotted a cave, and crawled in. Just beyond the entrance, a strange man and woman were crouched over a pit fire. They didn't look at him. They didn't speak. They were burning Verreaux's notebooks, methodically ripping out the pages of personal entries, but leaving the long lists of his field collections of animals and plants. He tried to scream "NO!" but his throat constricted around the sound, choking him awake.

Harry shoved the window shade up. Momentarily, he was blinded by the fierce light. They were over the Canadian Shield.

Labrador, according to the map on the monitor. Below, the solid wilderness of trees was slashed here and there by strip-logged streaks of land.

Liza met him at the airport curb in her red Jeep Cherokee. On the Parkway, through the snow showers falling on the cold, dark undulations of Pittsburgh, they didn't talk about Verreaux or Paris or Cape Town. Or about their own intimate entanglement. They stayed silent, as if words at that moment were the wrong currency for closeness. He did tell her what he suspected about Anna Storck and Gideon Gould.

She turned to gape at him, wandered across the dashed white lines into the oncoming lane, jerked the steering wheel, overcorrected, hit the brakes, and skidded off the road. Luckily it was along a stretch of the Parkway with a shoulder wide enough to fishtail and stop. He put his hand on her thigh and kept it there for the rest of the ride. On Orkney Street, she parked behind his yellow Toyota Corolla hatchback, leaned over, bussed his cheek, waited till he got out, and left.

Harry climbed the two flights of stairs, fell into bed, and slept on French time. He woke at two in the morning, wondered momentarily why the sun had not risen, and drifted back to sleep, realizing it still had six hours to wait for the Earth to turn.

At ten o'clock on Saturday, after coffee, a cigarette, and a few Bach preludes and fugues, Harry crossed the Smithfield Street bridge, found a parking spot on Ross Street, and wound through the Allegheny County Judicial Building to Detective Mazeroski's desk in the squad room.

"Przewalski," Mazeroski grunted. "Returned from the 1800s. Bring a perp back with you from France?" Technology had reached his desk: a computer, and a phone upgrade to a mobile handset. But fashion hadn't. Mazeroski was wearing a pink shirt with squiggles under a sport jacket with brown checks.

"Yeah, I brought something back. Patience for stupid questions. And the skull cap and teeth of a Neanderthal kid."

"Okay, you the one who stole it from that museum in Belgium? Interpol will be relieved."

"Very funny. No, but there probably was a plaster copy of it in the camel's belly. I'll give you the twenty-five cent version."

Harry briefed him on Verreaux's notebooks, the razored pages, the copy of the notebooks in the bird department in the Paris museum, and the bundle in the belly of the camel: Verreaux's cast of the Engis-2 fossil skull bones and teeth, and the mummified hand.

"Doesn't help us much with the perp. Any ideas?"

"Four people. Christine Dumoulin, the zooarchaeologist at the Paris museum. Marie LeBoeuf, the archaeologist at the Liège museum. Gideon Gould, the bird guy here at the Carnegie. And Anna Storck. They all had access to the original notebooks and the copy. They were all at the meeting in the Carnegie Museum in December. Christine and Marie—they're an item—stayed with Gould and Storck." Harry got up. "I got money on Gould. He knew about the bundle. Talked to him yet?"

Mazeroski lifted his eyebrows. "Okay, Przewalski, sit down. You think you know something I don't and I want to know what it is. Yeah, we talked to Gould. After his wife took the dive at the museum. What about him?"

Harry pulled the chair back and sat down. "Not sure. He and his wife went back and forth to the museums in Paris and Liège. That's when he came across the ornithology department's copy of Verreaux's notebooks. He made his own copy after he saw the entries about the bundle. I'm betting he showed it to Storck. In July, Gould bunked with Dumoulin in Paris when Storck was off in Liège. There were shenanigans. He tried to jump her one night. She fought him off. Then Storck decides to cash it in smack in the middle of the symposium that she's organized, two days after the camel driver business."

Mazeroski rubbed his face. "I'm not hearing much, Przewalski, except stuff for the gossip rags." He pointed at his desk phone. "See that? It works. New phone, old number. Call me when you're doing more than chasing dirt. If you're smart, you'll chase that nice lady, Liza, from the Carnegie. She called and told me you were working the case in South Africa and France. The last lady you fooled with at the Carnegie turned out to be a murderer. You might have lucked out with this one."

Harry fished a sheaf of papers from his backpack and tossed it rudely onto Mazeroski's desk. "There's all the dirt I chased down.

The bird department in the Paris museum let me copy their copy of Verreaux's notebooks. Like they did Gould. You got a copier here?

Mazeroski scowled at him. "Yeah, smartass, were in the right century."

Harry grinned. "Here, have someone feed the machine. It's just Verreaux's entries that bear on the case, including the razored pages about the bundle and what's in it."

Mazeroski wandered off for a few minutes, then came back with Harry's copy and tossed his own on the desk. "Thanks for the bedtime reading."

"Yeah, well, you'll probably need a dictionary. Verreaux uses the term 'cranium.' It means your noggin, which only keeps getting harder."

Mazeroski told him to quit parading his education and take a powder. "That means vamoose, scram, skedaddle, and get the hell outta here."

Harry took the Boulevard of the Allies to Squirrel Hill and the nursing home. His mother didn't recognize him. She stared straight ahead past his eyes into a distant place. It was a place, Harry knew, created by brain cells coated with plaques and choked with tangles. He wanted to believe they acted as hallucinogens, her outward blankness hiding a new, inner, Technicolor revelation. But he couldn't. He was a prisoner of empirical reason, even for that peaceable moment when he took his mother's face in his hands and held her.

Outside, snow had begun to fall in large, oblong, flattened chunks. The Corolla coughed, as if it had contracted the cold vapors. He drove up South Dallas Avenue past Homewood Cemetery and wound his way to East Liberty and his father's retro bike shop. The "E" in "*Velo Europa*" on the window had eroded to an "F" and created a new continent.

Inside, his father nodded at him and turned back to his customer. The guy was sporting a Cinzano jersey and a cycling cap with the Italian flag. He'd seen Breaking Away and wanted a bike like Dave Stoller's steel, lugged Masi. He'd come to the right shop. Harry's father imported old, steel frames from Europe, reconditioned them, threw on a Campy group set and Vittoria tires, and hung the finished bike on the long rack below the black and white shots of Merckx, Coppi, Anquetil, Moser, Gimondi, and Bartali.

He brewed espressos for Cinzano and Harry on the DeLonghi behind the counter, then proceeded to recount the cycling errors in the film. The worst was Stoller drafting down a highway behind a semi at 60 miles per hour, spinning in the small chainring instead of the large one. Harry had heard it before. For his father, it wasn't a coming-of-age flick. It was about the bike being the metaphor for life, how the purity of the machine revealed our failings.

53

Pittsburgh
Monday, February 7

Gideon Gould looked like a dapper gnome: short and burly, with an egg-shaped head and expensive clothes. Premature baldness and flattened ears made his head seem more pointed. He stared at Harry through wire-rimmed glasses. The thick lenses distorted his face, bulging the eyes and surrounding skin like a magnifying glass. He sported a monogramed pale blue shirt, a red bow tie, and dark blue suspenders.

"Nice office," Harry commented. It was a former exhibit gallery on the third floor with the accompanying benefits of neo-classical architecture: spacious; a marble floor; high ceiling; and tall, arched windows that opened onto the museum's inner courtyard. It was a few hundred yards down the long arm of the L-shaped corridor from Storck's former office.

At one end of the office, twenty white specimen cases were stacked two-high, back-to-back. One of them was open, with a drawer halfway out. Harry could see a bunch of small birds arrayed in orderly rows, all lying on their backs, beaks pointing up, as if it were a communal ornithological nap. Only death and taxidermy and anatomy and genomics could fix Darwin's frustration with species variation: "... all Nature is perverse and will not do as I wish it." Carnegie mammalogists, Harry remembered, would deliberately disdain studies of bird variation. "There are really only three kinds of birds in the world," they would scoff, "big brown birds, little brown birds, and medium-size brown birds. What about the Great White Egret? A big brown bird."

At the other end of the office, Gould had assembled a make-shift research laboratory: a long, handsome mahogany table, a dissecting scope, a compound scope, specimen trays, bags of sawdust, collection tags, scalpels, gloves, computer, large flat screen, and four stacks of papers held together with black binder clips.

"Nice table," Harry added.

"Salvaged from the Carnegie Library," Gould stated, "from the old Reading Room. But Mr. ..." Gould paused to look at Harry's card, "Przewalski—do you know that's the extinct horse?" He pronounced it correctly.

"Yeah, I do. And it survives in zoos. A salvage job. Like your library table."

Gould leaned back in his chair. His desk, at the center of the office, backed toward the windows. The daylight from courtyard framed his large oval head, like one of the Romanovs' Imperial Easter Eggs on an exhibit pedestal.

"Right," Gould said, a smug tinge in his voice, as if he resented the intrusion. "But you didn't come here to discuss my office furniture. Liza ... Miss Kole ... called to schedule you first thing this morning. She said you wanted to talk to me about the Arab courier exhibit ... the vandalism last December. I told her I don't know anything about it."

He leaned forward and put Harry's card back on his desk. "Now I'm telling you the same. I'm in the Ornithology Section here, not exhibits, not anthropology—or whatever discipline that thing ... that diorama ... belongs to."

Gould, Harry thought, was up front with his conceit. "Well, the vandalism might be about ornithology. And archaeology. Last July you were at the Paris museum to study the bird collection. And again in October. You worked with Jules Verreaux's notebooks—

actually, the copy the Paris museum ornithologists were using to verify his localities and digitize the data. You made a copy of their copy. I'm betting it's lying on that table over there. I see four large binder clips holding thick reams of paper."

Gould slowly sat upright. "Okay, I get it. A couple of weeks ago I showed Miss Kole our collection of Verreaux's birds. Apparently, she informed you about it. I wondered why an administrative assistant in the museum's front office had developed a sudden interest in stuffed birds. Commendable, but still curious."

More conceit, Harry thought. Gould pointed at the open case. "Andrew Carnegie bought a bunch of Verreaux's birds from a dealer in Paris in 1898. See that drawer? That's some of them. From South Africa, around Cape Town. Anyway, yes, I went to the Paris museum for my research. I needed the data on the rest of Verreaux's birds in the Paris collection. There have been biogeographic shifts in those bird species since the 1820s, when Verreaux made his collections, given the climate and habitat change in the past 184 years. I'm forecasting their future ranges. Ecological niche modeling. You probably would not understand."

"Let me give it a shot," Harry said. "Computational modeling of a bird species' suitability landscape, based on the time and place Verreaux collected the bird and the environmental conditions, like average temperature, average rainfall, plant cover. You then overlay NASA's, NOAA's and the IPCC's future climate scenarios to see the predicted effects. The birds species' habitat shrinks or expands or disappears. The species thrives, or moves elsewhere more suitable, maybe up the mountainside or to higher latitudes and cooler climes. Or the bird becomes extinct. Does that about cover it?"

Gould's eyes bulged. "I'm impressed." He looked down at Harry's card again.

"Yeah, it says 'private investigator,' but I'm a quick study. I read 'Biogeography for Beginners' on the way over here."

"Very funny." Gould reached up to his neck and tugged at his shirt, as if it were suddenly too tight. "But I'm not sure how any of this bears on the Arab courier exhibit. Isn't vandalism a police matter? I've already talked to one of them about … about Anna. What's his name. It's Polish, like yours." He opened a top drawer, rummaged around and found the card. "Detective Mazeroski."

Harry nodded. "I gave you the bird connection. Here's the archeological one. You read Verreaux's notebooks. He mentions two archaeological specimens from a cave near Liège, remains of a Neanderthal child: skull bones and teeth; and a mummified hand."

Gould raised his eyebrows. "Very interesting, but news to me. I was only working with his lists of specimens. I guess I'll have to read the rest of his notebooks."

He either didn't know about the bundle, Harry thought, or had taken lessons in method acting. "It gets more interesting. Someone razored two pages out of the original notebooks. After the Paris ornithologists made their copy, which tells us what was in the missing pages. So does your copy. The first missing page is an April, 1832 diary entry. The second is from November, 1867."

Gould shrugged. "Why would anyone do that?"

"To get at the Neanderthal specimens. And hide the information from anyone else. Verreaux tells us that the Paris museum was going to chuck the Neanderthal material as worthless. So he squirreled it away in the belly of the camel. Anna would have realized that the mummified hand was a scientific bonanza—a complete sequence of the Neanderthal genome. It was her area."

Gould jumped up and clutched the edge of this desk with his hands until his knuckles turned white. "Are you mad? How dare you. You're implying that my wife broke into that exhibit downstairs to steal a specimen from the camel's belly. I'm afraid our discussion is over."

Gould rounded his desk, marched over to the office door, opened it, and motioned for Harry to leave. Harry couldn't help notice that Gould's suspenders were attached to dark blue dress trousers with cuffs and a sharp crease.

"I'm implying that you knew all about the mummified hand from Verreaux's notebook entries. You told Anna. Or showed her your copy of the notebooks. Maybe also to Christine at the Paris museum. And to Marie, at the Liège museum."

Gould put his hands in his pockets, slowly circled back to his desk, and sat down. "I did nothing of the sort."

"You do know Christine Dumoulin and Marie LeBoeuf."

"Of course! Anna's colleagues. They stayed with us during the archaeology meeting here, when Anna ..." His voice trailed off.

Harry decided to squeeze Gould's conceit. "You stayed with Christine in Paris in July. And crawled uninvited into her bed one night. Attempted rape are the words that Detective Mazeroski would use."

"Is that what she …" Gould began, then caught himself.

"And you would have tried to bed her again when you stayed there in October. Trouble is, Anna was also there."

Gould clenched his jaw. Red blotches appeared on his throat and crept up to his face. "Your insinuations about Christine and me are complete fiction. And slanderous. How dare you!"

"It's my business. Anna and Christine went to the Neanderthal conference in Liège. Remember that? You joined them on the last day, a Friday, for the farewell reception. That's when the Engis-2 cave material was lifted from the gallery."

"What? I don't know anything about that. Or about some cockamamie story of specimens in a camel's belly. Your business appears to be fiction masquerading as detection. Good day to you." He waved his hand toward the door.

"Well, Mazeroski is putting stock in my fiction. So is Interpol." Harry got up, walked over to the library table. "I'm betting that these four stacks of paper with the binder clips are your copy of Verreaux's notebooks." He picked up the second and fourth stacks. One page in each stack had the top right corner turned down. He didn't have to check the dates on the entries.

"Hey!" Gould cried out, leaping out of his chair. "I protest! Put that down! That's my property! You have no right to examine it."

"Protest away. I'm also betting that these two dog-eared pages are the ones you or Anna razored out of Verreaux's notebooks."

Gould marched over, yanked the papers out of Harry's hands, and stacked them neatly back on the library table. "I have half a mind to file a harassment complaint with the authorities. Now please get out of my office."

Harry shrugged. "Call Mazeroski. Use the other half of your mind to tell him what you did with the Neanderthal material you cut out of the camel last December. His number is on his card."

54

Pittsburgh
Monday, February 7

Harry took Fifth Avenue downtown from the Carnegie Museum, crossed the Smithfield Street Bridge over the Monongahela River, turned up East Carson, and parked the Corolla on the gravel cinders behind the rusted steel mill. A realtor's sign promised that the building was the future site of upscale condos overlooking the river, ten minutes from the Golden Triangle, twenty from the museums and universities in Oakland.

He tried to take the four flights of stairs to his office two at a time, but quit, winded, on the second landing. There was two weeks of mail in the steel bucket outside his door. Utility bills, a couple of bike magazines, two issues of The Economist, an invitation to an evening event from a vendor of hearing aids, and an offer from the Monroeville Toyota dealership to trade in the Corolla shitbox for a new model. But no notice yet from the realty company that he was being kicked out.

There was a bouquet of flowers on his desk beginning to wilt. No note. Liza, he guessed, although he wondered how she got the landlord to let her in. He took in his office: the salvaged steel desk;

the cracked, red leather sofa chair; the grungy windows; and the blurred outline of the PPG building across the river. Hell of an impression for a client, he thought.

Out front, the shrill siren of a police car screamed down East Carson and waned. A few minutes later a barge hooted, leisurely steaming up the Monongahela, laden with coal. Harry wondered whether the pace of life was inherent in its sound, what that sound might be in the nanosecond world of quantum particles piercing space at near the speed of light.

Harry took Liza and his father to the hockey game at the arena that evening and seated them together amid the raucous safety of the crowd. Better that for their first meeting than the bike shop and his father's phantoms.

The Canadiens beat the Penguins. But they got to see Mario Lemieux circle at center ice like a rangy shark, grab a pass, explode across the blue line, deke a defenseman, fake a shot to the left, and lift the puck over the shoulder of Jose Theodore, the Montreal goalie. By the third period, Liza and his father were in animated conversation, their words drowned out by the crowd. Harry hoped his father wasn't giving sermons about the bicycle. His favorite was about the bike being that *élan vital*, the vital essence of independence that quietly navigates us through the spaces of life like no other machine.

After the game, Liza told Harry to drive to *Velo Europa* in East Liberty. His father opened the shop, turned on the lights, and pulled a gleaming, steel, celeste green Bianchi from the rack. It fit her. He told her to find a dry road outside of Pittsburgh and do at least 30 miles. He gave her a folding metric bike tool with eight different hex keys, and showed her how to tweak the handlebar and saddle position to her comfort during the ride. No sermon. Just the story of how Eddy Merckx would adjust the height of his saddle on the fly while riding in the peloton, because he could detect whether it was a millimeter too high or too low. Then Nicholas advised Harry to do something useful and go riding with her.

Later, at his place on Orkney, Harry briefed Liza on the Greef trial, Elisabeth's baby, the rumored Wylde infant, Verreaux's four notebooks, the razored pages, the skull and teeth of the Engis-2 Neanderthal child, and the mummified hand. He handed her the copy of the notebooks he'd made in Paris. She sat cross-legged on the bed, the sheet nonchalantly over one bare shoulder and breast, then reclined on her side, not aware how her long, languid legs swept across the cotton space to the edge. She was buried in the words, pausing only to sip from her tumbler of scotch. She reminded him of Manet's Olympia, the sensuality and art of the confident nude.

"So now we know," she said, sat up, shivered, and wrapped herself tightly in the sheet, as if the revelation had brought on a fright. "Who would have cut the camel open for Verreaux's stuff? Who knew about this?"

Harry poured more scotch and told her about the uneasy co-incidences: Christine, Marie, and Anna attending the archaeology meetings in Liège and Pittsburgh. Gould at the Paris museum for the IOU meeting last July, and for his research in October.

"Gould copied the notebooks from the one made by the Paris ornithologists."

Liza, skeptical, narrowed her eyes. "But he wouldn't care about Neanderthal remains. He studies birds!"

"Yeah," Harry answered, "but he also knows genetics. And all about the genetics of Neanderthals—from Anna. I'm sure he realized the scientific potential of DNA from the hand of a Neanderthal. If he didn't, Anna did. They break into the exhibit, sequence the mummified tissue, and co-author a paper in *Science* or *Nature* that make their reputations. She helps salvage his career—and their marriage."

"I don't know." Liza wrinkled her forehead. "It makes no sense. Why commit a crime? Why break into the diorama? They're staff. They could have just gotten permission for the exhibit people to open it up, unstitch the camel's belly, and retrieve the bundle. Hell, the Carnegie could have promoted it as an exposé, a live television event. Has part of a mummified Neanderthal child been secretly hidden in the belly of a stuffed camel for 150 years? Like what's-his-name a few years ago … you know … the guy who pimped the on-air excavation of the grave of Jimmy Hoffa."

Harry nodded. "I wondered about Gould and Storck doing it legit. But they would have had to reveal how they found out about it—Verreaux's notebooks. Which would implicate Gould in the razor job, a crime in Europe. Then there's the legal stuff. The Paris museum would go to court here in the U.S. to claim original ownership of the mummified hand. Maybe also the Belgian government. They'd get an immediate injunction to prevent DNA sequencing or any other analysis. Like the Native Americans in the Pacific Northwest did with Kennewick Man—the 9000-year-old skeleton of the Paleoamerican found along the Columbia River in Washington. That case dragged on for nine years. Instead, Storck and Gould do the sequencing, publish the results, get worldwide headlines, and deal with the legal backlash later."

"I guess so," Liza said, still skeptical. "So why would she commit suicide two days after she and Gideon got away with the break-in?"

"Who knows. Maybe she was overcome by guilt. I asked Mazeroski about it after our meeting in Stewart's office. He said the suicide seemed planned, deliberate. She was carrying a cup of coffee when she walked out of her office into the gallery hallway and "took a dive over the railing." That's verbatim. Sounds like she was set on doing it."

Liza bowed her head and clenched the tumbler with both hands. At that moment she looked like a Buddhist monk, wrapped in the white sheet, still, silent, meditating. Just the wrong gender. Harry deliberated whether to tell her about Gould's philandering.

She frowned at him. "You've got that screwy look you get on your face. There's something else you're not saying."

Harry was glad she could read him. He told her about Gould invading Christine's bed in Paris, about his professional jealousy of Anna, and their marital discord.

"I'm not surprised," Liza stated, almost business-like. "He's tried to put his hands on me more than once. Last time was in his office, when he was showing me Verreaux's birds. He kept brushing up against me. I told him if he wanted a rubbing of a woman he should pack paper and charcoal, get a ticket to Verona, and sidle up to Juliet's statue."

Harry grinned and grabbed the bottle of Highland Park. There was enough left for a third refill. He emptied it into their glasses. "The stuff in the bundle is probably hidden in Gould's lab. Or at his home."

"You want to search his office suite?" Liza suggested. "I have a master key. Middle of the night. No problem."

Harry dipped his finger in the scotch, brushed it across her lips, and kissed her. "Thanks, but it'll get you fired. I'll work on Mazeroski. At least to pull Gould in for a grilling. He can start with the razor job on the journals."

"Got any other suspects besides Gould rolling around in your head?"

He downed the scotch and put the glass on the floor. "Yeah, but they've got more friction. Christine. Marie. Gould could have shown his copy of the notebooks to either one of them. Or they saw it by accident. Or Anna told them. Both would know the impact on archaeology of the Neanderthal child's hand."

"From what you've said about Christine, I'm surprised you suspect her."

"This is cynical territory, Liza. My father often told me the proverb, 'lock your door ... or suspect your neighbor.' I'm in the business of suspicion, not locks."

She began motioning with her hands, one up, one down, as if they were on a teeter-totter. "Even me?"

"You're not my neighbor, Liza."

She finished her scotch, unwound the sheet, and held out her arms. "That's the right answer, Przewalski."

55

Pittsburgh
Tuesday, February 8

In the morning, the phone rang in his office. It didn't happen often enough for Harry to make a decent living. It was Mazeroski.

"He's filed a complaint. Your friend, Gould. Harassment. Even got the Carnegie Museum mouthpiece involved."

Harry shrugged. "Good. I egged him on. It worked. Gives us a shot at the bastard."

"Okay, get yourself down here this afternoon. I got the gist of Verreaux's notebooks and the goddamn trouble he's made. It's not often a guy gets to set the ticker to go off in the future. Looks like Verreaux did, with this business of a bundle in the camel. Anyway, Gould will be here. We'll play nice and make up. He'll kill the complaint. And maybe he'll confess."

Four hours later they were in the interrogation room in the Allegheny County Building downtown. It hadn't changed much. Still windowless. And still furnished for discomfort: a metal table, two metal chairs on one side, one for the perp on the other, and a hard, linoleum floor. An observation camera had replaced the two-way mirror. And the hospital green walls were now painted a submarine gray.

Mazeroski rubbed his face. "Okay, Dr. Gould, we appreciate you coming down here. I read Verreaux's notebooks. A copy. I hope you have no objection to Mr. Przewalski sitting in. It's his copy. He brought it back from the Paris museum, where he's just spent a week. He's on the Carnegie Museum's dime. He's helping with our investigation into who vandalized the Arab courier exhibit. And why. Once you understand the situation, we hope you two will make peace and you'll drop the harassment complaint."

Mazeroski got up, took off his brown checked jacket, and hung it on the back of his chair. Today he was sporting a tan shirt with blue squiggles.

Gould squirmed and nodded. Harry was willing to bet that the chair was a custom job, a few inches higher than the others to keep the perp's feet dangling off the floor. Gould's feet were dangling.

"I don't see how I can help you," Gould said, immediately sounding indignant. "I don't know anything about that overwrought exhibit." The first half came out as squeak, the second half an octave lower. He had swapped the light blue shirt for a black one, with a yellow bow tie, tan trousers and matching suspenders.

"Okay, let's see about that. Przewalski here tells me that two pages were cut out of Verreaux's original notebooks. French police confirm that. Also Interpol. The perp used one of those retractable razor-blade knives. Defacing archives is a crime in France. Here too. What might you tell us about that?"

Gould opened his mouth, then closed it. He looked up at the camera, started to get up, then sat back down. "I might tell you what I told Mr. Przewalski yesterday. It's fiction. I never saw those notebooks. I didn't even know about them until I came across the copy in the ornithology department at the Paris museum. It was in July. I was doing research there. They gave me permission to copy it. Anyway, France is out of your jurisdiction. I'm a scientist. If you pardon the expression, our bullshit detectors are set to high."

Mazeroski frowned. "Congratulations on your detectors, Mr. Gould. But Interpol is interested in our conversation. Interested enough to have the FBI send an investigator here, if necessary. One question they'd have is whether you showed your copy of the notebooks to your wife, Anna. That would have seemed a natural thing to do. So, you can talk to them or talk to me. Przewalski here will tell you that a smart scientist would choose me.

Gould seemed unfazed by the threat. "I'm sorry to confound your expectations. I didn't share the copy of the notebooks with Anna. There's nothing very exciting about lists of animals and plants from Verreaux's expeditions."

"Okay, Mr. Gould, here is what Przewalski thinks. And he's convinced me that it's what you scientists would call a 'viable hypothesis.' You read the notebook entries, not just the lists of specimens. You discovered Verreaux put a bundle in the camel's belly. You understood the scientific importance of what he'd wrapped up in that bundle: plaster casts of the skull bones and teeth of that Neanderthal kid; and the mummified hand, likely from the same kid; plus a note about the remains. Przewalski says you naturally wanted Anna to get at that bundle before anyone else did. And keep it a secret. So you—or you and Anna—got into the Paris museum archives and razored out the pages."

Mazeroski got up, walked around the table and stood behind Gould. "If your wife was involved, it might bear on understanding her suicide."

Gould craned his short neck to look at Mazeroski. "Surely, you can't be serious. My wife was depressed. Her work on the Neanderthal finger bone turned out to be contaminated. She was stressed by the archaeology meetings. And our ... our marriage. Never mind. My wife's suicide is a private matter. Please respect that."

Mazeroski nodded and assumed his fatherly voice. "I do. We all do. And I am sorry again for your loss. Verreaux's bundle came along at the right time for the two of you. You'd stumbled onto a great discovery. Of course you would show her the notebook entries. Anyone in your shoes would have."

"An interesting scenario," Gould said. "Fiction, nonetheless. Tell me this is a hypothetical."

"Sure, that works," Mazeroski allowed, and circled back to his chair. "Let's say the two of you thought about breaking into the exhibit to get the bundle. You break the glass, carefully make a small incision in the camel's belly, get the bundle, put back the stuffing, sew the camel's belly back up again, and no one is the wiser. Carnegie would report the crime. All we'd be looking for is some nutcase who smashed the glass front of a diorama."

Mazeroski paused, took a toothpick out of his shirt pocket, stuck it in his mouth, and waited for Gould to react. He didn't. Gould sat still, his egg-shaped head motionless and mute.

"Okay," Mazeroski continued, "let's say you thought about doing it during the week of the archaeology meetings at the Carnegie museum in December—just in case something goes wrong. There would be lots of archaeologists for the cops to chase down. In either case, you get the mummified hand, Anna takes it to that lab in Germany, it does the genetics, you publish the results. Headlines made. Careers and marriage saved."

"Fiction," Gould repeated. "The kind that would never sell. Even if I knew about the mummified hand, why break in? We work at the Carnegie. We could have gotten permission to have the exhibit opened and the bundle removed. Any legitimate professional could."

"Well, the DAs tells me it's not that not easy," Mazeroski said. "Property law. Przewalski agrees. Hypothetically, of course."

"Right," Harry broke in. "The Paris museum would sue immediately to get the mummified hand back. Probably also the Liège museum. It would get mired in the courts. The authorities would sequester the specimen. As they did Kennewick Man. I'm sure Anna told you about that episode. No specimen, no sequencing, no paper, no fame. There's your hypothetical."

"Let's keep this friendly, gentlemen," Mazeroski said. "Mr. Gould, we're trying to get an answer to a simple question: Did you show your copy of the notebooks to anyone else? This archaeologist at the Paris museum, Christine Dumoulin, thinks you did. She knows about your copy of the notebooks. She in on this caper too?"

"How the hell did she—" Gould stopped himself, took off his glasses, rubbed his eyes, fidgeted with his bow tie, and put the magnifying lenses back on. "Well, I imagine Christine could have seen my copy when Anna and I stayed at her place in July or October. I must have left it lying around. We never talked about Verreaux, or his notebooks, or his bundle."

Harry decided to raise the temperature. "Christine imagines you told Anna. We can call her. And Marie. It's … what, seven hours later there?" He checked the clock on the wall. "Nine o'clock in Paris and Liège. They might even be together."

Gould's shoulders sagged, as if the air had suddenly escaped from his bravado. He looked around at the gray walls, up at the camera, and adjusted his bow tie. "Well, I'm sure you will understand. Like I said, I was working on the long lists of Verreaux's specimen data. Between those pages were his personal journal entries. I started reading them. There it was."

Mazeroski nodded. "Okay, understandable You showed it to Anna."

Gould held his hands up in self-righteous innocence. "How could I not! It would be like her not telling me about coming across an undiscovered specimen of *Archaeopteryx*. I was so jazzed. I thought it would make Anna more— Never mind. But we never even thought of vandalizing the exhibit."

Mazeroski went out of the room, came back with three cups of coffee, and slid one over to Gould. "Who do you think would?" he asked, almost nonchalantly.

"Christine," Gould spurted out. "By herself … or with Marie." He started fuming. "She is, what is termed, a bitch, in the full sense of the word. In July, she'd prance around her place in shorts and those sheer chemises, her nipples showing through. Marie and Christine might be lovers, but Marie confided in Anna that she suspected Christine of lifting the original Engis-2 bones during the meeting in October at the Liège Museum."

Harry leaned back in his chair, pulled out his pack of Drum tobacco and a Zig-Zag paper, rolled a cigarette, and laid it on the table. "Why would Christine do that? She could easily have borrowed the specimens?"

Gould shrugged. "I don't know. You'll have to ask Marie. Seems to me you have a lot more to find out over there."

Mazeroski took out his toothpick, looked at it, and stuck it back in his mouth. "Okay, we appreciate your coming clean now. And wanting to protect your wife. But why didn't you come forward with all this right after the vandalism in December. You want harassment? I've a notion to slap you with a charge of hindering a police investigation."

Gould straightened up in his chair, unfazed. "I apologize. I had the best of intentions. I refrained from speaking about this out of concern for Anna. And I hate dealing in hearsay. But, that said, there is one more thing. In Pittsburgh, in December, Marie and Christine stayed with us during the first half of the meetings. Anna told me that Marie had warned her about Christine, that she'd half joked about breaking into the exhibit for the mummified hand."

With that, he slid off the chair, grabbed his wool overcoat, and headed for the door. "Of course, all of this is just fiction. Hypothetical. If you can turn it into evidence, be my guest."

Mazeroski took the toothpick out of his mouth, broke it half and swore, "Fucking pompous ass. I might make that egghead for this job. No wonder Storck jumped, coffee cup in hand, cool-headed to the end. Married to that guy, it might have been be a relief."

He got up, left the room, and came back thirty seconds later with an open box of Dunkin Donuts. There were three left: one chocolate, one with pink frosting and sprinkles, and one that had begun leaking crème around the edge, like stuffing spilling out of a crack in the hide of a taxidermied mount. Mazeroski shoved the box toward Harry. He passed.

"Okay," Mazeroski muttered. "Gould's pompous but he's right. All we got is a bunch of notebook entries from a guy 150 years ago, a stack of copies, and gossip. Interpol is nowhere on this. We're nowhere. The lieutenant is saying this smash-and-grab is taking too much police time. And Carnegie has already repaired the exhibit."

"You could check his office for the specimens. He'd be conceited enough to hide them there."

Mazeroski shook his head. "Forget it. No chance we'd get a warrant." He grabbed the crème donut and took a bite. The stuff squirted onto the sleeve of his shirt. "Shit!" he muttered, grabbed a napkin, and smeared it into the fabric. "Okay, what about this Dumoulin woman?" He pronounced it 'Doomooleen.' Harry didn't correct him, figuring Mazeroski was still pissed about the stain on his shirt. "You know her, Przewalski, you stayed with her. Did she prance around?"

"No, she didn't. Gould's making that up to justify assaulting her in the middle of the night last July. Anyway, it isn't summer. No sheer chemises in February in Paris. Seriously, I don't make Christine for any of this. I don't think she read the Verreaux notebooks—or the missing pages—until I showed them to her. Anyway, Christine wouldn't have the stomach for the razor job or the bundle job. Or enough lack of ethics."

Mazeroski downed the rest of the donut and wiped his mouth. "Doesn't matter. In law you're guilty of committing a crime. In ethics, you're guilty of thinking it. Someone said that."

"Immanuel Kant."

Mazeroski waved a hand at him. "There's that education you keep telling me you got."

56

Pittsburgh
Friday, February 11

Three days later, Harry stood at the grungy window in his office. The sky was a dirty gray and overcast, threatening snow. The Golden Triangle across the Monongahela was smeared in fog. The river looked almost still, the water barely moving past dirty white piles of snow on the south bank. Maybe it was just the window, the years of soot from the foundry annealed to the glass.

Wednesday afternoon he'd briefed Preston Stewart and Samaontha Mayer at the museum. The meeting was short. He told them about the Greef trial in Cape Town, Verreaux's entries, and the contents of the bundle. He didn't tell them about Gould, Christine or Marie. Stewart grumbled that he'd wasted good money on airfare, hotels and expensive meals. Harry told him the case wasn't done. And that he wasn't going to charge The Carnegie for a marketing idea for *Arab Courier Attacked by Lions*: Produce high-end facsimile editions of Verreaux's notebooks—the diary entries, the drawings. A coffee-table version for the tourists. A folio version for the art historians, philosophers and naturalists. Mayer liked the idea. Stewart dismissed it. No one, he said, would be interested in the scribbling of a 19th century taxidermist, grave-robber, and stuffer of people.

On Thursday the sun broke through long enough to raise the temperatures into the low forties. Harry and Liza loaded her Bianchi loaner and his Calfee into her Jeep Cherokee, drove north and east to the Clarion River, and did thirty miles on Miola Road through forests and croplands to Cooksburg and back. Nicholas had given her a *Velo Europa* jersey. It matched the celeste green sheen of the Bianchi.

Harry tweaked Liza's saddle height and the tilt of the handlebars three miles into the ride. He showed her how to clip in and out of her Look pedals, how to angle her knee and lean the bike into fast turns, and how to feather the brakes on steep descents. He rode beside her, watching her turn the pedals in fluid circles, and take a perfect line through an imperfect bend in the road. She told him she marveled at the bike's silent whisper of speed across the landscape. The ride back was into the wind, into the cold chill of the air. The low sun refracted through the crystals of snow on the side of the road, turning light to liquid.

She left the Bianchi in the trunk when they parked in front of *Velo Europa*. There were five customers, lured to the shop by the splash of sun and the illusory smell of Spring. Harry's father broke away long enough to welcome her hug, smile broadly at her exuberant description of the bike ride, and wink at Harry. He threw in a frame pump with the purchase.

At noon on Friday the phone rang. It startled Harry, who had started to nod of in the red leather chair in his office. It was Mazeroski. He told him to stay put, he'd be there in twenty minutes. Harry opened the office door at 12:20 and heard him stomping up the four flights of stairs. When he walked in, he was breathing hard and sweating in his police-issue blue parka, scarf and heavy mitts.

Mazeroski looked around. "Okay, Przewalski, I always wondered what your cheap digs were like." He motioned at the grimy windows. "If you wanted to crap the view, you succeeded."

Harry pointed at the two Eugene Smith black-and-white shots of Pittsburgh on the side wall—*Smoky City, Dance of Flaming Coke*. "That's what crapped it. And every other building in the city. I could hire a guy with a cherry picker, chemicals and a water blaster, but it'll have to wait till I collect from Stewart. And a few other clients. Anyway, a better view will only make the landlord raise the rent."

Mazeroski allowed himself a guffaw. "Okay, the realtor's sign out front tells me you're gonna be paying rent somewhere else soon. Or not, if you continue to be lousy with women."

He took off his parka, stuffed his mitts and scarf into one of the sleeves, looked around, and tossed it on the floor. "You need one of them wooden coat racks."

Harry rolled a Drum and lit it. "What's more important, my reading of women or getting a coat rack?"

"Women. Specifically this Dumoulin woman. Interpol got a tip. They searched her flat. Then her office. Guess what they found. In one of them specimen cabinets. The stuff stolen from the Liège Museum. And Verreaux's casts of the stuff stolen from the Liège Museum. And the mummified hand. She's been taken in for questioning. They have a good system over there—perps have fewer rights than here."

"I don't buy it," Harry countered. "Who tipped off Interpol?"

"No idea. Call from a phone booth. In Maastricht, they think. It's in Holland, Przewalski—I also got an education."

"Yeah, but an incomplete one. Maastricht is the place with the rock strata that define the Maastrichtian, the last geologic stage of the Cretaceous, when dinosaurs became extinct."

"Okay, smartass." Mazeroski got up and gathered his parka from the floor. "Anyway, they still have pay phones over there. I told them about the exhibit break-in, the bundle in the camel, Storck, and the suicide. They'll follow up with Dumoulin. Looks like it's over. We'll know soon enough. I got connections there."

"What do you mean?"

Mazeroski chuckled. "I got relatives in Europe. All over. Fled Poland during the war—the big one, WW2. One of 'em, a cousin sixteen times removed, is in Interpol, in Brussels. How do you think I'm getting this info? The cousin is on the team."

Harry stubbed out the cigarette. "I'm impressed. But not convinced."

"I told you, Przewalski, you're lousy with women. Forget her. It's done. Case closed."

"Maybe. But I'm going to talk to her. A last gambit. That's a move—"

"Watch it, I played chess in the Pittsburgh league. My favorite was Anderssen's Opening with the Polish Gambit."

Harry grinned. "I'm impressed again. We should have a game once this is over. My father taught me. Used to spot me a queen and win.

57

Paris
Saturday, February 12

Liza got Harry on the Friday night flight to Paris, a middle seat in economy at the back of plane. He tried to sleep, but every bump of turbulence jostled him awake. It didn't help that the seat back was jammed and refused to recline. He felt he was strapped into a cubic straitjacket. Finally, at two in the morning, with the first hints of light edging over the eastern horizon, he drifted off. Two and a half hours later the US Airways attendant woke him for breakfast at 35,000 feet over Ireland: orange juice, ham and cheese on a soggy bun, a dry croissant, and weak coffee. He passed. They landed in a soft rain at eleven in the morning, Charles de Gaulle time. By twelve-thirty, Harry was mounting the steps of the natural history museum amid bustling crowds on the Rue de Buffon. Liza had emailed Christine to meet him at the Frémiet sculpture.

She was there, waiting, in blue jeans, hiking boots, and a heavy black peacoat, unbuttoned, a pink scarf underneath. She looked distraught, nervously scanning the crowd, her forehead cramped into furrows, her spiked hair erupting at odd angles. She managed a feeble smile and led him to her office.

"You look tired, Harry. Jet lagged. Here's some coffee and food."

There was a thermos on her desk and a plate with two demi-baguettes, fresh camembert cheese, olives, and slices of salami.

"And you look as if the police harangued you for a while."

She grimaced. "Harry, you must know that this is crazy ... insane. *C'est foufolle!* I told the police I have no idea how the Engis-2 material got there." She pointed to a white, metal specimen cabinet in the corner. Harry couldn't make out the label in the slot on the cabinet door.

"Of course, they did not believe me. They're checking fingerprints. Marie's are on the real Engis-2 bones. No prints on the cast. Mine are all over the cabinet and drawers."

"What else is in the cabinet?"

"Animal bones from a site in France, La Quina, in Charente, around 32,000 years old. There's some human remains too—mandibles. Either very late Neanderthal, or early modern human. That stuff is being studied in the States. At Penn ... the University of Pennsylvania Museum."

Harry poured some coffee, broke off a hunk of bread, split it open, and sandwiched in a slice of camembert. "When was the last time you opened that cabinet?"

She thought about it for a minute. "Three or four weeks ago. I've been busy with a manuscript on the La Quina material. And on an archaeology display with the exhibit department. Anyway, I swear the Engis-2 stuff wasn't in any of the drawers then."

"Any visitors in the past month?"

"Almost daily. We had archeologists in the collections all last week. From Montpellier, Italy, Romania, Germany, Canada. And the US—from Penn."

"What about archaeologists who were at both conferences—the one in Pittsburgh in December, and Liège in October?"

Christine shrugged. "I don't know off hand. But I have the list Marie gave me. I'll check."

Harry finished chewing the hard bread crust and poured more coffee from the thermos. "Could any of them have gotten into the archives and skimmed the notebooks?"

"Sure. They're scholars. But why would they be interested in Verreaux? Or even know about his notebooks? You learned about the mummified hand by chance. So did Gideon. So did I."

"Check the list against your visitors in the past month. In my business, chance has a way of beating the odds."

Christine chuckled. "That makes no sense, but it's funny. It's the first laugh I've had in two days. You need sleep, Harry. Stay at my place. I have a spare room. My son is with his father for the week. Marie will be here this evening. To comfort me. I called her from the police station. I must have sounded deranged. She was just here a few days ago."

Harry thought about it and accepted. The hotel's bed was probably no larger than the son's. And the company would be preferable to solitary anonymity. "Sure, thanks."

He tried to stay awake during the drive through the rain in her mini Citroen to her flat near Place d'Italie, but the fog in his head succumbed to the rhythmic swish of the windshield wipers. When he woke, he was slumped down in the seat. The car was parked on a curb in front of a set of three steps, a tiny porch, and a red door.

Christine bussed him on the cheek. "We're here, Harry. Thank you for coming back. "You're a friend—actually a comrade."

"I'd rather be a friend. 'Comrade' makes me feel as if I ought to be wearing boots and singing the Internationale."

Christine laughed. "We will eat at Le Foumaillon tonight. You might be ready for a Trois Monts. But after you get some sleep."

Her place was cramped but workable. A small vestibule was lined with coats, scarves, and boots. It opened into a boxy living room, an efficiency kitchen, and a tiled washroom. The narrow stairs to an upper level looked like a recent renovation job. Christine led him past an alcove with a desk, laptop, and fold-out futon to the smaller of two compact bedrooms, her son's. His feet hung over the end of the bed.

Mazeroski had said he was lousy with women. He fell asleep thinking he didn't know why Mazeroski cared, but was glad that he did. Seven hours later he awoke to the chatter of women's voices downstairs. They were drinking red wine on the couch and snacking from a bowl of cashews. Marie rose and greeted him with a broad smile. Her blonde hair was striking against her black turtleneck, jeans, and knee-high, spiked-heeled boots. They bussed one another three times, the practice in Belgium and the Netherlands. The French stopped at two. In America, Harry told them, if he greeted a woman like that, it would get him a quick slap across the face.

They walked the few blocks to Place d'Italie. The rain had stopped. A warm wind from the north had chased the clouds from under the night sky. A few stars blinked through the street lights of Paris. At Le Foumaillon, they took one of the tables on the sidewalk under the awning, a few feet from the stream of cars speeding around the wide, three-lane traffic circle.

He asked them whether they had checked the list of participants at both archaeology conferences against recent visitors to the Paris museum's collection. They had. There were four hits: archaeologists from Tel Aviv, Madrid, Cape Town, and Philadelphia. Harry filed away the Cape Town reference. The El Negro angle had long since flat-lined to zero.

Christine motioned to the waiter and ordered the usual: three bottles of Trois Monts and pizzas. Harry rolled a Drum and offered her the tobacco. "Someone tipped the police to the specimens from Engis-2 being in your office."

"I figured." She rolled a cheroot in brown paper, lit it, and inhaled deeply. "Who would have done that?"

"Someone who thinks you stole them. Or wants the police to think you did."

"Clearly, that person must have been in my office," Christine concluded, suddenly hugging her shoulders with her arms. "They must have put it in the cabinet when I was out."

"Or had an accomplice do it."

"*Merde*! It could be anyone! Staff. A visitor. I even asked the assistants in the department whether a stranger had dropped off a package to put in my office cabinet."

The beer came. Harry stubbed out his cigarette and took a guzzle. "The tipster called Interpol from a pay phone."

Christine shifted uncomfortably in her chair. She and Marie looked questioningly at one another and then at Harry. "From where?" they asked, almost in unison.

"Holland. Maastricht."

"I know the archaeologist there," Marie declared. "At the Natuurhistorisch Museum. Aagje Kroos. She was at my conference in Liège. And I think also in Pittsburgh." Marie threw up her hands. "But she would not know about Verreaux's notebooks. Or the mummified hand."

Christine's face suddenly froze. "Maastricht? She slowly turned to face Marie and began speaking in rapid-fire French, quiet at first, then louder and accusatory, jabbing her with her finger. Harry couldn't make any of it out. Marie recoiled, stood up, and raised her hands in defense. "Non, non, non," she protested.

The rest happened too quickly for Harry to stop it. Christine kicked over her chair as she bolted up, seized Marie by the shoulders and began shaking her violently and shrieking into her face. At the edge of the curb Marie wrenched free, staggering backward from the momentum. The spiked heel of her boot appeared to catch in a deep crack in the cement. She teetered for a moment, her face aghast at what was happening, then fell without a sound into the outside lane of the traffic circle. There was a screech of brakes before the delivery van hit her front on. She rolled a few feet, her blond hair sweeping the street. She was dead before the ambulance arrived.

58

Paris
Sunday, February 13

It was midnight before the Paris police released Harry and Christine. There had been numerous witnesses. Diners at the next table. The waiter bringing the three pizzas. Pedestrians strolling by. A cyclist on the sidewalk who almost crashed into Marie. The police ruled it an unfortunate accident caused by a domestic quarrel.

They were silent in the police van during the drive to Christine's flat. She had begun shaking and couldn't stop. Harry found a bottle of cognac and poured two glasses. She held the snifter tightly in both hands, her face rigid, staring straight ahead. She asked him to roll her a cigarette. It quivered between her lips. He lit it for her, and watched the cognac begin to calm the trembling in her fingers.

When she finally spoke, it came out toneless, a dry recitation. Marie had betrayed her. Love meant nothing. Marie had come to Paris, to the museum, a week ago, on Tuesday, to work with her on the La Quina manuscript. They'd returned together to Liège on Wednesday, then went to Maastricht on Thursday morning. They wanted to see the new exhibition of Russian impressionist art at the

Bonnefantenmuseum. In one of the galleries, Marie had abruptly excused herself. She'd said she had to call her department chair at the University of Liège. She needed a pay phone. There was one just outside the museum. Her cell phone was dead. She said she'd forgotten to charge it the night before.

Christine stubbed out her cigarette. "I know now," she said in a hoarse whisper. "It was Marie. She used the pay phone to tip off the police—and frame me. She must have stashed the Engis-2 material in the specimen cabinet last Tuesday when I happened to step out of the office."

She clutched the snifter and asked Harry to roll her another Drum. He pulled two Zig-Zag papers from the blue packet and rolled one for himself and for her.

"It fits," he said. "Gould admitted showing his copy of Ver-reaux's notebooks to Anna and Marie."

Christine bowed her head to her knees. "Marie never told me. They kept it from me—Marie, Anna, Gideon. *Salauds*. Swine." She looked up at Harry, her eyes laced with the poison of betrayal. "They knew I would never agree to stealing the bundle from the exhibit. We could have just asked for permission to get the spec-imen out ... to test it. They must have broken into the exhibit at the Carnegie during the anthropology meetings there in December. How did I not know? I remember waking up in the night in the hotel. Marie wasn't in the room. I fell back asleep. She was in bed in the morning. I asked her where she'd been. She said she couldn't sleep. Nervous about giving her paper that day. She said she'd gone outside for a smoke and walk."

Christine downed the rest of the cognac, leaned over, took Harry's face in her hands, kissed him on the cheek, her lips linger-ing on his skin. "In the end, love means nothing," she murmured again. It was as much to herself as to him, he thought. Abruptly, she put out the cigarette, stood up from the couch, and climbed the stairs to her bedroom.

Harry was famished. He found some pita bread, hummus and cheese in Christine's refrigerator and wolfed it down. The police said they would return the Engis-2 skull bones and teeth to the Liège museum, and Verreaux's plaster copy to the Paris museum. The mummified hand was being held in escrow.

Christine had left a night light on at the top of the stairs. Habit for her son, Harry surmised. It was one in the morning, seven o'clock in Pittsburgh. He considered calling Mazeroski to tell him that Marie was the perp, that happenstance had become fate with its own death penalty. The call could wait, he decided. Mazeroski's cousin at Interpol would let him know.

Harry put a chair with a pillow at the foot of the bed to keep his feet from hanging over. He dreamt of Liza's long, lissome legs entangling his, her arm draped over his shoulder, her head nestled into his chest. He felt himself stir half awake and began to caress her. Christine, beside him, whispered, "Just hold me Harry. I need to be held." They slept until the first light filtered through the window onto the bed. In the distance, the two-tone blare of a Paris police van interrupted the quiet.

While he showered, Christine went out and came back with a bag of warm croissants and half a dozen tangerines. She moved about the kitchen as if from rote, deliberate, methodical, wordless. She made coffee in a large French press, laced it with shots from her Nespresso machine, and poured it into two café-au-lait cups. She hadn't put on makeup or combed her hair. The clumped spikes jutted out at the same disheveled angles that her life had suddenly protracted.

They ate in silence, perched on stools at the L-shaped bend of the kitchen counter. Christine rolled a cheroot, lit it, opened the window, and blew the smoke into a small back garden filled with clay pots and withered plants. She seemed meditative, almost brooding. Finally, she turned to Harry, her eyes somewhat bloodshot. "I cried too much last night. I'm sorry about ... your bed. I needed not to be alone ... at the moment when we are most alone. Stay ... if you can. For a few days. I would ... I would like that."

He bought time rolling a cigarette, waiting for the right words. "I know a police detective in Pittsburgh who tells me I'm lousy with women. And there's Liza. I don't want to be lousy with her. Or you."

She nodded, stubbed out her cigarette and bussed his cheek.

"This business is over," Harry said, "except for a few loose ends at the Carnegie.

She looked up. "What loose ends?"

Harry shrugged. "Gould. Anna. I'll let you know when I find them."

She drove him to Charles de Gaulle, climbed the curb outside the departure doors, and kept the motor running. "Thank you, Harry," she said, staring straight ahead, as if into a distance she no longer recognized. "If things turn lousy with Liza, give me a call. But I hope it won't be so." She turned to him, her lips pursed into a plaintive complaint. "I'm beginning to think that love is a Foucault phenomenon. It's merely a language construct."

Harry didn't tell her she was wrong. He let her take refuge in the philosophy of meaninglessness, as he once had. Ardor, passion, like all fuel, eventually gets used up in its space.

59

Pittsburgh
Monday, February 14

At eight-thirty in the morning on Monday the phone jangled him awake. He fumbled for the receiver, knocked it off the bed stand onto on the floor, groped around for it, and finally answered.

"Sounds bad, Harry," Liza said, without sympathy. "Go for a bike ride. Best way to beat the jet lag. If I were there, I'd help—I'd haul your carcass into the shower. Okay ... your sweet carcass."

Harry managed a foggy laugh. "Thanks. It would then be a bike ride delayed."

Liza chuckled. "It's good to hear that you can still think of the right words. Listen," her voice switched to officious, "I have news for you from Director Mayer.

Harry groaned as he got out of bed. "Shoot."

"The Paris and Liège museums are both claiming ownership of the Engis-2 Cave mummified hand. So are we. 'Hell, it's been inside our camel since 1899 when Andrew Carnegie bought the Arab courier exhibit.' That's a direct quote from Mayer. But all three museums have agreed to have the mummified hand sent to the

Max Planck Institute in Leipzig for sequencing. They're working out the details with Interpol."

Harry grunted. "Progress."

"Right," Liza declared. "Science marches on. Listen, march out of that bedroom and hit the shower." She hung up.

At ten o'clock, Mazeroski walked into Przewalski's office carrying a wooden coat rack. He was red-faced and sweating from huffing up the four flights of stairs. He set the rack against a side wall, took off his parka, stuffed his gloves and scarf into one of the sleeves, and hung it up.

"A gift, Przewalski. The lieutenant downtown was so grateful this camel driver business is over he let me swipe it from the squad room. It's the only piece of furniture down there that doesn't have a goddamn property tag on it. 'Repurposing,' he called it. Anyway, it goes well with the rest of the shabby deco you got here."

Harry scowled at him. "Thanks." He'd called Mazeroski and told him to come by if he wanted to know how Marie LeBoeuf had bought it.

"Okay," Mazeroski said, "my Interpol cousin sixteen times removed tells me the woman got hit by a van outside a restaurant. Fill me in. I'm listening." He sank down into the red leather sofa chair opposite Harry's desk.

Harry rolled a Drum, lit it, took out a couple of bottles of Iron City from a small fridge behind his desk, and handed one to Mazeroski.

"Pretty early, Przewalski." He took a long guzzle. "Still, taste's kinda good. Okay, I'm still listening."

"Here's the thinking. LeBoeuf had the goods, the Engis-2 Cave stuff: the original skull bones and teeth of the Neanderthal kid from her own museum, and Verreaux's plaster casts and the mummified hand from the bundle. She and Dumoulin were in Maastricht to see an art show. LeBoeuf invented an excuse to run outside to use a pay phone. She tipped off the police that the specimens were in the cabinet in Dumoulin's office. She'd been to see Dumoulin earlier in the week and planted the stuff."

"Fingerprints?"

"Nope. None. LeBoeuf was smart enough to wear gloves. After all, she's got a PhD."

"Never knew you were such a cynic, Przewalski."

"Yeah, well, life does that. You should know."

Mazeroski nodded. Neither mentioned Nicole. "Okay, no fingerprints. How the hell did this LeBoeuf get hit by a van?"

"When Christine was arrested, she called Marie, who came up from Liège. The three of us were eating at a brasserie off a traffic circle. I told them that the tip had come from a pay phone in Maastricht. Christine immediately made the connection—Marie, her colleague and lover, was the snitch. Christine grabbed her, screamed at her. LeBoeuf backed away and stumbled off the curb. It's a busy traffic circle."

"Okay," Mazeroski examined the Iron City label as if it had clues. "Sounds straightforward enough. Did you crawl into her bed, Przewalski? Dumoulin?"

Harry held up the beer bottle in mock toast. "You're becoming predictable. I figured you'd ask that. No. She crawled into mine. Nothing happened. But it got me thinking. All of a sudden last week, Marie gets desperate enough to tip the cops and pull the frame-up job. How come?"

Mazeroski took a last swig of beer and plunked the bottle down on the end table beside the sofa chair. "I know what you're thinking—the egghead. Gould. We had him downtown last Tuesday. He finds out that we know that he knew about the notebooks, about the stuff in the camel. And about him telling Storck and LeBoeuf about it. He panics. He calls LeBoeuf, his accomplice. He tells her that the cops are digging, but not to worry. He's taken care of it. He's fingered Dumoulin for the break-in. Perfect set up for LeBoeuf to plant the stuff in Dumoulin's lab, then call in the tip from that phone booth. Misdirection."

Harry ground out the cigarette butt, pushed the can of Drum to the other side of the desk, and emptied the ashtray. "Right. But I think there's something else. Something you won't like."

Mazeroski looked at his watch. "Okay, seems like I'm gonna be here for a bit. Run with it. I got a month. What'dya know that I don't?"

Harry told him. It took two minutes. "Like you said, misdirection."

Mazeroski sat back in the sofa chair and squinted at him hard until his bushy eyebrows came together above the bridge of his big nose. "I like you, Przewalski, kinda like a son gone bad. Like one I shoulda taught that opinions ain't facts. Quit the detective business. With theories like that you're primed for the nutcase conspiracy circuit. Listen, last I checked, she— Okay, never mind. I'll talk to the Lieutenant and get back to you."

Harry got up and walked over to his grimy window. Pittsburgh from here would forever be a smudge across the river. "They were a couple," he uttered, like a sad rumination. "Then again, there isn't much morality in our business. If there were, we'd be out of business."

Mazeroski levered himself out of the red leather chair and went over to the coat rack. "Yeah, well. We kill the things we love. The coward does it with a kiss." He put on his parka. "Someone said that. Show me your education, Przewalski."

"Oscar Wilde."

"Congratulations."

60

Pittsburgh
Wednesday, February 16

Two days later Mazeroski got back to Harry. "Okay, we got some stuff. Leave your yellow jalopy. Be outside your office. I'm in the cruiser. We're going up there to see him. I'll fill you in on the ride."

Mazeroski had the flasher bar going. He took East Carson to the Birmingham Bridge past the rusting hulks of extinct steel mills, museum pieces of Pittsburgh history. He crossed the Monongahela to Forbes Avenue and ran the lights through Oakland to the Carnegie Museum lot off South Craig Street. They wound through a couple of busloads of school kids in Dinosaur Hall, took the rear elevator to the third floor, passed the door to Storck's old office, turned down the L-shaped corridor, and strode into Gould's office without knocking.

He was standing at an open specimen cabinet examining some of Verreaux's birds. "The Polish duo," he cracked. "I wasn't aware that this was our weekly harassment appointment."

"No worries," Mazeroski reassured him. "I gotta admit we owe you. You came clean with us on the notebooks. You even fingered that Dumoulin woman. So we came up here to apologize for riding you pretty hard last week. Because they got her. Interpol got a tip. Anonymous. They searched her office and found the stuff in a cabinet in her lab—the stuff in the bundle. Also, the specimens stolen from that Liège Museum."

"Really?" Gould asked, circling back to his desk. "Christine's been arrested? Just as I predicted." He looked alternately at Harry and Mazeroski for confirmation.

Gould had quite a wardrobe, Harry thought. Today he was part of a barbershop quartet: deep red shirt with blue stripes, blue bowtie with red stripes, off-white trousers, white shoes, and blue suspenders.

"Yeah," Mazeroski answered, "last Thursday or Friday. I'm interested in clearing up a few details."

"Sure. Whatever." His face took on a look of disdain. "I told you she was evil. Kinda stupid, though, hiding things in one's office. It's the first place police would look." Gould leaned down, tapped one of the levers protruding from his high-tech armchair, and abruptly descended until half his torso disappeared behind his desk. Red-faced, he stood up, bent over, hit the lever, made the chair rise two stories, and sat back down.

"Well, it's funny how these things go," Mazeroski remarked. "Smart people make smart plans. Then when things go haywire, they get too smart and screw up."

"What do you mean?" Harry watched Gould pale.

"She used a pay phone. The tipster. In Maastricht."

"You said 'she.'"

"Yeah, that's right. Turns out you know her. What a coincidence!"

"Who is it?"

Mazeroski shrugged. "Your friend, Marie LeBoeuf. I'm sorry to say, she's dead."

"What!" Gould paled. His eyes goggled under his glasses. "I don't believe it! How did she ... what ... what happened?" He either didn't know, Harry thought, or he was ready for Broadway.

"Accident," Mazeroski said, matter-of-factly. "Got hit by a delivery van. In Paris, on Saturday night. Outside the restaurant where she, Dumoulin and Przewalski, here, were having beer and pizza. But we're thinking you already knew that. Dumoulin called you."

Gould looked perplexed. "I thought you said Christine was arrested and in custody of the police."

Mazeroski shrugged. "Yeah, I did. But they let her go. Not enough evidence."

"Really? Are the French police that incompetent? What about the stolen specimens in the cabinet in her lab? She obviously broke into the camel exhibit during the meetings here. Marie thought so. So did Anna."

Mazeroski shook his head and frowned. "Funny how police are wired. Skeptics by nature. Like you scientists. You'd think we were related. I got a distant cousin who works for Interpol. In Brussels. They let Dumoulin go. They also checked her cell phone. Lots of calls between you two since our chat last Tuesday. Also between you and LeBoeuf—while she was still alive."

Gould contorted his face, visibly digesting the news. "Of course I called them. To inform them of your questions ... and insinuations. They were Anna's colleagues. And friends.

"Whatever. Here's how the cops put it together. You and she—"

"Who?" Gould interrupted.

Mazeroski ignored him. "You and she cooked up a quick plan to frame Dumoulin. The pay-phone tip. She made the call from a booth outside the Maastricht art museum. She'd already planted the Engis-2 stuff in Dumoulin's office a few days earlier."

"This is news to me. I had nothing to do with any of it. Frankly, I'm surprised. I did not think Marie was nefarious enough to steal the bundle and then try to implicate Christine. But there you go. Now that the police are satisfied and the case is done, I trust that these weekly inquisitions will also be done."

Mazeroski got up and wandered over to the open drawer of Verreaux's bird specimens. "Can I pick one up?"

Gould waved his hand at the cabinet. "Sure. It's one of the birds Verreaux collected in Botswana. From his notebook record, I now know the exact locality."

Mazeroski picked up a small bird with a glistening yellow collar around the throat. When he turned it in the light the collar turned purple and green. "Interesting, this iridescence. Just needs a different angle of light to be revealed."

"Yes, so? What are you getting at?" Gould asked.

Mazeroski placed the bird back in the drawer, strolled over to Gould's desk, pushed aside the phone and planted half his backside on the corner. Gould pushed his chair back and looked up him, blinking madly behind the glasses, his eyelids magnified to wings.

"What I'm getting at," Mazeroski intoned, "is that the two of you planned the exhibit break-in and pulled it off. During the anthropology meeting here last December. Don't know which one of you did the actual smash-and-grab job. You have a key to get into the museum at three in the morning. She didn't. But you could have given it to her. How're are we doing so far?"

Gould sat motionless, his lips pressed tightly together.

"Okay," Mazeroski continued. "You hid the bundle temporarily in one of those cabinets over there—maybe even that one with the birds. I'll bet we'll find a few fibers from the bundle's linen wrap in one of those drawers. When the meeting ended, you gave her the bundle to put in her suitcase and take back to her museum. She could pretend that she'd found the long-lost mummified hand in the collections. No one could say otherwise. Because you or she took a razor to those pages in Verreaux's notebooks. Anyway, she was supposed to send the mummified hand off for the DNA work. It would be more credible coming from an archaeologist in Europe than an ornithologist in Pittsburgh. Pretty good plan you two hatched."

Gould rolled his chair forward and gripped the edge of his desk as if he were biting a pain stick with his teeth. "This is just fucking gossip. If you want to turn gossip into evidence, be my guest."

It was the first time Harry had heard him swear. Fear spoke a different vocabulary than arrogance. "There's one thing that wasn't part of the plan. You deviated. You weren't supposed to heave Anna over the railing."

"Wha—"

Harry held up his palm. "She got in the way. The morning after the break-in, Anna was in her office, frazzled. She knew it was you. She'd told you she'd report you to Mayer, or the police. That was the day she died. You either followed Anna out of her office, or were waiting for her outside the door. Then you—"

"FUCK YOU, YOU SON OF A BITCH." Gould lunged at him across his desk. Mazeroski grabbed him by the shirt collar and yanked him back into his chair. Gould's bowtie snapped off and flew onto the floor. It clicked like a gun firing on an empty chamber.

"Like I said," Harry continued, "Anna was in her office. She poured herself a cup of coffee and walked out to the gallery-hallway overlooking the atrium. She's drinking java, ostensibly occupied by the anthro meeting—that doesn't register as a suicide moment. She didn't jump. She had help."

Gould his mouth agape, turned and blinked at Mazeroski. "He's not the police. Are you accusing me of murdering my wife? She committed suicide! The police said it. The coroner said it."

Mazeroski shrugged. "Yeah, well, got to admit your wife's dive bothered me some. But there was nothing to go on before. Now there is." He reached into the pocket of his checked jacket, pulled out two sheets of paper, studied them, and handed one to Gould.

"You wanted gossip turned into evidence? Happy to oblige. That photo is black and white and fuzzy. Take a good look."

Gould studied the photo print. "What am I looking at?"

"It's a phone booth, the one outside the Maastricht art museum. The person inside is making a phone call."

"What?" Gould grabbed a magnifying glass from his desk drawer and examined the photo. "Who the hell is it?"

Mazeroski allowed himself a chuckle. "Why, it's Ms. Dumoulin calling in the tip to the police. Right time, right place. The Dutch call it *camerabewaking*. It means the camera is guarding the area. Kinda more lyrical than 'CCTV,' don't you think?"

Gould threw the photo on his desk. "I don't believe it. Makes no sense."

Mazeroski got up from Gould's desk, slid the phone back to its previous spot, and sat down in the chair beside Harry. "Nice piece of misdirection, Mr. Gould. Like that iridescence on the bird's neck. Dumoulin implicating herself in order to implicate LeBoeuf. Did she think of that? Or did you? Was that what you talked about during your phone calls last week? Anyway, it turns out you were right on both counts. Dumoulin was too smart. And LeBoeuf ... well ... she didn't quite have the gumption for theft and betrayal."

Gould took of his glasses, plucked a Kimwipe from the box on his desk, and wiped the lenses. "Are you done?"

"Not quite," Mazeroski said, and handed him the second sheet of paper. This is in color, an x-ray of a piece of carry-on luggage going through the scanner at our airport here in Pittsburgh. Wonderful machines for security. Terrible for privacy. They can take the picture, store it, and send it out. We think it's Ms. Dumoulin's bag. Right time. Right place. Look closely with that magnifying glass. See if you can make out the plaster skull bones and teeth, and the mummified hand of a human child. You don't have to be an anthropologist. Even police and ornithologists should be able to see it."

"Are you done?" Gould demanded again, raising his voice.

Mazeroski got up, circled behind Gould to the large arched window, and looked out into the central courtyard. It had begun to snow. A sparrow, all puffed up, was trying to burrow into a corner of the window sill.

"Just one more thing. Ms. Dumoulin won't be traveling much. They took her passport. She's too busy being questioned. And giving answers. She says it was your idea from the get-go, when you first showed her—"

Gould leapt out of his chair. "That lying dyke bitch. I should never have shown her the notebooks. She planned it, she executed it. She got it going in October when she lifted the original Engis-2 Cave stuff from the Liège gallery. There was a rash of museum thefts in Europe. It would be chalked up as one of them, she figured. In preparation for the camel driver. She did the break-in. Last week, on the phone, it was her idea to frame Marie that way. Followed by a convenient accident." He gestured at Harry. "You weren't supposed to be there."

"Yeah, I know," Harry said. Or in the bed she crawled into. "Looks like she's given you up."

Gould thrust his hands straight out, as if he were waiting to be cuffed. "God damn it, she's lying. She's a conniving, murderous bitch. She murdered Anna. I saw her that morning, just before I turned the corner to my office. Anna came out with her coffee cup. Christine was behind her, in the doorway. Christine just grabbed her around the legs and pitched her over. She should fry for this."

Mazeroski stood up and grabbed his parka. "Case closed, Gould. Call a lawyer. Murder needs a good one."

61

Pittsburgh
Friday, February 25

By Friday, Mazeroski had two signed statements on his desk. Christine Dumoulin and Gideon Gould admitted to vandalizing the Arab courier exhibit and stealing the bundle. Both accused the other of the murder of Anna Storck. A week later Mazeroski called Harry and asked him to come downtown.

They met outside on the Bridge of Sighs, a brick archway between the prison and the courts in the Allegheny County Judicial Building. It was a shade more pedestrian than the one in Venice. Mazeroski came out in his sport coat, scarf and big galoshes. It had been snowing all morning, long enough to cover the walkway. Harry rolled a Drum. Before he lit it, Mazeroski fished out a pack of Camels from his jacket pocket.

"Okay, seems only fitting, Przewalski."

Harry pulled a bottle of 18-year-old Lagavulin from under his coat and handed it to Mazeroski. "You're right. I'm lousy with women."

Mazeroski opened the pack of Camels and took out two cigarettes. "Yeah. Dumoulin. You trusted her. Understandable. But there's more to it than smarts and a warm bed. You oughta know that. There's a better bed for you up the road." He pointed east up Forbes Avenue toward Squirrel Hill, where Liza lived. "No nails."

Harry lit the Camel and leaned over the stone parapet. It hadn't been cold enough for the pool of water under the bridge to freeze over and hide the floating trash.

"Quite the gal, that Dumoulin," Mazeroski mused. "Steals the stuff. Kills Storck, her colleague. Frames her lover, LeBoeuf. Then kills her too. Gould would have been next. Too much of a liability."

"Hell," Harry scowled, "I'm betting the two of them tossed Anna over the railing that morning. Dumoulin isn't a heavyweight. She and Gould each took a leg."

Mazeroski nodded. "Yeah, could be. All for a lousy piece of science that isn't important to anyone."

"It was toDumoulin," Harry stated. "The mummified hand was worth killing for—the most comprehensive genome of a Neanderthal. Gould was the patsy. And too conceited to realize it. She crawled into his bed last summer, seduced him, or blackmailed him, or appealed to his ego. Maybe all three. They kept Anna and Marie out of it. Knew they wouldn't go along."

Mazeroski shook his head and sighed. "All I can say, Przewalski, is that it's way out of whack. Headlines, fame—hell, they come, they fade, they die. I'm not a romantic, but romance is supposed to be … the anchor." He reddened, turned away from Harry, and flipped his cigarette butt over the bridge. "Tastes like dried camel dung." He tossed Harry the pack of Camels.

"There's one more thing," Mazeroski added, his voice almost solemn. "My cousin in Interpol tells me that the Max Planck people sequenced the mummified hand. She got the preliminary results. Pretty interesting. You wanna know before it hits the anthro journals?"

Harry narrowed his eyes, wary. "Sure."

"The poor kid it belonged to isn't a Neanderthal. Not even close. She's was like you and me, a modern *Homo sapiens*. A thousand years old, maybe two. The Neanderthal skull and teeth belonged to a different kid. Both ended up in the same Engis-2 cave fifty-thousand years apart."

Harry looked at him, aghast. "All that … all that … It's madness! Fucking madness!"

Mazeroski patted Harry on the shoulder, tucked the bottle of Lagavulin under his arm, fished a slip of paper out of his shirt pocket, and handed it to him.

"Read it, Przewalski. 'The rage for fame infects both great and small.' That's John Wolcot. Daily quote on my desk calendar. There's your education for ya."

Afterword

Almost every novel begins with the disclaimer:

This is a work of fiction. Names, characters, and incidents are products of the author's imagination or are used fictitiously and are not to be construed as real. Any resemblance to actual events, locales, organizations or persons, living or dead, is entirely coincidental.

This is true only in part for The Camel Driver. The love affair between Elisabeth Greef and Jules Verreaux in Cape Town in 1827 was passionately real—their exchange of letters, her pregnancy, and the trial and verdict in the Cape Supreme Court in 1829. What happened to the child remains a mystery. There is no birth or death record of a newborn named Greef or Verreaux in the archives of the South African Commercial Advertiser. The newspaper carried a daily account of the trial. Mr. Fairbairn, its editor, fought to abolish slavery in the British colony, and legislate equal rights for the Xhosa native peoples of the Eastern Cape Province.

The venerable Muséum Nationale d'Histoire Naturelle in Paris is as described: millions of specimens of animals and plants in tall cabinets; tens of infants preserved in jars of alcohol in a musty sub-basement storeroom; hundreds of petrified skeletons marching forward in the Gallerie de Paleontologie; outside the gallery, Frémiet's sinister sculpture of an orangutan strangling, perhaps raping, a woman from Borneo; a top floor alcove with a window that opens onto the roof overlooking the Jardin des Plantes; and, nearby, the brasserie on Place d'Italie for devouring a pungent margherita pizza and washing it down with Trois Monts, a bière de garde.

Also real was Maison Verreaux, the premier natural history emporium in Paris in the 1800s. Led by Jacques Phillipe and his three sons, Jules, Édouard and Alexis, it conducted expeditions to Africa and Asia to collect specimens of animals and plants for museums and private collections. One of those expeditions, to Botswana, resulted in the infamous El Negro exhibit. A second, to North Africa, captured the Barbary lions, the dromedary camel¬¬—and possibly the human—for the diorama, Arab Courier Attacked by Lions.

After it was awarded the gold medal in the 1867 Paris exposition, Arab Courier was sold to the American Museum of Natural History in New York, which determined it was too theatrical for display. Andrew Carnegie promptly bought it for $50 in 1899 for showcasing in his new cultural palace in Pittsburgh, where it became the most popular exhibit after the skeleton of *Diplodocus*.

For much of the next 100 years, industrial pollution from the coke and steel mills—from what Carnegie liked to call "my dear old smoky Pittsburgh"—filtered into the museum and its exhibits, including Arab Courier. In 2016, when the museum undertook to clean, conserve, and restore the diorama, it made three stunning discoveries.

First, the dromedary's hide has a large, irreparable tear in the neck region, which may have occurred when it was shipped from New York to Pittsburgh. To conceal the tear, the position of the courier had deliberately been shifted forward on the camel.

Second, extensive x-rays showed that the mounts of the two lions and the dromedary still retain much of their skeletons. In retrospect, this is unsurprising, given the style of taxidermy practiced at the time by the Verreaux brothers.

Third, and most consequential, is the "courier's" head: the mannequin contains the skull and teeth of a human. Their origin is unknown—perhaps from the Paris morgue frequented by Verreaux and his friend, Frémiet; or plucked from one of the human skeletons lying in the Paris catacombs; or stolen from a plundered grave in North Africa, or elsewhere.

The museum is seeking to repatriate these remains, but cannot without knowing their origin—unlike El Negro, who was ultimately reburied in Botswana. As Harry tells Preston Stewart, President of the Carnegie Institute, "A dirty business, taxidermy. Not much cultural respect. Graves robbed. Bodies stolen and sold. People murdered. Humans stuffed."

Out of due respect, the institute deleted reference to an "Arab Courier" from the exhibit's new title, Lion Attacking a Dromedary, moved the diorama out of the natural history museum, and, amid continuing community concerns about the exhibit's racial and cultural representations, curtained off the big glass case from public view until it could be presented with new, interpretive information.

The diorama now sits in Carnegie's grand marbled foyer between its museums of art and natural history, embodying both. When unveiled, the dramatic desert scene will relate again the stories of how that very art and natural history, their past practice and prejudice, shaped the culture of Verreaux's creation.

Enjoy an Excerpt from

The Body on the Bed

by Leonard Krishtalka

Chapter 1

In the long-shadowed light of early morning, a man in a harness buggy rolled past her window. He slowed at the Ruthman house next door, glanced nervously over his shoulder, then continued on. She recognized him—Dr. John Medlicott, the Ruthmans' physician. He'd come past the Ruthman house often, but never at seven in the morning.

An hour later, she heard a loud commotion from inside the Ruthman home. It sounded like Belmont, Isaac Ruthman's fourteen-year-old stepson. She heard him shout "Father! Father!"

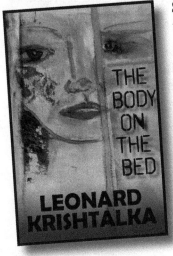

Suddenly, he came around the side of the house and began pounding frantically on his father's bedroom window. It was slightly ajar. He tried to raise it, but couldn't. He disappeared behind the house, returned with an ax, wedged the handle under the window, and managed to pry it up just enough to stick his hand in.

Why, she wondered, was Belmont trying to get in through the window? Had Isaac locked himself in his bedroom? Was he ill, unable to get up?

She watched Belmont move the curtain aside, then grope between the slats of the headboard that rested against the window. The white satin pillow caught the low, clear morning sun from the east. He pressed his face against the window pane then shrank back, turned, and dashed down the street.

Isaac must have been stricken, she thought. He'd seemed well yesterday evening. She'd spoken to him outside when he'd returned from work.

A few minutes later Medlicott's buggy pulled up to Ruthman's house. Belmont was with him. She quickly draped a sweater over her shoulders against the morning chill and went out to her front yard. The doctor looked pale. His hands trembled as he hitched the horse's reins to the post. Belmont ran up to the window, yanked the ax out, and handed it to Medlicott. He smashed the glass in the bedroom's adjacent window and climbed in over the sill. Belmont followed.

She heard muffled conversation through the open window. Abruptly, Belmont came tearing out of the front door of the house and raced past her up the street. Dr. Medlicott must be tending to Mr. Ruthman, she surmised. He's probably sent Belmont to fetch medicine, or another doctor.

She crossed the yard to Ruthman's front door. It was open. She found Medlicott in Ruthman's bedroom, leaning against a wooden dresser, reading a pamphlet. She could see the title in large block letters: MANHOOD! An Essay on the Cause and Cure of Premature Decline in Men. Startled, Medlicott jerked around and hastily put it back on the dresser.

Isaac Ruthman was stretched out on the bed, his body covered with a sheet, his face with a towel. She noticed the pillow, lying near the side of the headboard, stained with blood and spittle. There were shards of glass on the floor below the window from the broken pane.

"Is he dead?" she asked, lifting the towel. She didn't need to hear Medlicott's response. Ruthman's face looked like a leaf in winter. She wondered where the color drains to at the end, this ruddiness of life sapped from skin and veins.

"Yes, he's dead,"Medlicott said, placing his fingers on the side of Ruthman's throat. "But he's warm yet. Who are you?"

"Mary Fanning. I live in the next house. You might know me by my married name, Mary Apitz. I know you, Dr. Medlicott. I've seen you visit here often."

He blinked, seemingly taken aback. "I see ... yes ... Mr. Ruthman was my patient. Also Mrs. Ruthman. I've sent the son ... em ... Belmont to the county courthouse." He motioned north toward Henry Street. "The authorities should be here any moment."

"Yes, he ran past me. But I'm bewildered." She pointed to Isaac's body. "He seemed healthy yesterday evening. How did he die?"

Medlicott stepped away from the bed and shoved his hands into his pockets. "I honestly don't know."

She hesitated. "Do you think it could be suicide?"

Medlicott stiffened. "Why would you suggest that?"

"Why ... you had to break in here through that window. Belmont must have found the bedroom door locked. I assume Isaac locked himself in here last night. Why ... why else would he do that?"

Medlicott shrugged. "I don't know. The coroner will determine the cause of death."

She looked around the room. Four windows, two facing east, two north. A high-backed French bed. A plain nightstand. A chest of drawers. The most expensive piece of furniture was an upright piano in the corner. Last night, before retiring, Ruthman had folded his coat, vest, trousers, and shirt neatly on top of the piano. A last rite before suicide.

They stood in awkward silence waiting for the authorities. Medlicott kept checking his pocket watch. The dead, she thought, imposed this uncomfortable quietude, whether here in Ruthman's bedroom or in a funeral parlor, forcing us to stare at our own mortality—so feared, so private, so certain. And yet so uncertain. That we will pass, we know, but where to, we don't. It is how death begets belief. Faith assures us there is an afterlife when reason whispers there is not.

John Hutchings, the Douglas County Attorney, arrived first, on foot. He had a full head of short red hair. In the light it looked as if it had sprouted in patches. His cheeks and forehead were peppered with freckles that age had not matured away. He introduced himself, mumbled that the others were right behind, and checked the body on the bed.

"He's dead?" Hutchings glanced questioningly at Medlicott.

"Yes."

Three other men came into the bedroom. Mary recognized them. Andrew Carnes, the County Marshal, sporting a large, silver five-pointed badge on the front of his jacket. Charles Chadwick, judge and County Coroner. She'd attended his speeches in Lawrence in favor of women's suffrage. And Andrew Sharman, whose reporting in the *Lawrence Daily Journal* she thought was more recitation than journalism. Buggies pulled up outside the house. Dr. William Saunders and two other town physicians, Samuel Morse and Alonzo Fuller, hurried in, each carrying a leather medical bag.

Judge Chadwick yanked the sheet from the body. Ruthman's right hand was folded across his chest over his night shirt. His left hand still grasped the whiskers of his mustache. Saunders bent over Ruthman's face, then pointed to the froth around his lips and the blood and spittle on the pillow. He turned to Chadwick, motioning toward Mary with a quizzical, almost sheepish, expression.

"Judge, we … er … we need to remove his underclothes. Perhaps the lady should … er … be excused from the room." Saunders' round face turned red. He was short, slim, and had a stubble of yellow-blond hair that looked to Mary like a cropped hay field.

The other men stared at Mary, who was leaning against the piano in the corner. She folded her arms and flashed a defiant smile. "Gentlemen, I am Mary Apitz, married to Frederick Apitz. I've conceived two sons. And, although my name is also Mary, I assure you those conceptions were not immaculate. I know the nude male body. No part of Mr. Ruthman will be a surprise or seem indelicate. Please proceed."

Judge Chadwick nodded at her with a hint of admiration, then flicked his hand toward the bed. Saunders and Morse stripped the long night shirt from Ruthman's body.

"His skin is warm," Saunders remarked, "especially around the heart … almost lifelike to the touch. He appears to be dead, but strangely still animate. As if his eyes ought to open and his chest heave."

Hutchings, the County Attorney, ordered the doctors to try to resuscitate Ruthman. They applied heated bricks and hot water to his chest, then attempted to shock the heart to life with a galvanic battery. But Ruthman's eyes remained shut and his chest still.

"Judge," Saunders finally declared, "Mr. Ruthman is undoubtedly dead." He covered the corpse with the bed sheet. The shroud, Mary thought, that final, wordless verdict.

Heavy footsteps sounded on the wooden porch. A policeman in a blue uniform ushered six stern-looking men through the doorway.

"Good," Chadwick grunted, motioning to the policeman. "Dr. Medlicott, this is Deputy Marshal Jim Wright. He will take you to another room in this house where you will enjoy his company. And Jim, escort the good lady ... Mrs. Apitz outside to the porch."

Mary planted herself outside Ruthman's broken window, determined to witness the proceedings. Chadwick shook hands with each of the six men, asked them to raise their right hands, and swore them in as the coroner's jury. "For the record," he stated, "the inquest into the cause of death of Isaac Miles Ruthman is now in session."

Marshal Carnes and Hutchings began a methodical search of Ruthman's bedroom. In the drawer of his nightstand Hutchings discovered two boxes of medicinal powder. Carnes rummaged through Ruthman's clothes on top of the piano. Between the vest and the coat he found a memorandum book. Carnes adjusted his spectacles and paged through it.

"Ho!" He held up the memorandum book, triumphantly. "The last entry. It's a letter. Ruthman wrote it last night. To his wife."

Darling, the Doctor—I mean Dr. Medlicott—gave me a quinine powder Wednesday night April 26th. The effects are these: I have a terrible sensation of a rush of blood to the head, and my skin burns and itches. I am becoming numb and blind. I can scarcely hold my pencil and cannot keep my mind steady. Perspiration stands out all over my body, and I feel terribly. The clock has just struck eleven, and I took the medicine about

10:30 pm. I write this so that if I never see you again you may have my body examined, and see what the trouble is. Good-bye, and ever remember my last thoughts were of you. I cannot see to write more. God bless you, and may we meet in heaven.

Your loving hubbie, I. M. Ruthman.

Acknowledgments

The following sources provided invaluable historical and legal documents and information:

The *South African Commercial Advertiser*, South Africa's first independent newspaper, which started publication in January, 1824 by its founding editors, Thomas Pringle and John Fairbairn, and ceased publication in 1879.

Cases Decided in The Supreme Court of the Cape of Good Hope, Vol 1, 1903 [1828-1849]. J. C. Juta & Co., Capetown.

Scandal in the Colonies: Sydney and Cape Town, 1820-1850, by Kirsten McKenzie. Melbourne University Publishing, 2004, 210 pages.

Women's talk and the colonial state: the Wylde scandal, 1831-1833, by Kirsten McKenzie. Gender & History, April, 1999, volume 11, No. 1, pages 30-53.

Maison Verreaux—Animal Specimens of All Varieties. Catalogue of Organisms, blog by Christopher Taylor, February 25, 2002, http://coo.fieldofscience.com/2009/02/maison-verreaux-animal-specimens-of-all.html.

More notes on the Verreaux brothers, by Miquel Molina. Pula: Botswana Journal of African Studies, 2002, volume 16, no. 1, pages 30-36, and references therein.

El Negro of Banyoles, University of Botswana History Department, http://www.thuto.org/ubh/afhist/elnegro/eln0.htm

Africa Y La Historia, 2010, blog by Luis César Bou.

Diorientations: Spanish Colonialism in Africa and the Performance of Identity, by Susan Martin-Márquez. Yale University Press, 2008.

The Taxidermal Art, by Franklin H. North. Century Magazine, December, 1882, volume 25, pages 230-239.

Arab Courier Attacked by Lions, on exhibit at The Carnegie Museum of Natural History, Pittsburgh, Pennsylvania.

I am grateful to the following people who helped make this novel possible: Tanya Abrahamse, for introducing me to the Slave Museum in Cape Town and providing a learning tour of its history, exhibits and scholarship. David Bentley, Andy Bentley, and Henry April for enabling access to Cape Supreme Court documents from the Western Cape Archives and Records Service, Cape Town, South Africa. Steve Rogers, Carnegie Museum of Natural History, for information on the *Arab Courier Attacked by Lions*. Jerry Masinton, Martha Masinton, and the Write-On group for helping to fashion and edit the manuscript. My publisher, Maureen Carroll. And Aagje.

About The Author

Leonard Krishtalka is the author of award-winning essays and the acclaimed book, *Dinosaur Plots*. As a paleontologist, he has worked throughout the fossil-rich badlands of the American west, Canada, Patagonia, China, the Afar region of Ethiopia, and the Turkana region of Kenya.

In his Przewalski mystery series, beginning with *The Bone Field*, Pittsburgh private detective Harry Przewalski unearths sex, treachery, and murder buried beneath the science of petrified shards, skin, and bones. The second novel in the series is *Death Spoke.* The third is *The Camel Driver.*

OTHER BOOKS YOU MIGHT ENJOY FROM ANAMCARA PRESS LLC

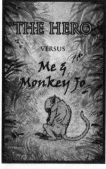

ISBN: 9781941237-08-3
$24.95

ISBN: 9781941237-33-5
$18.99

ISBN: 9781941237-30-4
$18.99

ISBN: 9781941237-13-7
$18.95

ISBN: 9781941237-18-2
$14.95

ISBN: 9781941237-14-4
$12.95

Available wherever books are sold or at:
anamcara-press.com

Thank you for being a reader! Anamcara Press publishes select works and brings writers & artists together in collaborations in order to serve community and the planet.
Your comments are always welcome!

Anamcara Press
anamcara-press.com